N.L. HOLMES

WayBack Press
P.O.Box 16066
Tampa, FL

Web of Evil

Quotes from "The Instructions of Any" from *Ancient Egyptian Literature* by Miriam Lichtheim, University of California Press (1976).

Cover art and map© by Streetlight Graphics.
Author photo© by Kipp Baker.

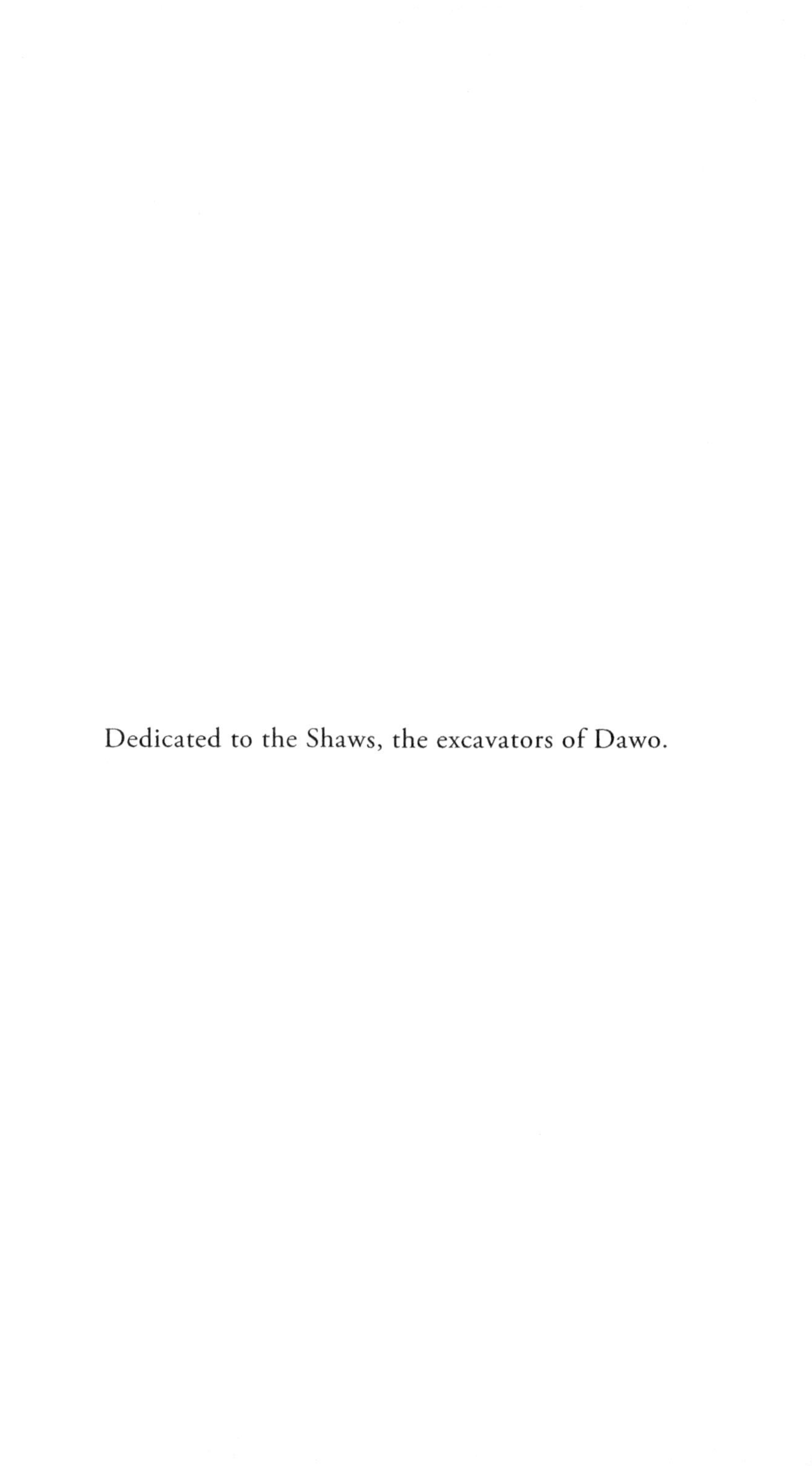

Dedicated to the Shaws, the excavators of Dawo.

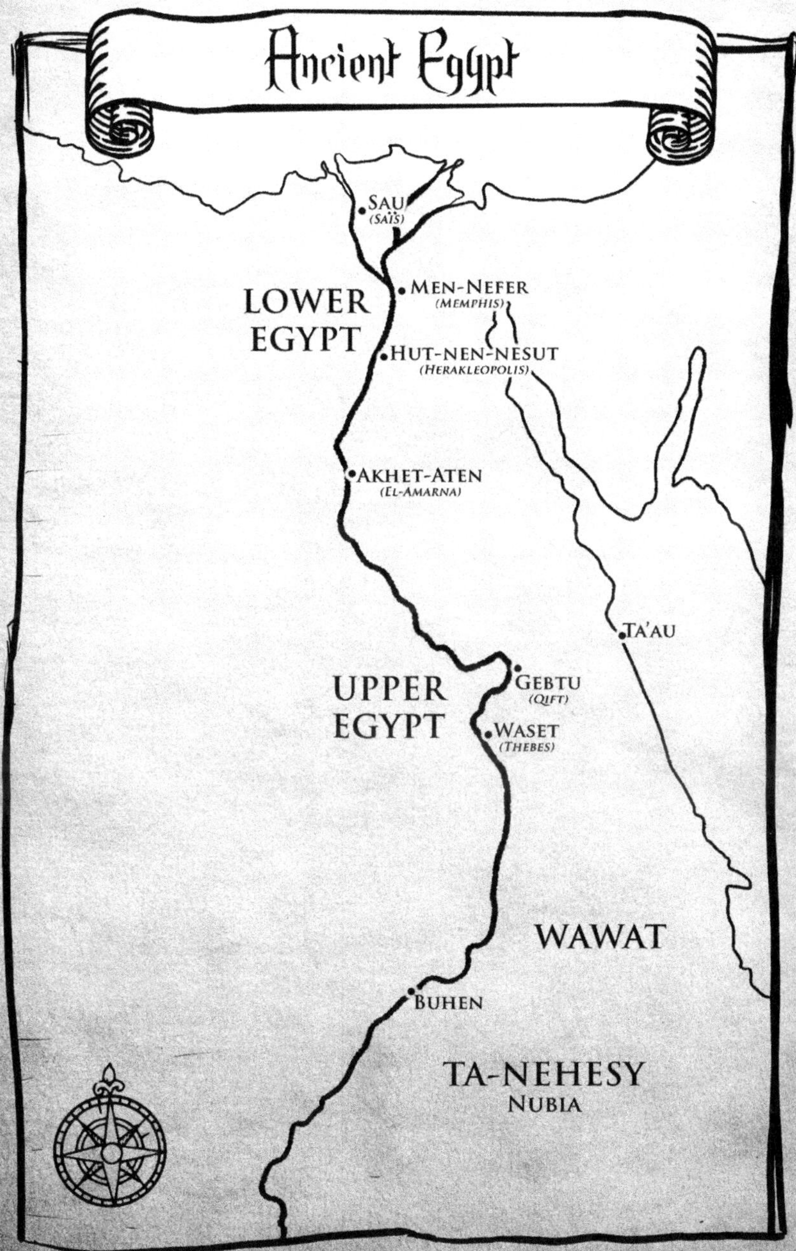
Ancient Egypt
SAU
(SAÏS)
MEN-NEFER
(MEMPHIS)
LOWER
EGYPT
HUT-NEN-NESUT
(HERAKLEOPOLIS)
AKHET-ATEN
(EL-AMARNA)
TA'AU
GEBTU
(QIFT)
UPPER
EGYPT
WASET
(THEBES)
WAWAT
BUHEN
TA-NEHESY
NUBIA

HISTORICAL NOTES

Our story takes place in ancient Egypt in the first year of Tut-ankh-aten(amen)'s reign, that is, about 1335 BCE. Although there was no Egyptian code of prescriptive laws, custom seems to have left it to the cuckolded husband to punish (or not) an adulterous wife and her lover, even with death. Thus, the form of the "law" presented in this book is oversimplified but essentially real. If that sounds barbaric, consider that Texas had a very similar legal permission until 1974! The difference is that in Egypt, adultery and its rectification were personal matters, and only the financial ramifications were of any concern to the community.

We do see examples where women served as village councilors or mayors.

In fact, despite the hierarchical society under an absolute king, there was a surprising degree of democracy at the local level, with elected officials and trial by a jury of peers. As in so many aspects of life, the Egyptians showed themselves to be miles ahead of their contemporaries. There were no professional lawyers, but the defendant himself or a friend might represent him in court. Thus, eloquence was considered a civic virtue. Any magistrate might sit as judge, with appeal to the king open to every defendant. One wonders how many awestruck "little people" would have dared to appear before the living sun god for a ruling!

The embalming ritual that helped to preserve the dead's mortal remains was an elaborate secret process presided over by the priests of Inpu (Anubis). The wealthier the person, the more extensive and successful—and expensive—his embalming. A high aristocrat might expect to rest forty days in the drying agent, natron. A poorer person might undergo a radically abbreviated stay or skip it altogether, with the poorest simply being buried rolled in a mat, trusting the heat and dry sand to desiccate them. To be thrown into the River to be eaten by wildlife rather than be buried with goods for the afterlife was a terrible fate. The mysterious smokeless flame Hani sees in the Pure Place would have had natron added to the combustibles. This might also be used in enclosed places like tombs when artists were at work.

The traditional Egyptian loom was the ground loom, stretched out horizontally, and women were the weavers. But in the New Kingdom, Egypt took on the vertical or warp-weighted loom from its Levantive vassals, and men became the users of this new high-tech commercial machine. The rest of the Mediterranean, including Keftiu (Minoan Crete), also used the vertical weaving style.

With the exception of the king's and certain gods', the Egyptians didn't celebrate birthdays.

CHARACTERS

(* indicates a historical personage)

A'a: Hani's former gatekeeper.

Aha: Neferet's oldest brother.

Ay*: Tut-ankh-aten's maternal grandfather and an influential counselor, probably a vizier.

Baket -iset: Neferet's oldest sister, confined to bed since a boat accident many years ago.

Bener-ib: the woman of Neferet's heart and her fellow physician.

Brute: a mastiff.

Cheetah: Neferet's one-eyed cat.

Dapurazo: a textile merchant from Keftiu.

Hani*: commissioner of foreign affairs in the north and Neferet's father.

Hapu-seneb: young scribe, son of Khnum-em-heb.

Heri-har: high priest of Inpu and Hani's childhood friend.

Hu-may: twelve-year-old orphan adopted by Neferet and Bener-ib.

Int-ef: a fisherman.

Iuty: Hani's gatekeeper.

Kem-sit: a weaver, widow of Pa-shedu, and mayor of the village.

Khnum-em-heb: owner of a large weaving network.

Mahu*: corrupt police chief, formerly of Akhet-aten, now of Waset.

Mangler, Faithful, and Hedgehog: three old dogs that guard Neferet's dispensary.

Maya: Hani's secretary and son-in-law, husband of Sati.

Mery-ra: Neferet's grandfather.

Mut-nodjmet: Neferet's cousin and sister-in-law, wife of Pa-kiki.

Mut-tuy: thirteen-year-old orphan adopted and apprenticed by Neferet and Bener-ib.

Neferet: Hani's daughter, a young sunet.

Nub-nefer: Neferet's mother, a temple chantress.

Pa-kiki: Neferet's second-oldest brother.

Pa-miu: Baket-iset's cat.

Pa-shedu: the former mayor of the village.

Pipi: Hani's younger brother.

Ptah-mes, formally called **Maya*:** Neferet's husband, Master of the Double House of Silver and Gold

Sat-hut-haru called **Sati:** Neferet's next-oldest sister.

Shu-roy: eight-year-old orphan adopted by Neferet and Bener-ib.

Sit-hut-har-iunet called **Iunet:** weaver and neighbor of Neferet and Bener-ib's dispensary.

Ta-em-resefu: Tjay's wife, a weaver.

Tiry: three-year-old orphan adopted by Neferet and Bener-ib.

Tjay: son of Pa-shedu, foreman and bookkeeper of Khnum-em-heb's weaving establishment.

Tut-em-heb: a neighbor of the dispensary and husband of Sit-hut-har-iunet.

Usret: sister of Tjay.

Web-khet: Maya and Sati's three-year-old daughter.

GLOSSARY

Ahhiyawa: Mycenaean Greece or one of its kingdoms.

Akhet: the season of Harvest, mostly late spring and summer.

Amen-Ra, the Hidden One: in the New Kingdom, when a Theban dynasty came to the throne, the local creation god Amen was merged with the sun god Ra to form a new national divinity.

***ba*:** a part of the soul that was thought to inhabit the tomb and fly out at night in the form of a bird.

Dawo: a port town in southern Crete, later known as Kommos.

Djehuty: Thoth, the god of scribes and judge of the soul after death.

Double House of Silver and Gold: the department of the treasury, although most of the kingdom's wealth was held in commodities.

Cloth Festival: a little-known Theban festival held soon after the new year.

Field of Reeds: the paradise in which the blessed souls lived after judgment, although they also aided Ra in rowing his barque across the sky.

Geb: god of the earth.

Golden Mosquito: Mery-ra's parody of the Golden Fly, an award for military valor.

Gold of honor: a: an award made by the king to a functionary who served him well. It included, among other things, a distinctive necklace of large lens-shaped gold beads (shebyu collar).

Hut-haru: Hathor, goddess of love, beauty, etc., who also welcomed the dead to the West.

Haru-lock: a braid worn by children to configure them to the child-god Horus.

House of Inpu (Per-Inpu): the temple of Anubis, with its embalming facilities.

Inpu: Anubis, the jackal-headed god of embalming.

***iteru*:** a unit of distance, approximately a mile.

Keftiu: the island kingdom of Crete.

Kemet, "the Black Land": the Egyptians' name for their country because of the rich black alluvium deposited by the Inundation every year. Also known as the Two Kingdoms.

khat: the mortal remains of the dead.

Khonsu the Traveler: the Theban moon god, patron of travelers.

Lovelies of Hut-haru: a bevy of divine girls who attended Hut-haru.

ma'at: the concept of truth, order, and justice. With a capital M, the goddess who personified it.

Men-nefer: Memphis, capital of the Lower Kingdom.

Mut: consort of Amen-Ra, queen and mother of the gods.

netjeri: natron, a naturally occurring salt used in drying food and embalming.

Osir: Osiris, divine king of the dead. All dead persons were thought to become Osir and hence might be referred to as an Osir.

Paisto: Phaistos, a palatial center on Crete.

Primal Mound: the original earth to emerge from the waters of chaos at the time of creation.

Pure Place: place of embalming, part of the Per-inpu or House of Anubis.

Sau: Saïs, a town in the Nile Delta where there was a temple of the goddess Sekhmet and a medical school.

Southern Kingdom: Egypt was historically divided into two kingdoms. The Upper Kingdom (that is, upstream on the Nile, which flows south to north) was also the Southern Kingdom.

sunu (m.), ***sunet*** (f.): scientific practitioner of medicine.

Tales of the Traveler: Maya's compilation of his and Hani's adventures abroad.

wanax and ***kiro*:** the Mycenaean and Minoan words, respectively, for *king*.

Waset: "City of the Scepter," Thebes, capital of the Upper Kingdom.

Weighing of the Heart: the judgment after death, in which the heart was physically weighed against the feather of *ma'a*t.

***weshket*:** a broad, decorative necklace that lies on the shoulders.

CHAPTER 1

Early in the season of Akhet, the Inundation, the precocious heat of spring had only intensified. Neferet and Bener-ib had been relieved to deliver the children to the farm to spend a few weeks in the relative cool of the open countryside. They themselves came nearly every weekend holiday, when Mama, Baket-iset, Sati and her children, and Mut-nodjmet and her brood were also likely to be around.

"This is perfect for the orphans," Neferet said, staring after the little ones, who had just run off amid a pack of overstimulated cousins. The baby crawled after them, crying, until the nurse scooped him up. "If this gang can't wear them out, nobody can."

"And maybe they'll learn some manners by example," grumbled Mut-tuy, the oldest of the orphans. At thirteen, she no longer considered herself a *little one*. Her Haru-lock of childhood had fallen to a rebellious chop of the knife a few months earlier, but the hair that would become her maiden braids still only stuck out about a thumb's length from her scalp.

It wasn't a good look, Neferet had to admit, considering the girl from the corner of her eye. Mut-tuy was tall, skinny, and flat chested. Her face promised beauty later in life, but at the moment, her appearance was dominated by awkward elbows and big feet. The ruthlessly cropped hair didn't help.

The women of the family sat in the grapevine-covered side yard of the farmhouse and shelled cowpeas while lunch simmered in the kitchen court, filling the house with a delicious smell of onions. At Bener-ib's feet lay Brute, the mastiff, who rarely left the two young *sunets*' side. Paws extended, tongue lolling, he resembled a brindled brown lion taking his ease.

"Maya keeps talking about buying some land in the country, but I almost hope he doesn't." Sat-hut-haru, Neferet's next-oldest sister, shook her skirt to empty the folds of accumulated pods. "I so love to come here. It reminds me of my own childhood. And there are always the other grandchildren around for the little ones to play with." Maya, Papa's secretary, was Sat-hut-haru's husband.

Mama smiled, her slim fingers expertly splitting a pod and reaming out the beans. "It makes me so happy to hear you say that. I've sometimes wondered if it weren't time to build onto the house, though. If everybody's here at once, it becomes rather like a barrack."

"No!" they all cried in chorus.

"Don't change anything," Baket-iset pleaded from her couch. "Leave it just as it was when we were children."

Neferet suspected that was more important for her sister Baket-iset than for anyone, since her childhood—before the terrible accident that had left her paralyzed—must have been the last truly carefree period of her life. Back then,

Baket could still dream of becoming a temple dancer for the Hidden One and having a husband and children of her own.

Neferet turned to the woman of her heart, who sat beside her. "At least they don't have to worry about you and me and Mut-tuy during the week. We can't leave the dispensary except on weekends."

"Should we not come so often, Lady Nub-nefer?" Bener-ib asked Mama. "We don't want to be a problem..."

Mama laid an affectionate hand on the young woman's shoulder. "No, no, my love. Don't even think that way. You girls are as welcome as anybody. You're all our troop of Lovelies, like the divine girls who attend Lady Hut-haru!" She beamed about at the group of young women who surrounded her.

And Mama, Neferet thought proudly, *the center of that bevy, is as beautiful as the goddess herself.*

Despite her name, Neferet wasn't sure she counted as a lovely. While her two sisters took after their mother, she resembled Papa—broad and sturdy, with small eyes and a square jaw. She didn't mind a bit. The youngest of the five children, she was especially close to Papa, and it was an honor to resemble him. She was smart like him too. She and Bener-ib were *sunets*, physicians, who had recently given up their position at the palace and opened a dispensary in the modest neighborhood of Maya's childhood home, a goldsmith's workshop. One might argue about how smart that was, but the two young women derived immense satisfaction from helping people who might not otherwise have access to a good doctor.

All at once, Brute jerked to attention, his eyes fixed on

the road that led from the farm to the bank of the River. The women's heads all swiveled as if they had been pulled by a string. Against the ferny greenery of the reeds that bordered the water, a group of men had appeared. From afar came excited shouts.

A shudder of uneasiness rolled up the back of Neferet's neck. She shaded her eyes with her hand, straining to see. "There's Maya—but where's Papa?"

The two men had gone out into the marshes that morning on Papa's little reed boat. And although the River was necessary to life, it could also be a vehicle of death. In its waters lurked crocodiles, serpents, and hippopotamuses. Sometimes, at night, she had heard the roar of the enormous animals right there in the backwaters near the farm.

"Oh no," Bener-ib murmured almost inaudibly. She had lost so many loved ones that she was always quick to expect the worst.

Everyone was on their feet now. Brute took off toward the men at a gallop, like a chariot horse heading into battle, with Neferet close behind. She wasn't ashamed to hike up her skirts in the interest of speed. A quick glance over the shoulder revealed that the other women trailed after her at a more ladylike pace.

Where is Papa? The question made Neferet's heart hammer as she pounded down the earthen road. *Great One, don't let anything have happened to him.*

Maya, recognizable by his short stature, was waving his arms at them. The other men huddled over the drop-off at the bank, some of them kneeling. They seemed to be pulling something up the slope. At last, a prone form slid onto the land and lay there, unmoving.

An anguished cry escaped Neferet despite herself, and she forced her winded body to give a burst of speed. At last, as she and Brute approached the men, Papa climbed up from the forest of reeds. Relief flooded through her, and she slowed down, daring to catch her breath.

"What's happened, people?" she panted, mopping at her forehead.

Apart from Papa and Maya, she didn't recognize any of the men who stood before her. They were deeply sun darkened, like people who worked outdoors every day, and were clad only in loincloths. The unfortunate who lay stretched upon the ground, on the other hand, was dressed in a kilt and a shirt that came to midcalf. He was a grisly sight, waterlogged and bleached by the River, starting to swell under the rays of the summer sun.

By this time, the others had caught up to Neferet, and Mama threw her arms around Papa. "Thanks be to the Hidden One that you're all right, my love. We saw Maya but not you, and I feared something might have happened."

"I was below in the boat, trying to lift this poor fellow up for the others to pull," Papa explained with an arm around his wife's shoulders. "These reed cutters had dragged him out of the water and asked if we could help them get him to the nearest habitation." With a smile, he turned to the four workmen and clasped their hands in turn. "We'll see to it the priests of Inpu get him and try to notify his next of kin. You're sure nobody recognizes him?"

"No, my lord," said the eldest. "Maybe he's a city man."

"Maybe. Thanks to you all."

Bowing and murmuring, the reed cutters made their way down the bank and onto their boats. In a moment, the soft plashes of their poles could be heard propelling the reed crafts away through the papyrus.

"Whew," said Maya, brushing down his kilt. He slipped an arm around Sati's hips. "A fellow just goes out for a quiet paddle through the marshes, and here comes a corpse."

"We need to get him out of the sun." Mama seemed quite unfazed by the unsavory deposit on their doorstep. "Mut-tuy, my dear, will you run back and bring one of the servants with the donkey cart and a sheet?"

For once, the adolescent obeyed without rebuttal. The rest of the family stood on the road, staring in uncomfortable silence at the dead man as Brute sniffed him with interest.

"What did he die of?" Neferet asked. "Clearly, no animal got him."

"We couldn't tell, my duckling. Perhaps you and Bener-ib can look him over and let us know. We need to find out who he is."

Neferet squatted at the man's side and lifted a water-shriveled hand. "He's been in the water for a while, but he's in pretty good shape. Maybe he drowned." She leaned over him and pressed down hard on his chest with both hands.

Everyone cried out, and Papa made a convulsive move as if to stop her. Pleased to have shocked everybody, Neferet said, "No, he didn't drown. He was dead when he went in, or else he'd have breathed in water, and his lungs would be full of it."

Bener-ib peered over her shoulder. "His hands aren't calloused. He's probably not just a workman."

Papa and Maya looked at each other in surprise. "I don't see any wounds," Papa said. "And he looks too young to have dropped dead of natural causes."

Everyone was crowding around curiously now, which helped to block the blinding sun. The man appeared to be in his thirties, his close-cropped curly hair still uniformly dark. It was difficult to make out the features, which had started to grow soft and blurry. Vitreous eyes stared up, unseeing. He was slim in build despite the ominous swelling of the abdomen that had begun, with plenty of hair on his chest and limbs.

Bener-ib continued to examine his hand. "There's just this callus on his middle finger. I think he might have been a scribe."

"Not very high position, though," Nub-nefer said. "His kilt isn't especially fine linen."

"Most observant, my dove!" Papa said. "If you ever decide you don't want to sing for the Hidden One anymore, I'll bet the *medjay* could make a spot for you on the police force."

But Mama gave a bitter sniff. "I'd rather die than work for that awful Mahu. Do we have to report this to him?"

"I shouldn't think so. We're a long way from the city of Waset. We can let them know in the village. The local mayor will have jurisdiction."

The clop of hooves and the rumble of wooden wheels betrayed the approach of the donkey cart. Mut-tuy jumped out, and Papa and the driver, with the help of Maya, heaved the dead man awkwardly into the little vehicle. An acrid odor of manure still floated about it.

Neferet spread the sheet over the corpse and tucked in the edges. "Somebody'll have to go back to the city to get the embalmer priests," she said, wiping her hands on her hips.

But Mut-tuy, looking smug under her effort at casualness, said, "The steward's already sent somebody. I told him what happened."

Papa gave her an amused glance. "Very enterprising, my girl."

"I'd be surprised if they send someone out this far," Mama said, watching the retreating wagon through hand-visored eyes.

Papa gave a chuckle. "Oh, I'm sure they will. The high priest is a fellow I went to school with when we were lads. I saved his honor with the schoolmaster once, and ever since, he's been more than obliging."

The others laughed.

Mama steered Sati and Mut-nodjmet toward the house. "Well, let's go back, girls. We left Baket-iset alone. She'll be wondering what happened."

"I told her." Mut-tuy looked satisfied, her smirk stretching from one corner of her cheeks to the other.

Neferet rolled her eyes. *That girl's getting above herself. She'll be telling us all what to do if we let her.* But she knew the adolescent was desperate to be part of the group—even more than most thirteen-year-olds. Her own parents had either died or abandoned her. Her brother, her junior by a year, took care of the little ones unless Mut-tuy was forced to. She seemed not to feel much kinship with her half-wild younger brothers and sister. She'd even refused to follow the path of her father and brother and apprentice as a goldsmith.

But there were more immediate problems than Mut-tuy's cockiness. As the three remaining young women trudged back toward the farmhouse, Brute at their heels,

Neferet said, "We need to find out who this dead man is so we can tell his family what's happened."

"Maybe they'll know in the village," Bener-ib suggested.

"That's what I'm hoping. Perhaps if we examine him more closely at the house before the priests of Inpu come, we'll discover how he died or find some clue to his identity."

The others had installed the dead man in the center of the salon, beneath the ceiling ventilator where any breezes that entered would blow over him. The thick mudbrick walls kept out the most ferocious heat, and Mama had heaped aromatic herbs around his body, but even so, it wasn't the time of year when one wanted a corpse around for too long.

The clatter from the kitchen made it clear that lunch was almost ready. Mut-nodjmet—Neferet's cousin and sister-in-law—and Sati were already carrying stools out into the yard and setting them up under the grapevine.

"We'd better do this now, before we have full stomachs," Neferet said resignedly.

She whisked off the sheet while Bener-ib retrieved the basket of medical supplies they always carried in case of accidents. With Mut-tuy's help, she turned the man on his face. There wasn't a great deal of light in the salon, but some things were clear. His back was covered in dried dirt where it had lain on the ground, and the blood was sinking, giving his nether half a sinister purple hue. There was no need to look further for a cause of death. A huge lump with tattered edges rose on the back of his curly-headed skull.

Bener-ib poked gently with a finger. "It's a bad depressed fracture. Somebody hit him a terrible blow from behind. There must have been a lot of blood, but it's all washed away in the River."

"I'll bet robbers got him and threw him in afterward to hide their crime." As usual, in the presence of murder, Mut-tuy's eyes were alight.

Neferet wasn't willing to let the thirteen-year-old guide the examination. "Or maybe he fell and hit his head, trying to get into a boat." She rolled the dead man onto his back once more and ran a finger under the waistband of his kilt. Nothing was tucked there against the tail of his long shirt—no purse, no papers, no writing implement. "After siesta, we can go into the village and ask around. There can't be that many literate people here."

"If he's from here," Bener-ib added pensively. "If he fell off a boat, he could be from anywhere."

Neferet replaced the sheet over the man's body just as Mama called from out of doors, "Girls? Where are you? We're ready to eat."

"Come on, people. Let's wash up in the kitchen. We have our task for the afternoon."

The tables were set up under the vines, where gourds as well as unripe grapes hung down. The cicadas were so loud it was difficult to hear what everyone said, but there was no mistaking the savory smells that rose from the platters of flat beans and stewed onions. Papa passed a big bowl of lettuce dressed with herbed vinegar.

"What did you find out about the cause of death, my duckling?" he asked as Neferet heaped the leaves on her dish.

"Somebody hit him on the head, or else he had an

accident. His skull is fractured. Pieces of it are pressed down into the brain."

Papa and Maya exchanged a look.

Sat-hut-haru said with distaste, "We're not going to have a report here at the table, are we?"

Neferet made a face while her sister's head was down. "Some of us are going to have to go back to the city tomorrow afternoon, so if we want to learn anything to tell his family, we have to do it as soon as possible." She turned to Papa. "Where exactly was the victim found, Papa?"

"As I understood it, the reed cutters came upon him floating face up among the papyrus down near the end of the little island—you know, where there's a kind of stream between the main bank and that hummock that's separated when the water is low. I've taken you down there before. It's all gotten flooded during the Inundation, of course."

"He could have floated there from somewhere else, then. How long would you say he's been dead, Ibet?"

"At least a day or two. He's no longer stiff."

"*Iyah.*" Sati sprang up from her stool and stalked away toward the house. "I'm going to eat with the children in the kitchen court."

"If that doesn't take away her appetite, nothing should," Mut-tuy said under her breath.

Maya gave her a dark look.

Mama turned to feed Baket-iset a spoonful of her food and said dryly, "Perhaps when they've sickened us all, the girls will have some nice emetic to offer us."

Neferet let out a big guffaw. "Funny you should say that, Mama. I cut an armload of castor beans and leaves out by the goose pen. I hope you didn't have any other plans for them."

"That's fine, my love. I never poison anyone till the middle of the week."

The others laughed, but Bener-ib gave her plate an uneasy glance.

"Perhaps I ought to… *ahem.*" Maya edged up from his seat, his eyes flickering toward the house.

"Go on, my boy. I'm sure Sati would appreciate your company." Hani chuckled. His secretary hustled off through the wide-open doorway, barely having to duck the rolled-up fly mat. Being a dwarf had its advantages.

"Well, people, we're going into the village to ask around about our dead man." Neferet rose from her stool and brushed out her skirts.

"I'll go with you in case there's anything I can add," Papa said. "Nub-nefer, my dove, if the priests come for our Osir, you know what to do."

"Of course, my love."

Papa and Neferet headed for the gate of the little low-walled yard. Neferet turned and held out a hand, smiling, and Bener-ib hurried to her side and clasped it. Together, they and Papa set off, Mut-tuy following them. Brute ambled along, matching their pace, with his calm, possessive stride. The little party set out along the path that crossed the fields, surrounded by a cloud of dust, while the sun hammered down on their heads and bare shoulders. Around them, the rich glebe sparkled with water it hadn't yet managed to absorb. The humidity was almost thick enough to push against the skin.

"This wasn't the best hour, probably," Neferet admitted. "Everybody may be sleeping."

"We can wake the mayor. A dead man washed up on the shore is his responsibility." Papa fanned himself with his wig. "You ladies are going to look like field workers after this noonday sun."

"We'll fit right into the neighborhood, then." Neferet snickered.

A quarter hour's walk brought them to the local village, a settlement of not much more than a hundred people. They shopped there occasionally and attended local festivities, but the girls didn't know it well. Neferet wasn't even sure of the name—all through her childhood, the family had simply referred to it as the village. It was mostly unwhitewashed brick the color of the encircling land, shaded with palms and figs and pomegranates. The packed-earth street, little more than a trail, was sprinkled with modest houses surrounded by yards, walled or otherwise. Pigs and geese wandered at liberty, foraging.

A trio of young children ran shrieking around a house until someone yelled from the doorway, "Quiet, you brats! People are trying to sleep!"

Papa chuckled. "I doubt we'll have to wake the mayor after all." He looked around then pointed to a solid-looking house a little back in a grove of date palms. "Last time I came here, the mayor lived right there. He's a man named Pa-shedu."

There were no garden walls. The trampled earth and bushes might or might not have belonged to the mayor, and the guinea hens that gobbled and pecked seemed to be the same ones that roamed up and down the village.

A donkey was hobbled in the shade of a fig tree, its head surrounded by a cloud of flies. It looked up in curiosity as the little troop passed, but Brute didn't dignify the animal with a glance.

The door stood open in the heat, the fly mat hanging. Papa called out softly, "Is anyone home?"

Almost immediately, a wiry little woman on the far side of middle age pushed aside the mat and said in a deep voice, "What can I do for you?"

"We're looking for the mayor, Pa-shedu, mistress. I hope we're not waking the household."

"Well, you won't wake *him*. He flew into the West more than a year ago. I'm his widow. It's me who's mayor now."

She turned and led the visitors into her unassuming salon. Brute, a gentleman if ever there was, dropped modestly into his place outside the door, sending the geese squawking for cover. The thought of a woman mayor lit a warm little fire of delight in Neferet's heart. She expected the widow to take her seat in a chair of office, with a scepter of authority. But apparently, village life was less formal than life in Waset. Instead, their hostess settled herself cross-legged on the floor and offered her guests the cushions strewn around.

Her expression was intense and businesslike. "My name is Kem-sit. How can I help you?"

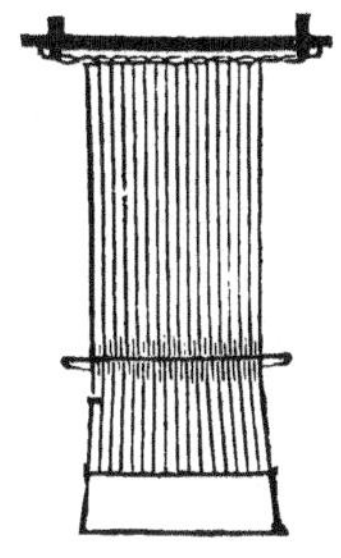

CHAPTER 2

Neferet and her father both started to speak at the same time. Papa, with a barely suppressed grin, gestured to Neferet to continue.

"We're from Lord Hani here's farm down the road," she explained.

"I know you. You come to the village sometimes, and you employ some of our people." Kem-sit nodded her approval at Papa.

"This morning, Papa was out in the marshes, and some reed cutters found a dead body floating in the River. Papa helped them bring him back to the house. My partners and I are *sunets*, so we examined the man and found he had been hit on the head—"

"Or fallen and hit it," Papa inserted.

"Anyway, he's dead. Very likely murdered." She shot a meaningful glance at Papa from the corner of her eye. "We called the servants of Inpu, but we wanted to see if the man lived here in the village. Somebody needs to notify his family."

Her eyebrows pinched, Kem-sit continued to nod as Neferet spoke, as if she had suspected all this. At last, she said in her deep, scratchy voice, "It must be Tjay. He's been missing for two, three days. What's he look like?"

"Early thirties. Slim. Curly hair. Probably good-looking, but it was hard to tell."

"That's him."

"I doubt if the servants of the Pure Place have arrived yet. If his family wants to reclaim the body, it isn't too late," Papa said.

"I'm gonna take it upon myself to say that they probably don't. He was estranged from most of them—only his sister was close to him. Better she just thinks we didn't find out about his demise until too late."

"He was some sort of scribe, wasn't he?" Neferet asked.

The possibility that Tjay had been murdered was growing. If he was such a disagreeable specimen that his own family disliked him, almost anyone might have shortened his life. She wanted to learn what she could before they had to return to the city.

"Right. He was the overseer and bookkeeper of a good-sized weaving establishment. How'd you know?"

"His hands were soft except for a callus on his second finger, as if he'd held a pen for years," said Bener-ib.

Neferet, carefully avoiding her father's eye, added, "What else can you tell us about him, Kem-sit? My colleagues and I would like to find his murderer. We've done this before. We feel it's only fair to the *ba* of the Osir. Otherwise, it's likely to go wandering."

Kem-sit gave a snort that might have been dry laughter. "He'd love that—annoying people and drawin' attention to hisself. Forgive me—shouldn't speak ill of the dead, but I've known him since he was a boy." She stared upward at the bars of dust-filled sunlight that streamed in through the high windows. Neferet was on the point of getting to her feet, but finally, Kem-sit said, "It'd probably make sense to talk to his boss or the people who worked under him. His wife, maybe, although she may not want to say anything. His sister'll tell you all the good things about him—mostly from her imagination. I can tell you this much. Tjay was from a family of weavers who work for a certain Khnum-em-heb. His employer helped him get a education and made him the supervisor and bookkeeper of his business. Tjay was a demandin', self-important man who nobody really liked, and I'm sure Khnum-em-heb musta regretted giving him even a little power over others. It was no secret that Tjay mistreated his wife and children."

Neferet exchanged a glance of disgust with Bener-ib. Behind the latter's shoulder, Mut-tuy looked thunderous.

"So, anybody could have gotten fed up with him and knocked him in the head," Papa said pensively.

Kem-sit tipped her head in reluctant agreement. "There was times when I'da liked to do it myself. Probably everybody in the village could say the same. I don't know about his friends in the city."

"We thank you, mistress, for your help." Papa got to his feet, and Neferet felt obliged to do the same. The others followed.

Kem-sit led them through the vestibule to the door, where a wave of heat hit them. "If you're gonna look up his wife, they live in that two-story place at the north end of the village." The mayor squinted into the glare. "His sister's down by the riverbank, where the reed boat's pulled up."

"You've been very helpful," Neferet said, taking her hand. "It's wonderful to see a woman mayor."

"Happens sometimes," the older woman said almost grimly. She looked as if she was on the point of saying more but thought better of it.

Brute arose from his spot in the shade of a tree and joined the little party as they made their way through the disorderly plantings, animals, and accumulations of village debris.

"Well, ladies," said Papa, "do you want to speak to his wife?"

"Of course, Papa. Even if he was a terrible husband, she deserves to know what's happened. She might be aware of somebody who especially had it in for him." *Although it sounds like everybody had it in for him.*

The village wasn't large—surely not much more than a dozen or fifteen households—but the dwellings were scattered, and it took a few minutes to make their way to the far end. Nobody was eager to walk fast in the sticky heat along the River's banks. Brute's liquid panting rhythmed the shuffle of their feet.

The dead man's residence was marginally grander than its neighbors, with a walled yard and fresh whitewash. The sound of children playing and shouting on the roof terrace broke the siesta-hour silence. Papa knocked on the gate, and a woman looked over the parapet.

"Who's there?"

"My name is Hani. Your neighbor downriver," Papa called. "It's important. May we come in?"

Her face stiffened in suspicion. "I'll be right down." Above the roar of the cicadas came the pad of hurried bare footsteps from within the court. The gate flew open. "Yes?"

"This is about your husband," said Neferet gently.

"Yes?" The woman looked tensely from the girl to her father.

"Some reed cutters found his body in the marshes near our farm," Papa said. "He'd been dead for several days."

The widow stared as if she didn't know how to respond, then she seemed to return to herself. "Please come inside."

They followed her through a skimpy yard with a few flowers and a little pond that needed refilling, then they entered a salon lit wanly by high windows. After the midsummer brightness of the out-of-doors, Neferet was blinded by the darkness. The widow offered Papa the only stool, and the women all seated themselves on the floor. Neferet cast an eye around as her vision adjusted. Someone had furnished the room with an aspiration to genteel living but on a small, rural scale. The walls were brightly painted, though Neferet detected little warmth or happiness in the place.

Maybe I'm just making this up. Baket-iset would have a better feel for it.

"What... what happened, do you know?" the woman asked.

"He was hit on the head hard enough to fracture the skull. Somebody killed him and threw him in the River." On seeing the woman's blank look, Neferet added, "My colleague and I are *sunet*s. We examined the body before turning him over to the servants of Inpu."

"It was sure to happen. I knew he was dead when he

didn't come back for days." The widow lowered her face and swiped at her nose wearily with the back of the wrist. She didn't strew her head with dust or begin to wail or tear her clothes, Neferet noticed. None of the usual gestures of grief. *Perhaps there is no grief.*

"Do you have any idea of who might have done such a thing?" Neferet asked.

The woman gave a bark of bitter laughter. "There's too many possibilities. Nobody liked him. He was hard on his workmen, arrogant to his peers. His family—none of them is close except his sister. And she's a little... I've never seen a stranger relationship."

"That's what the mayor said." Papa was observing her attentively.

"Did Kem-sit tell you he was her stepson?" the woman asked.

"Why, no." Neferet shot a glance at Bener-ib, who was drinking in everything with round eyes.

"Her husband's son by a first marriage. Tjay fought her for the office of mayor after Pa-shedu died. You get a sense of what people thought of him by the fact that they preferred to elect a woman. It finished off any goodwill anybody still had for him."

"*Iyah*," Neferet said with a lift of the eyebrows. Quite a picture of the man was forming.

Papa sucked his lip thoughtfully. "Is there anything we can do for you? My name is Hani, by the way. Your husband's body is at my farm a short way upstream, and it's possible the priests haven't arrived yet from Waset if you want to see him."

"No. Not after he's been in the water for days. He

wouldn't want me to see him like that," said the woman unemotionally. "He was good-looking, at least. I'll give him that. And vain."

She was attractive too—slim and fine featured. She looked no older than thirty. Her hands had the dry, calloused look of someone who worked, though, despite the relative prosperity of the household.

"My name is Ta-em-resefu." She gave a resigned half smile. "Since we're neighbors."

"My wife will want to pay her respects, I'm sure, Ta-em-resefu" said Papa. "I'm just sorry the circumstances are sad."

"I hope I won't shock you to say they aren't all that sad, Lord Hani. Anybody in the village would understand, and there's no need to play the hypocrite."

"Are you going to be under hardship now, mistress?" Neferet asked. "You have children, I think."

"Three, yes. But no, we won't suffer. I'm a weaver. Tjay made me stop, but in the last few days, I've set up the loom again. My brothers will help me. Kem-sit will help me."

"You're still close to her, then?" Neferet said, pleased.

"Yes. She never sided with Tjay, even though he was her stepson. She would take the children away when he was… in a bad mood."

Neferet found herself admiring the mayor more than ever.

Papa said, "We'll leave you now, mistress. Please call upon us if there's anything we can do. I'll notify you when the embalming is complete—someone will surely organize a funeral, won't they? Maybe his sister? At the moment, I suppose we need to notify her. And his employer."

"That would be Khnum-em-heb. He lives in Waset. The sister's named Usret. She's here in the village, down by the marshes."

They took their leave of the widow and made their way through the village to the isolated residence Ta-em-resefu pointed out to them.

Usret's house was a shabby pile of brick at the water's edge, screened from the banks by a row of skinny date palms. A bald man was piling armloads of reeds in the yard.

"Excuse me," Papa called. "We're looking for a woman named Usret. Is she home, do you know?"

The man looked up, smiled a gap-toothed grin, then returned to his work without curiosity. Papa waited, but no answer was forthcoming. Eventually, he shrugged, and the four left the bald man to his task.

I wonder if that's her husband or a servant. Neferet led the way to the door and yelled, "Is mistress of the house Usret in?"

Over the parapet of the roof terrace, a scarf-clad head appeared then an entire woman. "What, then?" she said brusquely.

"We have something to tell you, mistress. You may not want it yelled aloud in the street."

Usret disappeared then, a moment later, stood in the doorway, pulling off her scarf and fluffing her curly hair. She was a few years older than Neferet and Bener-ib, thin to the point of skeletal, narrow hipped, and flat chested. She had attractive features, but her cheeks were painfully gaunt, every movement of her mouth provoking a visible shift of the jawbones and muscles. Neferet felt uncomfortable looking at her.

Belying the curt impatience of her first words, her face had taken on an expression of doglike eagerness to please. "How can I be of service to you?" she asked with a fawning smile. Her eyes were darting from face to face as if trying to read the least sign of approval.

"I'm afraid we have some bad news for you, mistress. It's about your brother," Papa said.

Usret's fleshless features registered suspicion then fear then growing horror as the implications of this introduction penetrated.

Neferet continued, "We live on a farm near here, and this morning, Tjay's body washed up in the reeds. He's been murdered."

There was an instant of stunned silence. Then the young woman began to wail. She clutched at her hair, her mouth wide, and howled with grief. This was the conventional reaction one would expect from the bereaved, but it was so different from what they'd encountered that morning that Neferet was surprised.

Somebody, at least, loved Tjay. But that was far from a consoling thought. Neferet was genuinely confused. *Did the man really have two such different sides?*

Usret ripped at the neck of her shift and sank to her knees, sobbing and shrieking, smearing dust on her face and pouring it on her head. The messengers of bad news stood around uncomfortably. Mut-tuy watched, skepticism painted all over her face.

On the riverbank, the bald reed cutter looked up. Then he came running. The man squatted at Usret's side and put his arms around her. Neferet wondered if he wasn't her husband after all, despite the seeming difference in age.

"Tjay! Tjay!" the woman wailed. "He's dead! Lord of Souls, have mercy! What will I do?" She let herself be embraced, but the man's presence didn't seem to comfort her. He never said a word.

Neferet and the others expected questions, but the woman seemed completely wrapped up in her own eruption of grief. Eventually, they offered their condolences and slipped off.

"We can talk to her later," Papa said quietly, drawing Neferet away.

They rejoined Brute under the trees and made their way in silence to the road. Only when they'd set out through the flooded fields did they begin to speak.

"It's sad, isn't it, when somebody dies, and everybody in the whole village is practically jumping up and down with happiness. Imagine what sort of person he must have been." Neferet shook her head.

"That lady mayor didn't even want to be associated with her own stepson," said Mut-tuy in ghoulish awe.

Papa said sadly, "His sister seems to be the only person who even cares that Tjay has died."

"That was suspicious," Mut-tuy said in a cynical voice. "Can he have been such a different person with her than with everybody else?"

The question echoed perfectly Neferet's own thoughts.

Bener-ib shrugged, always willing to excuse people. "They were flesh and blood. Maybe after the father died, Tjay was the last family she had left."

But little as she wanted to admit it, Neferet shared Mut-tuy's suspicion. There had been something a little too theatrical about Usret's demonstration of grief. The fact was, Neferet hadn't liked the woman very well, although she couldn't have said why.

"We can come another time when she's calmed down," Neferet said. "Surely she'll want to know the details—what's become of the body and such. And we'll talk to this Khnum-em-heb as soon as we get back to the city tomorrow. One of our neighbors is a weaver, remember? She must have heard of him."

Neferet found herself getting more and more excited as she spoke. She was already picturing the sequence of interviews they'd need to carry out in order to narrow down the list of likely murderers. Bener-ib's dubiously cocked mouth didn't daunt her. The girl from Sau would come around, and nobody was more fearless than the timid-seeming Ibet when it came to the hunt. She had followed a desperate gang of smugglers to their lair only a few months earlier.

Papa made a throat-clearing noise that drew Neferet's attention. "I know we've had this conversation, my duckling, but the father in me feels it's my duty to say all this again. It could be extremely dangerous to—"

"I know, Papa," she said wearily. A steam of annoyance heated her face. "I was present when we had the conversation, you know. Though we carried it off rather brilliantly in the end, as I recall. Apprehended the killers. Solved a big case of contraband. Came out alive and well. Earned the king's gratitude." She shot him a look that sparked with challenge.

"And appeased the victim's *ba*," added Mut-tuy.

Dear gods, can the girl ever not have the last word? But Neferet thought it would be ungenerous to squelch her ally publicly.

Papa stumped on in silence, his lip thrust out and eyebrows knotted as if he were wrestling with himself. At last, he said reluctantly, "All right. You're adults. I can only beg you to be prudent. I remind you that most of Tjay's family doesn't seem eager to pursue the case, so you're going to have a little trouble justifying your involvement if the police ask questions."

"I bet Usret wants us to pursue it. Besides, the police don't have any jurisdiction out here anyway. It's the mayor of the village, you said. Remember? And besides, it seems that Tjay was just such a jackal prick that somebody took against him personally—he wasn't part of some sinister plot. I can't imagine his confederates are going to go after us. I don't see that there's any danger at all. Besides, we have Brute to protect us." The case sounded good when she spoke the words aloud. Even Papa should find it convincing.

He grunted.

They walked on, saying nothing further. The crushing heat licked up their perspiration as soon as it emerged. Neferet's shaven head, battered directly by the sun, felt like it was afire. Invisible cicadas roared in rhythmic waves, and Brute's panting was like the rasp of a saw. Even the birds had abandoned the sky and were holed up somewhere in the shade. Neferet saw the farmhouse, with its fringe of palms, shimmering like a mirage in the fields ahead, and her relief was an Inundation, a River in flood. The little group's steps grew quicker until they reached the house. Inside, it was noticeably cooler and as silent as the family tomb.

"Everyone's taking their nap, I see," said Papa, stretching

and yawning. "I think I'll go up on the roof and do the same. How about you girls?"

"I'm going to sit outside under the awning and start planning," Neferet said.

Papa gave her a penetrating look then squeezed her around the shoulders and set off up the staircase, which creaked under his weight. "Listen to the Hidden One in your heart, my girl. That's all I can ask."

When he was out of sight, Bener-ib said anxiously, "He's right, you know, Nef'et."

"Of course. I always listen to the Hidden One in my heart."

"No, I mean this could be dangerous. We were lucky last time. We could have been killed."

"But those people were real criminals. This was just a personal grudge. It sounds, in fact, like it was an act of virtue to clear that Tjay from the bosom of Geb." Neferet took her friend's hands in a cajoling gesture. *Come on, my girl. Don't make me drag you.*

"How do you know?" asked Mut-tuy.

Neferet gaped at her. "Whose side are you on?"

The girl shrugged with her usual affectation of indifference. "Ours. Only we don't have any evidence yet. How do you know this was a personal grudge?"

Neferet cast her eyes to heaven. "I'm speaking in generalities, Mut-tuy. You don't think Tjay's murder is part of another smuggling ring, do you?"

"No, but both of you always say not to jump to conclusions."

"And something else we always say is that young girls

should know their place. How about a little listening to your elders?"

"I do listen. And you always say not to—"

"Enough! *Iyah!*" Neferet clapped her hands over her ears.

The girl was impossibly stubborn. Although Neferet had much the same reputation, she had to admit. But there was a difference between standing by one's principles and being pig-headed.

"Well, I'm going out under the arbor to think. Join me or not as you like, people. Come on, Ibet," Neferet said, putting a fond arm around Bener-ib's shoulders.

They turned and pushed through the fly mat. She called to the thirteen-year-old over her shoulder. "Why don't you bring us that jug of tamarind drink Mama left cooling in the well, my girl? We're going to get thirsty." Mut-tuy shambled off with a roll of the eyes, and Neferet shot a martyred glance at her companion. "I'll be glad when she's grown out of this stage."

Bener-ib said, "She's had a hard couple of years."

"So did you, but you're the nicest person in the Two Lands."

Neferet drew her against her side tenderly. Every time she thought about how lucky she was to have found someone like Ibet, her heart melted. The two young women settled themselves on stools, pushing aside the basins of half-shelled cowpeas the others had left that morning, and Neferet began to think once more about the tasks that lay before them.

"Probably that what's-his-name, the weaving employer, is the most important person to talk to, but we can see him when we return to the city tomorrow. I'd like to take advantage of our presence here to talk to the mayor again. And try to find some of the weavers who worked under Tjay. Maybe one of them had a grudge against him."

Mut-tuy entered with a tray, upon which sat a sweating clay pitcher and three cups. She plunked it down on an unoccupied stool and took her seat, making no effort to pour.

"I think it's easier to drink from a cup than directly from the pitcher," said Neferet dryly.

Mut-tuy shrugged. "I'm not a servant."

With the sigh of one sorely tried, Neferet poured each of the three a measure of the drink. A tart, sweet fragrance that set the mouth watering arose from the cups. She handed one to each of the others then took up her own and snuffed deeply before lifting it to her lips. "Ah! The perfect drink for a hot afternoon. To our new case, ladies!"

CHAPTER 3

THEY SIPPED IN APPRECIATIVE SILENCE. Rather than planning their next investigation, Neferet found that the heat and lazy silence of the afternoon loosened her mental acuity. Little by little, it became hard to keep her eyelids open.

She jumped to consciousness from a kind of half slumber when the sound of footsteps shuffled up. Before her stood four men with a stretcher—the two priests of Inpu and their servants.

"Is this Lord Hani's farm?" asked one of them, mopping his forehead.

"Yes, it is. I'm his daughter. Mut-tuy, go get Papa, please, and tell him the priests are here." She and Bener-ib led the way into the salon, while the adolescent galloped up the stairs to the roof terrace.

Tjay lay in dimly lit solitude. The sickly-sweet reek of death had begun to hang heavy in the room, and a noisy storm of flies hovered over the sheet-draped figure. The elder of the two priests drew aside the sheet and considered the corpse with a professional eye. Neferet, too, examined his pale, bloated face. He had heavy, round-arched eyebrows that gave him a frank expression and a matching dent in his chin and the tip of his nose. However disagreeable he'd been in life, there was none of that written in his features. His expression was mild and a little surprised. She noticed now what she'd failed to see earlier: a big scar on his wristbone, as if he'd been cut badly in his youth.

Poor man. He had a history, like everybody else. Perhaps something happened to him that turned him bad. That's what Ibet always says.

Heavy footsteps came clumping down the stairs, and Papa appeared, tying his kilt. He brightened at the sight of the priests. "Ah! Thank you for coming so promptly. Our unexpected visitor is starting to wear out his welcome."

"Who is he, do you know?" asked the older priest.

"Tjay, son of Pa-shedu, son of our local mayor, and a scribe with a weaving establishment. But we'll be paying for his embalming. Nobody in his own family seems much interested."

The girls left Papa and the priests to conclude the transfer of the body, and before they'd even returned to the yard, heavily scented incense smoke had begun to curl from the men's censers.

"Your father shouldn't have to pay for this," murmured Bener-ib as they took up their seats under the arbor. "It's the family's duty to take care of their own, and they didn't seem poor."

"We might drop a little hint when we go to see Kem-sit."

"*Are* we going to go see her?" Mut-tuy asked.

"Yes, my girl. And the widow and sister too. Before we

have to go back to the city tomorrow. Then we'll look up that Khnum-person."

The idea of trudging back to the village in the heat of late afternoon was almost too formidable to confront. But it was the only way to get the information they needed. The men had emerged at the front door, the servants carrying between them the red-draped stretcher with Tjay's body.

Neferet gestured at her father and mouthed, "We're off to the village."

He nodded, distracted by the business of handing off the corpse, and the three young women set out along the path through the fields, pausing only for Neferet to dodge back and snag one of the basins of shelled peas.

"What's that for?" Mut-tuy asked curiously.

"Just a little gift for a bereaved family. We don't have any flowers."

But Bener-ib had spotted some in the dry weeds beside the path, and little by little as they walked, her miniature bouquet grew larger.

The dusty trees and ill-kempt houses of the village offered a welcome shade. Life was just beginning to reawaken after siesta when the three arrived, sending a gaggle of geese scattering noisily. Before they'd even reached the mayor's house, they saw Kem-sit in the yard, emptying a pan of dishwater over a patch of straggling onions. She looked up as the trio approached and straightened, a hand on her hip.

"You forget something?" she asked, a quirk of humor in her deep voice. She was a wiry woman with her graying hair in tiny braids—more a working-class country housewife than a figure of officialdom.

"Do you mind if we ask you some more questions

about your stepson?" Neferet asked. "We thought it might be easier to talk woman to woman, without Papa present."

Kem-sit heaved a weighty sigh, and when she spoke, there was relief in her voice. "You found out he was my stepson, I see. I say 'was' and not just because he's dead. It's because I completely disowned him after Pa-shedu's death. There was a bitter struggle over the inheritance and the office of mayor—maybe Ta-em-resefu told you." Kem-sit led them toward the house. "She's here, by the way."

"Oh, good. We wanted to talk to her too."

The mayor led them around to the side of the house and up the masonry steps to the roof terrace. There, they found her daughter-in-law on her knees, bent over a floor loom with another set up beside it. She looked up, brushing her hair from her eyes, as the visitors emerged.

"Who was—oh, hello again." She smiled as Neferet, Bener-ib, and Mut-tuy followed Kem-sit onto the terrace and sat back on her heels.

"They want to talk about Tjay," said Kem-sit.

"We want to find out who killed him, and anything you tell us about him could be a clue," Neferet said, crossing her ankles and sinking to the floor beside the weaver.

Kem-sit gave a bark of caustic laughter. "I want to give whoever it was the gold of honor. He's done us all a service."

"Was Tjay so bad?" Mut-tuy's eyes were round with a gourmet's appreciation of evil.

"Ta-em-resefu is the one who could answer that best." Kem-sit looked closely at Neferet, who was carrying a basin of peas, and asked wryly, "What's them peas for?"

"A little present of condolence. We didn't have any flowers. Except, well, Ibet found some." She gestured

Bener-ib forward, who shyly presented her handful of wildflowers.

"Why, how very kind," the widow said, taking the basin and the bouquet. "You didn't have to do this. You knew we weren't as sorry as all that."

"We'll celebrate when we eat the peas." Kem-sit took the basin from her daughter-in-law and laid the flowers carefully atop the legumes. "Ta-em-resefu, my girl, they ask if Tjay was 'that bad.' Tell 'em what your life's been like." She reseated herself at the foot of her loom and began to push the shuttle through the warp.

Neferet noticed that both women were working with very fine bleached-linen thread, fashioning gauzy strips about as wide as a man's outstretched arms. Somebody was going to pay top price for this exquisite fabric.

"It's not like he hit me very often," the younger weaver said, her face bent over her loom, expressionless. "But I was like a prisoner. He controlled everything I did—what I wore, who I talked to. He was always belittling me, saying I was fat or ugly or a bad mother—after a while, a girl starts to believe it."

"Fortunately, he couldn't stop her from talking to me, not as long as his papa was alive," Kem-sit said. "She could see her sisters-in-law here sometimes. Of course, that infuriated Tjay, and he'd take it out on her and the girls. I never seen a sicker jealousy. He guarded her like that gaudy *weshket* collar he always went around flaunting. He said it was because he loved her, but love don't act like that." Kem-sit snorted in disgust. "I'm not sayin' Pa-shedu had no guilt in the raising of that piece of shit, but it was his mother that made him what he was."

"You knew her?" Bener-ib asked.

"Everybody knows everybody in a village this size. She was full of pretensions—gods know why. She wasn't no better than any of us. Made him a damned monster, thinkin' the whole world was here just to set him off to his finest. And her daughter's just the same. Usret practically burns incense to her big brother."

"What exactly did he do for Khnum-em-heb?" Neferet prompted.

"He kept the man's books for the weaving, like. And went around to pick up the piecework and keep everybody on schedule. Oh, he loved that, I'm sure." The dead man's stepmother gave a bitter baritone chuckle.

"That's why he didn't want me to work," said Ta-em-resefu. "He wanted to be above all that piecework business that's supervised. He fancied himself a superior, like the master and his son."

Neferet cocked her head in curiosity. "If the master has a son, how come *he* didn't do the supervising and bookkeeping? Sounds like our Tjay rather replaced him."

"Oh," Ta-em-resefu said casually, keeping her eyes lowered, "he isn't interested in the business. He wants to be a real scribe, not just a weaver's supervisor."

Neferet exchanged a glance of incomprehension with Bener-ib.

But Mut-tuy said sagely, "Not everybody wants to follow in their family profession, you know."

"So, Khnum-em-heb had Tjay trained to read and write? That was quite an honor." Neferet lifted her eyebrows, thinking of Maya, who was forever bound to her father by gratitude for much the same favor. Literacy was the ultimate gift. It lifted a man into the ruling class.

Kem-sit hooted rudely. "And don't think it didn't go to his head. He held his own father in contempt because *he* was so much better. After all, Pa-shedu was just a poor weaver, and *he* was literate. Even his master—rich maybe but not literate. I bet Khnum-em-heb rued the day he'd had that idea."

"It sounds as if any number of people might have been angry enough at him to hit him on the head. Maybe not even really trying to kill him, just pushed to lash out in a moment of frustration," said Neferet pensively.

"He was hit from behind, Nef'et," Bener-ib murmured reluctantly.

"Could Tjay and his murderer have fought?" Kem-sit sent her shuttle through in the other direction and beat the fine thread down tight.

But Neferet thought an accidentally fatal blow was unlikely. Someone had delivered a real whack to the man's skull. Someone had wanted badly to send Tjay posthaste into the afterlife. "Any chance Khnum-em-heb's son might have been jealous?"

"Oh, no," Ta-em-resefu said quickly. "He isn't that sort of person. And he didn't really want Tjay's job."

Kem-sit shot a penetrating glance at her daughter-in-law.

"Where is the son?" Neferet asked. "Does he live here or in Waset?"

"Waset." Ta-em-resefu dropped her eyes. "But he's not even here right now. His father was going to send him on a business trip to the northern capital."

"So he had something to do with the business after all." Mut-tuy's voice held a triumphant note.

The widow started to answer, but Kem-sit interrupted. "Ain't it about time you collected the children, Ta-em-resefu, my dear? You're going to have to tell them about their father." She got to her feet, and the younger woman hastily did the same. Neferet and her colleagues had no choice but to follow. It seemed their interview was over.

"Thank you for all your information," Neferet said earnestly to the mayor. "We may be back as we have other questions."

"How come you're so interested in this business? Tjay's own family don't care so much, except Usret." Kem-sit ushered them to the staircase. They thudded down in a rumble of bare footsteps. Ta-em-resefu, looking nervous, smiled and peeled off toward the gate before Neferet could even answer.

But something about the widow's manner made Neferet's ears prick up. She called after Ta-em-resefu, "When did Khnum-em-heb's son leave for Men-nefer, mistress?"

Ta-em-resefu quickened her pace, glancing over her shoulder with a frozen smile. "Oh, two or three days ago, my lady. At least three, surely."

The others stood at the foot of the stairs in silence as she hurried through the yard and away. *Something funny is going on here.* Neferet stared at the shadows where the young woman had passed a moment before. Eventually, she realized she still needed to answer Kem-sit's question.

"As I said earlier, we're *sunet*s," Neferet said. "We take care of people's bodies. But once they're dead, we can't just leave their souls floating around unavenged. We want *ma'at* to be done for every person we treat. And anyway, you people are our neighbors."

They were almost the subjects of Neferet's family, given the usual relationship between the peasantry and affluent landowners like Papa. But Papa, the least pretentious of men, had certainly never sought that role, nor was Kem-sit at all servile.

The older woman nodded, her eyes narrowed in thought. "I suppose it's my responsibility to deal with this, as mayor. And as family, of course, we'll pay for the embalmin'. Tell your father."

"I will, mistress. May the lord of the horizon give you a good afternoon."

The three made their hasty goodbyes, with Kem-sit appearing strangely pressed to be rid of them. As the young women tramped away from the village under the increasingly oblique rays of evening, Neferet said, "Did you notice what was going on? Ta-em-resefu seemed *very* eager to steer us away from the master's son as a suspect."

"I bet he did it," Mut-tuy said with conviction. "He supposedly left just about the time that Tjay was killed. Notice how she made it sound longer than the original two days."

"And Kem-sit suspects, doesn't she? She was open to our questions at first, but once Ta-em-resefu began to act strange, she started closing up too." Even Bener-ib was excited. "Is she trying to protect her daughter-in-law?"

"You're right, Ibet. Maybe it's Ta-em-resefu who did it! She certainly had provocation. Kem-sit may be afraid that we'll turn up evidence."

"But, Nef'et," said Bener-ib, stopping in her tracks.

"Who are we doing this for? It's Kem-sit's legal responsibility. If she doesn't want to pursue it..."

"Don't we want to see *ma'at* done?" cried Mut-tuy, as aggrieved as if someone had just taken her dinner away.

"I mean, let's say we find out who the killer is. Who do we tell if not Kem-sit?" Bener-ib was the most logical of women. Sometimes to the point of annoyance.

Neferet waved her hands helplessly. "Do we have to tell anyone? The Lady of Truth will know."

"She already knows," said Mut-tuy in automatic contrariety.

Neferet stared at her incredulously. "Which side are you on, my girl? Do you want to stop our investigation before we find the murderer?"

"No, I—"

"Then stop sounding like Papa."

Bener-ib hung her head. "I... I don't know, Nef'et. It just seems pushy to do this for our own pleasure."

Neferet grabbed her hands. "It's not for our pleasure, though. It's for the sake of *ma'at*. Even," she added in the interests of that *ma'at*, "if we do enjoy it. I mean, something doesn't have to be painful to be the right thing to do."

"All right. You know best." Bener-ib looked doubtful.

Neferet could see that the lady of her heart was less than enthusiastic, although she would have sworn that only a minute ago, the girl had been full of interest. Ibet was just too logical. It made her a good doctor but a reluctant investigator.

"Would it make you feel any better if Papa is favorable to our inquiry?"

"I guess so. He knows about such things," Bener-ib said.

But Mut-tuy looked up, her mouth open. "*Is* he favorable?"

"Of course," said Neferet, hooking Mut-tuy's eye with a meaningful stare. *He will be when I've talked to him.*

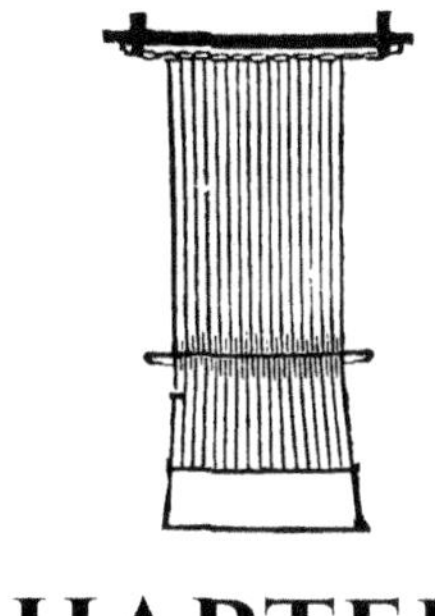

CHAPTER 4

HANI AWOKE REFRESHED FROM HIS nap to find that Nub-nefer had already slipped downstairs. He lay for a moment, enjoying the faint hot breeze tempered by the shade that danced across his pallet on the roof terrace. *Ah, the lazy afternoons of late summer*, he thought with a sense of delicious well-being. Tomorrow, he'd have to head back to the suffocating humidity of the city and the endless minor complaints of the northern vassals, but it was sweet, for the moment, to enjoy doing nothing in the country—here on the terrace where he'd passed so many luxurious siestas as a lad.

He heard a burst of youthful feminine laughter from the garden below. The girls were sitting outside the house, taking advantage of a quiet moment before the children awoke from their nap. It warmed his heart to see how the youngsters loved the farm. Too bad Father hadn't been able to join them this weekend, as he usually did—his lady friend was hosting a big party for her nephew, who had been promoted at the Double House. But the old walls were still bursting with the happy chatter of children and grandchildren, savoring the cooler air of the countryside. He heaved himself to his feet and stretched voluptuously, yawning with a roar.

From below, he heard Baket-iset say, "Papa's up."

He chuckled and stumped down the stairs, scratching his belly. In the shade of the arbor, Nub-nefer and her court of daughters and daughter-in-law were braiding tresses of onions to store. The orphan boys, under the eye of their nursemaid, played chariot battle under the palms across the yard. Three-year-old Tiry and Sati's youngest, Web-khet, stuck flowers over the ears of Brute, who sat with patient benevolence at Neferet's side. Around them, the cicadas roared in sleepy chorus.

"Guess what we found out this afternoon, Papa?" Neferet called.

Hani settled himself on the ground beside his wife, and the girl proceeded to tell him about their second visit to the village. "But just when Ta-em-resefu was starting to reveal something new, Kem-sit hustled her away. We're almost sure either she or the master's son committed the murder and Kem-sit is trying to protect them."

Hani made a noncommittal noise.

"We need to talk to Khnum-em-heb next," said Mut-tuy, a fierce light in her eyes.

It was unsettling how the sullen girl came alive on the trail of some wrongdoer. He wondered if tracking down a murderer helped assuage her sense of helplessness in the face of her own father's murder. Hani knew who had killed the goldsmith Ipy, but he could never reveal it, even to the victim's daughter—Lord Ay, the king's grandfather, was still alive and in power. The truth could carry a heavy price. Hani had told himself he would nag the girls no more, but anxiety sat heavily on his shoulders when he thought about the dangers their mania for investigation exposed them to.

He eyed the young orphan. She was barely thirteen. And tiny, fragile-looking Bener-ib didn't seem much older, although she was Neferet's age, twenty-four. Then there was his little duckling, a sturdy, energetic young woman but so much smaller than the rough and ruthless men she was likely to encounter while investigating a crime. And innocent. She'd grown up surrounded by goodness and love, and he wondered if she really grasped what malice was about. *All you Great Ones, look after these children.* I *certainly can't talk any sense into them.*

"I'm sure you'd agree we need to pursue this, Papa," said Neferet, staring at him in a meaningful way as if she could pressure him with a look to give her the answer she wanted. "It would be wrong to let a crime go undiscovered, wouldn't it? Even if the victim was mean and rotten—I mean, his *ba* would like nothing so much as to bang around, demanding justice and scaring people. We have to send him on to the Weighing of Souls and let the Lord of Judgment take care of him, don't we? Like you always say: 'Djehuty sits by the scales.'"

Nub-nefer flicked him a quick, knowing glance. Her lips were pressed together as if she, too, were trying to control the warnings of an anxious parent.

Hani said helplessly, "My duckling, you're adults. I can't tell you what to do."

Neferet shot a triumphant glance at her friend. "That's settled, then. Since Papa is in favor, we proceed."

Nub-nefer, who knew her daughter's powers of manipulation, smothered a snort of laughter. Hani could feel his face growing hot. Honest men didn't stand a chance against the wiles of girlish tyrants.

"What's for dinner tonight, my dove?" he asked his wife, transparently changing the subject.

She held up the braid of fat onions in her lap. "Lots of these. And rabbit."

Neferet nearly blew a laugh out her nose. "That sounds vewy dewicious." She was making a reference to her recent investigation into a crime involving a man nicknamed Rabbit, who had a speech impediment.

The clever little rascal. Hani's heart expanded with affection.

"But," she continued, rising, "I think we need to get back to the City. We have some interviews to carry out. Right, Ibet?"

Bener-ib and Mut-tuy surged dutifully to their feet.

"You're not even staying until the end of the weekly holiday?" Sati cried. "I think you're becoming obsessed with this silly hobby."

"We're just doing our duty as good subjects of the kingdom and devotees of the gods, my girl," her sister answered primly. Neferet, Bener-ib, and Mut-tuy trooped out, leaving the others staring at one another, nonplussed and, in some cases, annoyed.

"I've given up," Nub-nefer said. "Just as I've given up trying to get her to wear a wig."

"She's always got to be different, to draw attention to herself." Sati's face had grown crimson with pique. "She adopts all those orphans and then leaves them here all week while she goes off to Waset to play policeman."

Hani said mildly, "In all fairness, my swallow, the girls do have jobs. And it's better for the children to be here in the summer than cooped up in the city. That's why you've brought your own."

But Sati snorted. "Oh, Papa. She doesn't have to work, you know. Her husband is as rich as the king, almost. It's just another eccentricity."

Sat-hut-haru is pregnant, thought Hani tolerantly. *She's bothered by everything, which isn't her usual nature.*

As was so frequently the case, Baket-iset saved the good humor of the afternoon with a sweet smile. "Neferet is just Neferet. You don't have to worry about her. She'll do fine, and so will the orphans."

My little oracle. Hani gratefully squeezed her shoulder and got to his feet. "I'm going to find Maya. He must be up by now."

The following morning, while most of their neighbors were still asleep on the final day of their weekly holiday, Neferet gathered Bener-ib and Mut-tuy in the salon of the dispensary. The four dogs sprawled at their feet, panting and thumping an occasional tail in lazy pleasure at the mistresses' return. Cheetah lay curled up in Bener-ib's lap.

"We need to talk to Khnum-em-heb. He probably doesn't even know his supervisor is dead," Neferet said.

"Where does he live?" asked the logical Bener-ib.

"Let's check with our weaver neighbor. She may know."

"You mean the bodyguard Tut-em-heb's wife? Her name is Sit-hut-har-iunet. They call her Iunet."

Neferet stared at the lady of her heart in admiration. "How do you know all that?"

"I went back to their house a few times to see how their little girl's arm was doing."

Neferet beamed with pride. "You're such a good *sunet*, Ibet. I stand in awe."

Bener-ib dropped her head modestly. "You'd have done the same."

So that would be their first visit. Everybody among their working-class neighbors would be at leisure for a change. The three young women waited a little longer to give people a chance to wake up on one of their few days of repose then walked in a brisk body down to the corner of the block where the bodyguard and his weaver wife resided. The shrieks and laughter from behind the wall told them that the children, at least, were up and about.

Iunet opened the door at the first knock, her face brightening at the sight of the neighborhood healers. "My ladies, welcome. What can I do for you?"

Neferet launched straight in. "We have a question to ask you. I know you weave—do you happen to know a man named Khnum-em-heb? He has a weaving workshop and sends things out for piecework."

"Of course—I work for him. A lot of people do, here and in the country. He has a very big network."

Neferet grinned with delight. "What a coincidence!"

"Not really," Iunet said. "Almost every weaver in this quarter does piecework for him. His is one of the biggest workshops in Waset. What do you want to know about him?"

"Where does he live? His foreman has been killed, and we need to notify him."

The weaver's eyes grew round and—Neferet would have dared to say—delighted. "Master Tjay? Dead? Gods be praised!"

Neferet and Bener-ib exchanged looks. "That's what everybody has said. He must have been a real turd."

"Probably, he wasn't really evil. Just a pompous, hard-hearted son of a jackal. And always a little too familiar with the girls." But despite her virtuous attempt to give the Osir the benefit of the doubt, she looked as if she could have danced in relief. "Anybody Master Khnum-em-heb hires to replace him will be better."

"So where do we look for Khnum-em-heb?"

"I can take you to his workshop, but nobody'll be there today. I think he lives there, too, though, come to think of it." Iunet drew her oldest toward her. "Tell Papa I've taken the doctors to visit Khnum-em-heb and I'll be right back."

The four women set off cheerfully through the narrow streets toward the temple district and its weathered old neighborhoods. Although the heat was mounting fast, a faint early-morning coolness still lingered and a freshness full of promise—once the Inundation blessed the Black Land, summer was almost over. A striped cat rolling in the dust of the street stopped long enough to fix them with a curious eye.

They stopped finally at a modest walled workshop east of the temple of Mut. Iunet seemed suddenly shy and let

Neferet knock on the heavy gate. An elderly gatekeeper appeared, rubbing his eyes and yawning.

"Is your master up?" Neferet asked in an appropriately serious voice. "I have some news to give him about his foreman."

The gatekeeper melted silently back into the enclosure, leaving the young women standing in the street. A moment later, a short, well-upholstered man in middle age opened the gate once more. His curly graying hair stood out as if he had yet to run a comb through it, and his cleft chin was ill shaved.

He eyed them up and down apprehensively. "My name is Khnum-em-heb. You say you have some news of Tjay?"

"I'm Neferet daughter of Hani and Nub-nefer. Our family owns a farm next to the village where he lived. Yesterday, my father and some reed cutters found his body floating in the River. We got an identification from the mayor of the village and from Tjay's wife. I'm afraid he was murdered."

Neferet was braced to see the man burst out in joy, but he looked troubled. "That's inconvenient," he said with feeling. "My son is out of town. I'll have to find a replacement right away, or the business will stop." Then he roused himself from his preoccupations and gestured the women inside the gate. "Forgive my lack of courtesy. Please come in."

They followed the master of the house into a bleak work yard, where several looms were stretched out on the ground, unwarped, propped on big stones. Ahead of them, a low building with a large closed door suggested a studio of some sort. To the left, an unassuming two-story residence rose, with the fly mat hanging in the doorway.

Khnum-em-heb faced the four girls. "What happened to him?"

"He was either hit on the head from the rear hard enough to smash his skull, or he fell and knocked his head on something with a great deal of force," Neferet said. "My colleagues and I are *sunet*s, and our professional opinion is that he was murdered, though."

Khnum-em-heb nodded sorrowfully. "I guess that shouldn't surprise me. He seemed to make a lot of enemies."

"We've heard the same thing from everybody, including his wife and his stepmother."

"He was… abrasive. But good at what he did. Tjay had a way with the books. He kept everything perfectly, down to the least little transaction. If only my son were interested in bookkeeping."

"Your son is literate too?" It occurred to Neferet that this was the son the widow had started to defend. Another suspect. "Tjay's wife said he didn't seem to have anything to do with your business."

"True. Tjay was the son of a couple of my piecework weavers. He was smart and about the same age as Hapu-seneb. I had both of them trained together at the House of Life, but Hapu-seneb has never been interested in commerce. He wants to be a literary scribe, an archivist, a… a poet. I don't know what fantastical thing he wants, frankly. But it doesn't have anything to do with helping his father. When I die, I guess my widow will have to sell the workshop." His voice shook with the intensity of his disappointment. "Oh, I make him work for me, but his heart isn't in it. It's because he doesn't have a family to support. Otherwise, he'd hustle a little harder. Can you imagine? He's thirty-two and still unmarried. No sense of grown-up responsibility. Just a big, dreamy child. I sent him off to Men-nefer to negotiate an order because I had to—Tjay couldn't be everywhere at once."

"When did he leave for Men-nefer?" asked Bener-ib.

"Two days ago. What day does that make it? He won't even have gotten there yet. I don't know whether to call him back or just find somebody else to take over from Tjay." Khnum-em-heb scrubbed his face wearily with his hands.

I ruined his weekend, Neferet told herself with regret.

"I've put all my hopes in Tjay. Overlooked his faults. Treated him like the son my own son refuses to be. And now..." The weaver heaved a great sigh. "Our lives are in the hands of the gods. What about the body? Is it still at your farm? Did his family take it?"

"The priests of Inpu have it. My father was going to pay for him to be embalmed, but Tjay's stepmother said the family would take charge of that. Talk to her if you want to be part of it."

"Ah, Kem-sit. She's a good woman. One of the best. I'll offer my condolences. I can help them with the funeral."

"Forgive me asking," said Bener-ib tentatively, "but why isn't your son interested in getting married? Is it possible he, er, doesn't like women?"

Khnum-em-heb was quick to reply. "No, no. Nothing like that. He says the girl he's set his heart on isn't available—I take that to mean she's married. And he swears he won't wed anybody if it's not her. You see what kind of childish nonsense the boy indulges in."

Bener-ib nodded, expressionless.

She's got something in mind, Neferet thought. "Well, we're sorry to be bringers of bad news. We'll leave you to your morning," she said brightly. "Iunet, here, is one of your piecework weavers. If you have any questions, get word to us through her."

The man thanked them for bringing him word of his employee's death and shut the heavy gate behind them. They stood for a moment in the street. Neferet was itching to ask Bener-ib what she was thinking, but there was no need to involve Iunet. So they walked slowly back to their neighborhood, each lost in thought, and left the weaver at her gate.

Once alone, Neferet burst out, "Why did you ask about his son's interest in women, Ibet? You're onto something, aren't you?"

"I think he and Ta-em-resefu are lovers. Remember how she started to defend him until Kem-sit steered her away?"

All at once, the obvious signs began to make sense. "Of course!" Neferet cried in delight. "You're brilliant, my girl! And that means they both had a strong motive to kill Tjay. They could never be married until he was out of the way. Why, this must have gone on for years!"

Mut-tuy's expression, usually one of disinterest, had caught fire. She added breathlessly, "Did you notice? Hapu-seneb left for Men-nefer two days ago, not three like Ta-em-resefu said. He would still have been around when Tjay was killed, and then he took off right afterward. I'll bet anything it was him."

Neferet's heart did a little jig of excitement. Things were starting to move along nicely.

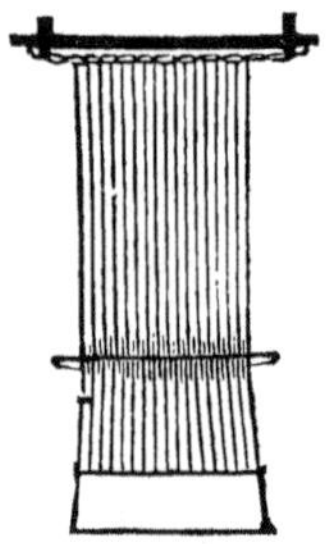

CHAPTER 5

"I THINK WE NEED TO TALK to Ta-em-resefu again. Or somebody who would know about her. I wonder who the village gossip is. Surely, if Ta-em-resefu's involved with the master's son, there will be people who've noticed." Neferet pushed open the gate of the dispensary, and she and her companions trooped in. The old dogs greeted them joyously, while Brute, who hadn't been invited on their morning's mission, maintained a discreet professional distance. The guard looked up from his seat in the shady yard, where he was whittling something, and when he saw it was the doctors, he settled back onto his haunches.

"But we can't leave our practice during the week. It will have to wait until next end-of-week holiday," said Bener-ib, ever logical.

Neferet felt a surge of stubbornness. "That's too long. They could have coordinated their stories by then. We need to investigate this right away."

"You go, then, Nef'et. I'll take care of patients. You can certainly go and come back in a day."

Bener-ib had selflessly made just the offer Neferet had hoped for. Neferet squeezed her hand. "Thanks, my Sweet Heart. I'll be back by evening if all goes as planned. Muttuy, stay here to give—"

"No," said the adolescent. "I want to go too."

"You aren't much of an apprentice, my girl," Neferet said sourly. "All right. But we need to get moving. There's no point in heading all the way back to Lord Ptah-mes's house to get the smaller yacht. Let's just grab a public ferry."

The two of them set off at a brisk pace through the streets. Bener-ib waved from the gateway, with Mangler, Faithful, and Hedgehog circulating at her feet. Brute hesitated then came trotting after Neferet.

"You want an adventure, do you, big fellow?" the girl said, scratching his wrinkly forehead as she walked. "You can protect us, then, if the village gossip gets too aggressive."

Their two sets of feet slapped rhythmically on the earthen lane, accompanied by Brute's panting. The embarcadero was quiet. The usual commercial traffic was stilled, and only family outings seemed to be afloat. They easily found a small sailboat for hire and directed the young boatman downriver, and in not much more than an hour, they were tying up at the landing of the farm. One of Papa's little reed crafts was pulled up on the bank, and the doors of the boathouse were open.

"Anybody in there?" Neferet called.

Grandfather stuck his head out the door of the cabin. "Why, Neferet, my girl. What are you doing here? Nub-nefer said you had left yesterday evening. Where's Bener-ib?"

"She's at the dispensary—somebody had to take care of patients, and like the perfect woman she is, she volunteered.

We missed you over the weekend." She paid the boatman and scrambled up the bank to where Grandfather stood in the doorway of the boathouse. There she hugged him exuberantly. "We had gone back to the city, but then I realized we had some things to ask back in the village. Did Mama tell you about our murder case?"

Grandfather waggled his eyebrows. "Well, she didn't call it that. She said your father had found a dead man among the reeds and you'd gone with him to the village to identify him."

"He was murdered. And we think we know who did it. Right, Mut-tuy?" Neferet said smugly.

"Right," the orphan confirmed with a forceful bob of the head.

"I was going to clean up the boathouse, but it can wait. I'll walk back to the house with you." Grandfather closed the door and propped it shut with a rock. "Tell me what's going on with this murder."

"We're going to go to the village first, though, Grandfather. We'll say hello to everybody afterward and then head back to the city right after lunch."

"I'll go with you, if youth and beauty will make room for gray hairs and wisdom."

"We can always use a little more wisdom." Neferet linked her arm through her grandfather's, and the three of them set off down the path toward the village.

They slowed their pace to accommodate Grandfather's puffing, blowing progress, and it was nearly midday when they arrived. The settlement was quiet. *Everyone is probably preparing for lunch—maybe the one nice meal they get all week*. But Neferet's target was more affluent. No doubt Ta-em-resefu had servants to help her.

With Brute trotting at her heels, she led the way to the ostentatiously whitewashed house at the end of the village, where a cacophony of honking geese sounded from inside the wall. Neferet knocked.

Grandfather gazed around him as they waited, his hands on his hips. "Been a while since I was in this village. The mayor was a weaver named Pa-shedu."

"He's dead now. It's his wife who's the mayor."

"Woman mayor, eh? That's unusual."

"Apparently, there was a bit of a civil war after Pa-shedu died. His son and his—"

But the gate opened before Neferet could finish, and a dull-eyed young woman, her hair tousled and dusty, said, "The mistress is at table. Can I take a message?"

At least they're observing some semblance of mourning. "Tell her it's Neferet, please. From Lord Hani's farm."

After a moment, Ta-em-resefu herself stood in the doorway. She'd strewn some decent dust on her head, but there were certainly no tear-stained eyes or clawed cheeks in evidence. "My lady, how can I help you?" she cried, her expression both glad and uneasy.

"This is my grandfather, Lord Mery-Ra." Neferet indicated Grandfather with a gesture.

The woman bowed. "My grandparents have spoken of you, my lord. Your generosity is legendary around here."

Neferet stared at Grandfather in surprise. He grinned and blushed and caught her eye with a twinkle as if to say, "I'll tell you about that later."

"Ta-em-resefu, I have a few questions I'd like to ask

you. I, er, I've spoken to Khnum-em-heb, and he said his son and you were in love."

The young widow's face went chalky pale. She clutched at her throat and stared at Neferet with stunned eyes. "He knows? Oh, dear gods. He'll fire me for sure."

Neferet had exaggerated the information Khnum-em-heb had given her in order to flush the woman out, but she felt suddenly that perhaps she'd overdone it. "Well, he didn't use your name. Is it true, though? You're the one?"

Ta-em-resefu hung her head. "I know he's above me socially, but you don't pick the person you fall in love with. And I don't think I could have survived all those years with Tjay if I hadn't had somebody who really loved me." Her voice had grown thready with tears.

Neferet put a compassionate arm around her. She knew what it was like to love someone society said you couldn't have. "But it doesn't matter anymore, does it? Because you're a widow now, and you can marry anybody you want!"

"Yes!" The weaver's tear-sparkled eyes grew brighter. "The Great Ones have heard our prayers. I just hope..." She trailed off, and her face fell from joy back into anxiety. She gnawed at her lip.

"What, my girl?" prompted Grandfather.

"I just hope Hapu-seneb had nothing to do with Tjay's death, is all," Ta-em-resefu murmured, her brow puckered with fear. "I mean, I don't think he did. He wouldn't. He's a good man. A gentle man. It's just—he disappeared about then, and I—"

"His father sent him to Men-nefer, remember?" Neferet assured her. "He doesn't even know about the death yet, I'm sure."

"Did Khnum-em-heb really send him away because he wanted to keep him away from this lady?" asked Mut-tuy.

Neferet shot her a fierce look. *Quiet, you puppy—he doesn't actually know about her.* She turned back to the weaver. "Don't worry about anything. It's all in the gods' hands. And so what if he fires you? You won't need to work anymore, anyway, once you and Hapu-seneb marry."

"That relieves me so much. Thank you, my lady." The weaver gave a nervous little laugh. "Because I can hardly settle down to the loom, I'm so excited. I just want to run around and talk to friends—except I hardly have any anymore, after Tjay cut me off from them all for so many years."

"Why don't you come to Waset and visit us?" suggested Neferet kindly. "Bring the children. They can play with ours. And one of your colleagues who works for Khnum-em-heb lives on our block. Do you know someone named Iunet? She's about our age. You'll like her."

Ta-em-resefu's pretty face grew more and more eager until she was all lit up with hope and anticipation. "Oh, that would be wonderful! How can I thank you? I feel I just want to get out of the house. It's been like a prison. If it weren't for Hapu-seneb and Kem-sit, I don't know what I would have done for these seven years."

"Things will change now—you'll see." Neferet beamed. "You can go anywhere you want and meet all the people you like."

"If only Hapu-seneb were here. I want to share this moment with him."

"He'll be back in a couple of weeks, surely. Then you'll have the rest of your lives to share."

The weaver broke out into a laugh of delight that sat strangely with her conventional signs of mourning. "How can I thank you, my lady? Your family is full of goodness." She cast shy eyes at Grandfather.

"Well, we'll be going now." Neferet hugged Ta-em-resefu in sisterly solidarity. "I meant it about visiting us. We're in the dispensary every day."

She gave the other woman directions for finding their clinic in Waset. Then they extracted themselves from the widow's goodbyes and set off back up the lane of the village.

Grandfather, who had listened in silence, finally said, "What if she or her lover is the murderer?"

"Or both of them?" added Mut-tuy.

Neferet was silent for the space of several footsteps. *What if?* It was almost a certainty. She decided some things were more important than strict justice. "Tjay deserved to die. I, for one, am discontinuing this investigation. If the lovers are guilty, I don't want to know about it."

Grandfather blew an appraising whistle, but he didn't say "Good for you." "Your mother and father will be relieved."

Neferet decided to change the subject before she was called upon to give a rationale for her decision. "What is it you did that made the villagers so grateful, Grandfather?"

"Oh, I had a well dug when their old one ran dry. That was a long time ago." The old man tried not to look too proud of himself. "That sort of thing was considered the duty of the local landowner back then. No particular virtue on my part."

But Neferet slipped her arm through his and gave it a

squeeze. "You see how a kindness is rewarded? They still remember you fondly."

"Hani would have a maxim about that, I suppose," said Grandfather with a grin. "Set your goodness before the people. Then will you be greeted by all."

"Did Papa say that? Maya made me memorize ten thousand of his maxims when he took over my scribal training from you."

Grandfather chuckled. "I think he said it—or else it's something I used to tell him when he was a boy. Even Hani can't remember everything he's written."

"Weren't we going to visit the sister? To tell her details about Tjay's death?" Mut-tuy said.

"Oh. I guess we should if she wants to hear." Neferet found herself reluctant to confront the woman again, but it did seem to be the decent thing to do.

She headed toward the riverbank, where the reed boat still lay upside down, propped on a pile of bricks. The bald man had by now assembled a massive pile of fresh reeds and was in the process of constructing another boat under the gaze of two small boys. He barely looked up as the young women approached his door. Neferet knocked, and almost before the sound had died away, Usret stood in the opening, wiping a hand on her skirts. She had a mourning scarf tied around her disheveled curls.

"Good morning, mistress. I don't know if you remember me, but I'm Neferet, of the family that found the body of your brother. I wondered if there was anything you wanted to know about... you know." She found herself uncomfortable in this woman's presence, although she couldn't have said why.

Usret forced a mournful smile. Her eyes were red but strangely untouched by either mourning or smile. "That's so kind of you, my lady. Kem-sit said how nice you've been to her and Ta-em-resefu. She's told me everything." Her voice began to tremble. "So unless there's something new, I guess not." She put her face in her hands briefly then lifted it as if trying to be brave. "But I have something to tell you."

Neferet exchanged an excited glance with Mut-tuy. *Is it possible Usret has a clue about the killer?*

"Nobody else may say this, but I want you to hear it. Tjay wasn't the mean person everybody has probably told you, especially Ta-em-resefu. I mean, she's a nice girl, but she really wasn't the right wife for Tjay, and so they never got along. Tjay was a noble soul, my lady. He was so much above the rest of us here in this village that people didn't understand him. He was refined, sensitive. I grew up with him, and I can tell you he was a special man. A soul among ten thousand. The gods have seen fit to take him from us, and a light has gone out of our lives. They'll find out how much they miss him now, you'll see—all those people who didn't like him." Tears were dribbling down her fleshless cheeks, but she didn't wipe them. Her voice had grown exalted as if she were speaking of a god—as if she were mourning the Lord Osir on his feast day.

Neferet said kindly, "That's good to know. I'm sure you'll see to his funeral, right? My father will tell you when the embalming is done."

"That's so generous of you." Usret's shoulders shook with tears, but her lips were smiling.

It seemed like a good moment to escape. Neferet

murmured words of condolence, and the three took their leave. She felt a lively sense of relief as they drew away from the River and into the shade of the village trees.

"So, who's telling the truth about him?" Mut-tuy asked as they walked past the mayor's house. The donkey watched them pass with its melancholy, submissive eyes.

Grandfather said mildly, "Both, I suppose. He must have shown his sister a different face than he showed his wife. Nobody's all good or all bad."

"No, but Usret's almost idolatrous. I find something strange about her."

Grandfather shrugged. "She seems to want to give you what you want. I've met people like that."

"What do you mean, Grandfather?"

The old man stroked his chin as though the gesture might help him find the right words. "Some people don't seem to know by instinct how to feel about things the way most of us do, my girl. They try to learn by watching those around them. But in the end, their emotions always seem a little overdone, a little fake. I don't think they really are fake, just inexpert. And they're never sure they've done it right, so they watch to see how you react. Does that make any sense?"

Neferet nodded pensively. Perhaps that was why she'd felt so uncomfortable with Usret's demonstrations of grief. *Grandfather's not stupid. We don't give old people enough credit.*

They continued up the path until the village fell behind them, and their steps took them through the fields, most still shimmering with the water of life deposited by the recent Inundation. A few workmen, tiny figures under a molten sun, were repairing the floodgates of an irrigation channel in the distance.

"Tomorrow's a holiday," said Grandfather. "The Cloth Festival. Time to roll out the banners and hang them off the roof."

"Another holiday? It's a long weekend, then. We needn't have rushed back to the city."

"But you're here. Why don't you just stay?" Grandfather asked.

"Ibet's not here."

If they'd still been investigating their murder case, Neferet would have sent a message and, in fact, remained at the farm. But there was no point now. They would pass a quiet holiday at home. Neferet's husband, Lord Ptah-mes, might or might not be with his children. If not, it would be a nice gesture to eat with him. The truth was, Neferet was a bit put out with Sati and didn't relish a whole day spent under the hail of her complaints. Things would be better after the baby was born.

But Sati was in her normal sunny mood again, and Neferet and Mut-tuy lingered over lunch with the greatest of pleasure. The cowpeas they'd helped to shell were certainly worth the work. Mama had directed the kitchen servants to prepare them with onions and garlic and a bit of tasty pork fat, and they were more delicious than anything the king ever ate, Neferet was sure.

It was late in the afternoon when the two girls and Brute finally entered the gate of the dispensary. Bener-ib greeted them from the doorway, just as they had left her, with the oldsters swirling at her feet.

"Did you find out anything?" she said.

"I'll say. Ta-em-resefu admitted to being the lover of that Hapu-seneb. She half suspects he may have killed Tjay but doesn't want to acknowledge it even to herself. I, uh, I think we should abandon the case."

"Without finding the murderer?" Bener-ib asked in surprise.

"We probably know who he is, don't we? And I don't want to have to decide what to do with that fact. In the eyes of Ma'at, he's done the world a favor."

Bener-ib, who was always quick to grasp such moral subtleties, nodded. "You did the right thing, Nef'et. We have nothing but suspicions, and it's none of our business anyway." She stepped back from the threshold to let them pass inside. "Have you had lunch?"

"We ate at the farm. I invited Ta-em-resefu and her children to come see us. She's all itchy to get out of the house where that awful Tjay almost imprisoned her."

"But what if it's *not* Hapu-seneb or Ta-em-resefu who did it?" Mut-tuy objected.

Neferet shot her a glance of annoyance. "You were just arguing that it *was* them. Who else would it be? They had a very strong motive."

"I don't know who, but it could be anybody. It could be Khnum-em-heb. He'd given Tjay all the favors of a real son, then he started seeing what an unworthy dog turd he was."

Neferet cast her eyes to heaven.

"Or Kem-sit. Tjay had become an unbearable pest. And

maybe he was bitter after he lost the mayor's race, and she was afraid he—"

"We'll never know, will we? Because we aren't going to investigate." *Really, the girl's impossible. She'd attack her own statement just to get an argument going.*

Mercifully, a knock sounded at the gate, and Bener-ib flew to answer it. At the door stood Papa and a man with long hair and a colorful kilt that came to the middle of his thighs, bound at the waist with a wide belt. On his feet were the cutest short boots, laced tight around the ankles. One of Papa's foreigners.

"Good morning, girls. I present to you my guest, Dapurazo. He's here from Keftiu as an agent for his king, who's interested in importing fine Egyptian linen and even bringing in workers who can produce it in his country."

The man bowed. He was in his thirties, Neferet judged, and clean-shaven, with pleasant, strong features and wavy dark hair as long as a woman's. His humorous, twinkling eyes the color of marsh water were what pleased her best.

"Come in, my lord," she said, smiling. "We have nothing to do with weaving, I'm afraid, but any friend of Papa's is a friend of ours." Then it occurred to her that he might not understand what she was saying. She caught Papa's eye. "Does he speak Egyptian?"

"I do," said Dapurazo, baring his teeth in a mischievous grin. "Although I sometimes pretend not to because I hear more interesting things that way."

She led the two men into the salon, where they seated themselves on the stools and beds.

"I've told him about your medical practice," Papa said. "But it occurred to me you also seemed to know something about the weaving networks here in the city. You mentioned someone who had a lot of piecework weavers, remember? Only I couldn't recall his name."

"*Iyah*, of course. Khnum-em-heb. They say he has one of the biggest businesses in Waset. We can take you to his house if you want."

"That would be wonderful," the man of Keftiu said gratefully. "Needless to say, your king has given his blessing to this. Thanks to Lord Hani, I have all the documents this fellow might want to see." Despite his accent, Dapurazo spoke excellent Egyptian. He reminded Neferet of some of the Hittites Papa had hosted over the years.

"Do you want to go right now? Everything will be closed tomorrow," Neferet said.

Papa winked. "I was hoping you'd say that."

"The others can stay and man the infirmary," she said with a pointed stare at Mut-tuy.

The girl was gazing with a moony expression at the handsome foreigner and trying to comb her chopped hair into some order with her fingers. *Gods preserve us from thirteen-year-olds.* Usually, it was Lord Ptah-mes's good-looking son who seemed to hypnotize the orphan. *Was I ever that way as a girl?* But Neferet had met the woman of her heart at thirteen, and that had been that.

It was Papa's official duties that called her away, and even Mut-tuy could find no excuse to tag along, so Neferet and the two men set off down the street toward the neighborhood where Khnum-em-heb lived and worked.

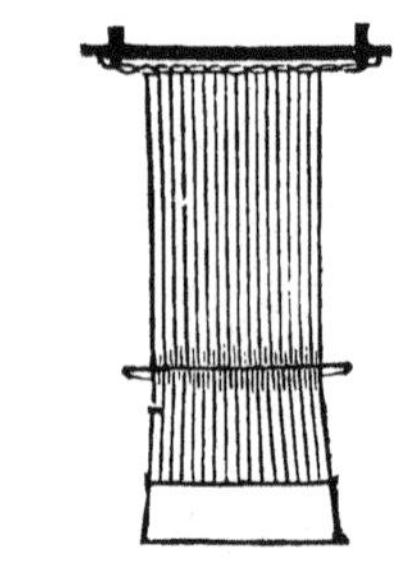

CHAPTER 6

"I KNOW KHNUM-EM-HEB'S PEOPLE PRODUCE VERY fine, gauzy linen," Neferet said enthusiastically as they walked along the lane, "because I've seen it on the looms. Two of the pieceworkers in our village make it."

"That sounds promising. I'd be glad to have a woman's evaluation of the fabric," the man of Keftiu said with a nod.

Excellent. He's a civilized foreigner. There are some who wouldn't give a rotten fig for a woman's opinion on anything.

Papa said nothing, just beamed benevolently. He could probably guess what she was thinking, however—and was no doubt relieved that she didn't say anything. He always seemed surprised that she'd actually learned to weigh her words, as if a person didn't mature with age.

Just to let him know she was onto him, she said, "I could say more about some people who *don't* care about a woman's opinions. But I won't."

Papa's smile curled up to his ears, and he lowered his eyes so he didn't have to face her. Dapurazo seemed not to have heard anything tactless and strode along contentedly in his cute boots. The closer to the River they drew, the more oppressive the humidity became, and it was with a sense of relief that they reached the gate of the weaver's workshop. Neferet hammered on it with the heel of her hand.

An elderly man appeared. "Shop's closed this afternoon. Come back after the festival."

"Already? That's not until tomorrow," Neferet protested.

Papa stepped forward and said in his most persuasive and authoritative voice, "I'm Lord Hani of the foreign office. I have here a representative of the king of Keftiu, who may be interested in placing a substantial order with your master. I think Khnum-em-heb might be very displeased if you didn't let us in, my man."

The old man backed up hastily and admitted the threesome to the bleak court. "Wait here, my lords. I'll see if the master is available." He scuttled off into the house.

"I don't know how we ever get anything done in this country," Neferet said, shaking her head. "We never seem to work."

"And yet your accomplishments are known throughout the earth," the foreigner said gallantly.

A brief moment later, Khnum-em-heb burst into the court, still wiping his hands on a towel as if he'd just popped up from his table, despite the late-afternoon hour. "Forgive my servant, my lords. He's a little protective. Tomorrow is the Cloth Festival, you know, and our guild always has duties to prepare for it. How may I help you?"

He was all complaisant smiles and nods—the words "substantial order" had certainly been the magic formula. Papa summarized the situation and its business potential, and the weaver listened with growing interest. He and Dapurazo discussed bast fibers and weft and hand and pick and sleying until Neferet felt her eyes were spinning.

"Would you like to see our big vertical looms, my lord?" he finally said. "No one is at work at the moment. We use these for coarser textiles, mostly, like sailcloth or sheeting. The gauze is produced by women doing piecework on our traditional ground looms." Khnum-em-heb led the visitors toward the door of his workshop. He was as eager as a child with a new toy.

Inside the vast barnlike studio, lit with a twilight uniformity by high windows in every direction, five towering looms were propped against the wall. They were as wide as a man was tall, their warp held taut by a row of small weights dangling at the bottom. The fabric was forming at the top of the web, where it had been rolled backward to clear the warp for more work. Shuttles wound full of thread had been tucked between the strings, awaiting the next work session. Neferet thought the looms had the look of some strange musical instruments—cloth-harps, she decided to call them. Into others of the walls were driven odd configurations of heavy pegs, some already wound in labyrinthine patterns of linen thread.

"As you see, we warp the thread here too," explained the weaver proudly.

"These look like our looms," Dapurazo said in approval.

"They're copied after the looms of Kharu and Djahy. Men work them, often in pairs to permit a wider weft. If you want to see gauze, the best pieces are in a village not far from here. We have women on traditional looms make it because their fingers are finer passing through the shed, and they can control the tension by hand."

"This is beautiful stuff," the man of Keftiu said, stroking the forming cloth with a finger. "But it's really the gauze I'm thinking about. I would even be interested in hiring some of your women to teach my workers how to weave it."

"I'm sure we could arrange something." Khnum-em-heb was almost comically enthusiastic. Neferet expected him to rub his hands together in the universal gesture of greed. "But it's rather late to go to the village at this hour..."

Papa said, "In fact, we had intended to go down to my farm this evening and pass the holidays with my family. It's right next to the village—only about an hour away from here. There's plenty of daylight, if you wouldn't be too inconvenienced."

"That should be feasible," the weaver said. "Give me a few minutes, and we can grab a ferry."

"I have a boat at the quays. If you'd like to spend the night at our farm, you're more than welcome. That would take the pressure off you to get back before dark."

"That's most generous, Lord Hani. Let me notify my wife that I'll be back tomorrow morning, and I'm all yours."

He returned shortly with a small wicker toilet chest under his arm, beaming widely, and with a fraternal slap on the back of the foreigner, he inserted himself between Papa and Dapurazo. The men set off toward the River three abreast, with Neferet trailing them. She wasn't sure whether she needed to accompany them to the farm or not, but she wanted Khnum-em-heb to realize it was through her that this opportunity had come to him. Besides, although she'd backed off from investigating the murder of Tjay, a teeny-tiny part of her was still curious. Khnum-em-heb might reveal something that would confirm her suspicions. But it would die there, she swore. She would tell no one except Ibet.

At the quay, she found a boy who was hanging around, hoping for a commission, and she paid him to take a message to Bener-ib: "Going to the farm with Papa. Back tomorrow morning." Mut-tuy's nose would be out of joint, but too bad. The girl was getting way above her place. On further thought, she directed the lad to Lord Ptah-mes's house afterward with the same message.

In front of her, the weaver was saying in a loud, jovial voice, "Normally, I'd have my own boat here, but my son took it to Men-nefer. I sent him to conclude a big order in the northern capital. We do business all over the country and even beyond."

"Master Khnum-em-heb," she said to his back, "you'll have to get him more involved in the business now, won't you? With all the new engagements and all."

He half looked at her over his shoulder, but his words seemed to be aimed at the men at his side. "That's right. Do him good. And I'll hire another agent. Our young foreman just died," he explained to Dapurazo. "But don't worry. It won't slow us down."

They made their way up the gangplank of Papa's small yacht. It was a cheerful little vessel painted in red and green, with an impish, grinning head of the god Bes at the prow. Papa had bought it from Uncle Pipi, who'd impulsively put a down payment on the boat without being able to finish paying for it. It was nothing like the luxurious boats of Lord Ptah-mes, one of the richest men in the kingdom, but

Neferet rather preferred it. It had personality—and a saucy one, at that. The crew busied themselves hauling in the stone anchors and pushed away from the River's edge into a swirl of water as green as bloodstone.

She stood at the gunwales, leaning her elbows on the wicker barrier, while the three men gathered not far away, chattering on about weaving. *This could get boring*, she thought, stifling a yawn. Suddenly, Khnum-em-heb broke off in midsentence and stared across the water toward the shore.

"What is it?" Papa asked.

"I would swear that's my boat anchored there." The weaver pointed at a modest yacht disappearing behind them in the forest of masts and sails clustered along the embarcadero. "But obviously, it can't be. I guess someone else has one just like it. That's annoying." He gave a bark of laughter that sounded more irritated than amused. Neferet noticed that his gaze remained fixed on the boat until they'd pulled out of view, and even then, with his eyes narrowed in thought, he continued to stare.

He probably paid for a unique paint job, Neferet thought with a mental snort.

The River was still running high, and the distance downriver was devoured in less time than usual. Already, the afternoon shadows were long, and there wouldn't be many hours left to meet with the pieceworkers in the village before dinnertime. They anchored directly at the village, among the little fishing boats and reed crafts drawn up on the shore, and while the sailors settled down on the deck to wait, the party trudged through the cicada-filled evening toward the mayor's house.

Kem-sit appeared at the doorway, looking surprised and a bit suspicious. Her eyes darted from face to face. "Master Khnum-em-heb. Lord Hani. Lady Neferet. How can I help you?"

"Don't worry. It's something good, Kem-sit," Neferet reassured her in an undertone before the men could speak.

Khnum-em-heb explained that their distinguished foreign visitor wanted to see the gauze being woven, and Kem-sit led the way back out of the house and up the stairs to the roof terrace in a clumping procession. The two looms were still stretched out side by side. Ta-em-resefu was talking to her three little girls, who stood around where she sat on her heels beside her web.

When the visitors entered, she looked up then scrambled to her feet, her eyes wide with fear. "Master Khnum-em-heb."

She thinks he's here to berate her for her affair with his son, Neferet thought with a guilty pang that flushed her face with heat. She wished she could take back her deception.

"First, my condolences on the loss of your husband, mistress," Khnum-em-heb said in a voice throbbing with compassion, which Neferet would have sworn was sincere. Then he turned to the others. "Her husband was my foreman and bookkeeper. A most valuable man."

He went on to describe once more why they were there. The two women stepped back and let their visitors inspect the growing expanses of diaphanous gauze stretched upon their looms. Dapurazo seemed fascinated. He fingered the warp threads and touched the delicate finished fabric with a respect bordering on awe. Ta-em-resefu watched him with the wary attention of a half-tamed animal approached by a harmless-seeming human.

Dapurazo looked up and caught her eye. His expression was full of admiration. "You women are real craftsmen. Do you think you could train some of my people to produce such work?"

Ta-em-resefu glanced uncertainly at her mother-in-law, who said in her mannish voice, "I don't see why not, my lord. If Master Khnum-em-heb is agreed."

"He's more than agreed, because Lord Dapurazo is also going to order a shipload of this beautiful product for his king. Am I right, my lord?" Khnum-em-heb beamed at the foreigner, who gave a little nod but directed the gesture at Ta-em-resefu.

"You'll need to train spinners, too, master," Kem-sit said. "Everybody can spin, but something this thin isn't easy."

"Absolutely right, my good woman. We'll calculate all that in the final price, right, Lord Dapurazo?"

He's as excited as a child with a big sesame treat in his hand. Neferet almost snickered. She rather liked the weaver for his enthusiasm, even if it was oriented toward silver.

After a few more moments spent watching and admiring, Papa shepherded the men outside with Neferet at their heels. She whispered to the two women as she departed, "I meant it when I said to come for a visit." With a conspiratorial wiggle of her fingers, she slipped through the doorway and out into the road with the others.

A dim shade had settled under the palm trees. The geese had waddled off, and only the donkey still stood patiently hobbled, switching his tail. A fisherman plodded up the bank from the River, a basket of eels on his back. He eyed the strangers curiously as he passed.

Leaning toward Neferet, Lord Dapurazo said quietly with a charming smile, "And what is the woman's opinion of that fabric? Would you wear it?"

Neferet tried without success to picture herself swanning about in a voluminous sheer caftan such as the rich ladies of the day affected. "Oh, *definitely*, my lord."

"It's a short walk to the farm from here," Papa told his guests. "We probably have an hour left of daylight. Shall we get underway?"

"You know," said Khnum-em-heb, "since I can do it before darkness falls, I think I'll just head on back to the city. Could your men possibly take me home, Lord Hani?"

"Of course, my friend." Papa seemed a little surprised that anybody wouldn't prefer to stay at the farm.

It struck Neferet that this might be a chance to ingratiate herself with Khnum-em-heb if she should ever decide to return to the murder case—if the culprit should somehow turn out not to be one of the finally liberated lovers. Because of course, no matter what she had told herself, she was still curious.

"I think I'll go back too," she said.

"Very well. The crew knows you, my duckling. They'll take orders from you, so I'll say goodbye here." Papa clasped forearms with Khnum-em-heb in his friendly way and kissed Neferet.

With a wave, the two passengers strode down to the River's edge, where the yacht lay bobbing on the quiet, darkening waters. At the top of the slope, Papa and Lord Dapurazo turned in the other direction and disappeared into the village. Neferet hailed the sailors, and they stretched out the gangplank. She and Khnum-em-heb climbed up and onto the deck. The weaver could hardly keep a grin from breaking out on his face. Neferet heard him humming a happy little tune under his breath.

"It turned out to be a profitable day for you, eh, master?" she said with an innocent smile.

"What? Oh yes, my lady. And I thank you for any role you played in directing the foreign gentleman my way."

"Skill should be rewarded. I hope Mistress Kem-sit and Mistress Ta-em-resefu will do well in the deal too."

"Definitely. Definitely." Khnum-em-heb's beatific expression sobered. "Not that it makes up for the loss of her husband, but at least something nice has happened to the poor woman." He heaved a sigh. "As for me, I'll have to find another foreman and bookkeeper—and fast. If you know of anyone, tell them I'm looking."

"I will—I swear by my mother's *ka*. We see a lot of patients in the course of the day, and you never know when an unemployed scribe will come by."

"Patients?"

Neferet smiled smugly. "Yes. My partner and I are *sunet*s. We're literate, but we've chosen to take care of the people of our neighborhood, including your weaver Iunet."

"Well, well. Women mayors, women physicians—what next? And why not, after all? I'll send any of my people down there who might need treating. Weaving's not all that dangerous, but I've heard the ground loom is hard on the back."

She snorted. "And I guess you could drop the weights on your foot if you're using the cloth harp."

He looked confused for an instant and then threw back his head and laughed. "Cloth harp! I like that!"

The pair fell silent, but Khnum-em-heb continued to chuckle to himself for several minutes. He was clearly in what Papa would call an effervescent mood.

After a decent time had passed and the weaver's merriment had expended itself, Neferet said in a guileless voice, "Have you had any thoughts about who might have killed Tjay?"

Khnum-em-heb pursed his lips in reflection. "No. I can't say that I've thought about it, frankly. I don't know anything about the man's personal life. He might have had all sorts of enemies."

You don't know much about your son's personal life either, my boy. "No rivalries at work or anything, I suppose?"

"Not really. His position was unique. The only other person I employ who even *could* have done his job is Hapu-seneb, but he certainly wasn't interested. There's no sense in which you could call them rivals."

Neferet nodded, but she couldn't help thinking, *That's what* you *know.*

As they angled across the stream for their descent into the embarcadero, the sun cast a brilliant-orange glare into their eyes, setting afire the water and washing with gold the high walls and obelisks of the temples. In the time it took them to disembark, though, the fires had banked in the shadowy streets, and a soft purple twilight was settling on the quay.

"Have a good evening, Master Khnum-em-heb!" Neferet called as she started inland, but he seemed preoccupied, staring at the line of pleasure boats anchored at the water's edge.

"That *is* my boat," he murmured. Neferet raised her eyebrows at him, and the weaver gave a bleat of laughter tinged with pique. "My son must have taken the ferry. He hates anything that smacks of the privilege of wealth. We've, er, we've had differences over this before. I think he's sending me a message." Khnum-em-heb stared back at the cluster of anchored boats in tense silence. Then he sighed. "You know how young people are."

But it was no longer any of Neferet's business.

CHAPTER 7

NEARLY A WEEK PASSED BEFORE Neferet saw Ta-em-resefu and Kem-sit again, although she didn't pay much attention to the unrolling of the calendar—there was a flurry of patients needing care. That often seemed to happen in the lead-up to a long festival—the forces of Chaos were always hoping to sidetrack the kingdom's pious activities. When Sutesh was on the prowl, no wonder if children got earaches and workmen fell off scaffoldings. And soon, the Ipet festival would begin—eleven days of celebration in honor of the Hidden One in his greatest shrine, a celebration dear to the people of Waset and pleasing to the king of the gods.

The young doctors had just seen out the last patient of the day, one of the dyer's little ones who had a soured scrape on his knee. Neferet leaned with her back against the gate and let out a big sigh. "*Iyah*, I don't think we've sat down all day. Did we even stop for lunch?"

A timid knock on the gate announced the arrival of Hu-may, his day at the goldsmith shop ended. In the courtyard, the nurse was gathering the rest of the orphans for their daily parade home. Neferet heard loud wails and an angry shriek.

"That's mine!" Shu-roy bellowed.

Neferet thought with a guilty sigh that it would be a pleasure to send the children off to the farm again.

Bener-ib let Cheetah into the house and propped open the cat door so he could get out when the wanderlust seized him. The three old dogs were fed and watered. The girls would check in on them every morning, even though the dispensary would only be open for emergency cases. This time of year, there was a glut of festivals, but she was eager for a long slice of doing nothing but relaxing at home and eating the traditional dishes. They could go down to the country again for a longer stay, too, with no pressure to get back.

As they trooped out the gate, she waved to the guard, who would continue his watch in their absence. And on the threshold, they ran right into Ta-em-resefu and Kem-sit.

"Oh, you're leaving," cried the younger woman, looking distraught. Her coppery Theban complexion was downright pale.

Kem-sit said in a strained voice, "I was afraid of that. We were late getting away."

"Come in, come in." Bener-ib, rallying first from her surprise, stepped back through the gateway and gestured the two women inside.

The nurse herded the children off down the lane, but the *sunet*s turned back with their guests. Mut-tuy hesitated then dodged into the court after them. Together, the five made their way into the dispensary, and Neferet offered them stools. She was disappointed at their timing but glad the two weavers had taken seriously her invitation to join them in the City of the Scepter.

"How nice of you to come," Neferet said with a big welcoming grin. "You didn't bring the children? I guess that's just as well, since ours set off for home not a moment ago."

"This isn't exactly a social call, although it started out that way," said Kem-sit. Her face was strained and pale. She shot her daughter-in-law a significant glance. "Ta-em-resefu has something to report to you. About the murder."

The younger woman looked from one face to another, her features tense. "I… I just saw Tjay's ghost." She twisted her hands nervously in her lap.

Neferet's stomach plunged to her feet. It was usually the long-unburied ones who stalked the living, begging for a proper home of eternity, and Tjay hadn't even been embalmed yet. But everybody seemed to agree that Tjay's *ba* would take perverse pleasure in harassing those he had known in life. And here he was, already at it. She pictured him as a malevolent bird swooping down on his widow.

"What happened?" she asked, almost afraid to hear the answer.

"We had barely landed in the city and had set off inland, following your directions how to get here, when—" Ta-em-resefu broke off in a hiccup of tears and clapped her hands to her face. "When I saw him in the street. He froze as if he was as shocked as I was, then he took off running. Oh, Mut, the mother of us all, won't he ever leave me alone even now?" she wailed.

Neferet and Bener-ib exchanged a look of confusion.

Neferet had never seen a ghost and wasn't sure if they could experience surprise, but as apparitions went, this sounded strange. "Did he make noise when he ran?"

The young weaver stared up with frightened, teary eyes. "What do you mean, my lady? He never said a thing."

Kem-sit said through clenched teeth, "If he starts hounding the children, I'll kill his damn ghost."

"I mean," Neferet said, "did his footsteps pound on the ground when he ran?"

"I… I don't know. There were people all around. There was lots of noise."

"Maybe you could show us where this happened," Neferet said, rising.

The two women led the way back out into the street, and despite some uncertainty, they backtracked as far as a seedy neighborhood in the vicinity of the quays. Sailors and longshoremen pushed past the five women—and other shifty-eyed figures of less identifiable professions. *I'll bet this place is crawling with thieves.* Aggressive females yelled to the passers-by and even followed them, their dress straps peeled down to expose the wares. It was a quarter seething with noise and crime that Neferet always took pains to avoid when she had need of boarding a boat. At her side, Mut-tuy gaped around with goggle eyes.

Ta-em-resefu led them resolutely to a corner where a wall had partially fallen down, leaving mudbricks spilling into the street. There she stopped. "I'm sure this is it."

Kem-sit nodded. "This is it, all right. He was comin' from that direction, around the corner." She pointed. "Then he seen us and froze and fled back up the same street."

Bener-ib stared at the scene intently. It was clear her thoughts were working hard.

"What are you thinking, Ibet?"

"Are you sure he was dead?" the girl asked diffidently. But of course, the question was exactly the right one.

The two weavers looked at each other with uncertainty.

"No," said Kem-sit. "If I didn't know better, I'da assumed he was alive. He looked the same as anybody. Except I know he's *not* alive."

"How do we know what a ghost looks like?" Mut-tuy asked.

The women ignored her and fell silent. The crowd swirled around them, cacophonous and dirty, elbowing them, jostling. People smelled like sweat and garlic and unwashed clothes. They radiated heat. Their footsteps thudded on the earthen street, their joints crackled, their breathing hissed or rattled—a *ba* without a body would do none of those things.

"I don't know what to say," Ta-em-resefu said hesitantly. "I'm sure it was him." She looked so distressed at the thought of her late husband coming back to curdle her life again that Neferet's heart clenched in pain for her.

"You never actually saw the body we fished out of the River, did you? Either of you?"

"No," Kem-sit said. "But you described him, and Tjay had disappeared. What else could we have thought?"

"Of course. It's exactly what anybody would have thought. But what if it wasn't Tjay after all?" Neferet said.

"Oh no! All you Great Ones have mercy!" Ta-em-resefu pressed both hands to her mouth. "Say he isn't still alive!"

"Describe him to me in detail, my girl," Neferet urged.

"Thirty-two years old. Medium height, slim. A squarish jaw. Curly dark brown hair and black eyes. Thick eyebrows." Ta-em-resefu waved her hands helplessly. She must have realized such a description could fit a good many young men. "Ears stuck out a little, but not too much. Uh… uh…"

Neferet tried to pull up before her mind's eye the corpse from the River, with its bleached, bloated face and surprised expression, but the details were already retreating from her memory.

"Nothing distinctive?" she prompted.

"Not really. He was nice enough looking but nothing that stood out when you describe it like that," Kem-sit said. "It was his expression I was always conscious of. Contemptuous like."

"Any scars?" asked Bener-ib.

"Just little ones here and there, like everybody." Ta-em-resefu was almost in tears. "Oh, say he's really dead."

But Neferet had just remembered something genuinely unusual about the corpse. "No big scar on his wrist? An old one, I'd say."

The younger weaver grew paler. "No. He… no."

The five women stood silent in the jostling crowd as the implications of this sank in. Neferet shot Bener-ib a look and asked in a sepulchral tone, "Then who is the dead man?"

⁂

The first shadows of the long summer evening were stretched out across the fields. Hani was sitting at his ease under the grapevine at the side of the farmhouse, watching a pair of magpies contend a jujube fruit, when Neferet, Bener-ib, and the troop of orphans came tumbling up from the River like a line of agitated ducks. Brute paced sedately at their side, a good marshal of the parade.

From afar, Neferet cried out, "Papa! We have some terrible news!"

Hani sprang from his stool, his heart pounding. *The entire family is here at the farm, and all the orphans seem to be accounted for. Surely, no one has ransacked the girls' dispensary again. Could something have happened to Lord Ptah-mes?*

"What is it, my duckling? No one hurt, I hope?"

"No, nothing like that," she said as the little army approached in a cloud of dust, chatter, and laughter. "But the dead man isn't Tjay."

"Well, well. How did you find out?" His stomach eased back out of his throat.

The nurse led the troops off into the farmhouse while Neferet and Bener-ib and the inevitable Mut-tuy approached and greeted Hani with a hug. They all drew out the stools and settled themselves with Brute at their feet. Neferet wiggled excitedly on her seat, her heat-rouged face aflame with excitement. "His family never actually saw the corpse, of course, and we all jumped to conclusions. But this afternoon, the two weavers showed up at the dispensary. They'd seen Tjay's ghost in Waset. Only it wasn't a ghost, we figure—it was the living Tjay. And when I gave them a fuller description—that scar on his wrist, for example—they recognized that the corpse wasn't him after all. So poor Ta-em-resefu. She thought she was free to marry her man friend, and now she finds she's still married to this jackal turd."

"But if he's run away, isn't that the same as divorce?" asked Bener-ib.

Hani had to admit to ignorance. "I can find out. Somebody at the chancery will know."

He stared in pensive silence at the ground, trying to decide how much responsibility he had in this matter. They'd made a good-faith effort to identify the corpse—it could be anybody at all now that the possibility of familial links to the village had evaporated. Undoubtedly, Kem-sit would no longer be willing to pay for the embalming, but Hani had already prepared himself for the expense anyway. He could afford it, and it was the only decent thing to do since the man had intruded, albeit involuntarily, on Hani's property.

"So we've eliminated the village," Neferet said with a businesslike manner. "That means he comes from the city or farther away."

"But he wouldn't have floated upstream from Waset. He was either killed to the south or in the vicinity of the farm," Bener-ib said shyly. "Or else was carried there from the scene of the crime."

"*Iyah*, you're right, my logical girl. So, maybe we need to expand our interviews in the village instead. Somebody else may have lost a loved one, or maybe they heard or saw something that might have been a murder or people dragging a body into the marshes."

Hani, who knew the marshes rather better than his daughter, thought it unlikely that any nefarious business carried out in the secret embrace of the reeds would have been noticed by anyone. But he said, "That's a good idea. Perhaps they've reported to Kem-sit by now."

Neferet looked sly and punched his arm playfully. "Have you changed your mind about us investigating, Papa? It's not so dangerous now?"

Hani laughed. "You're not talking about finding a murderer, my little duck. Just identifying the corpse. Which is very appropriate, I think, considering that we were more or less the ones who found it." He hesitated, weighing how much he wanted to encumber his vacation with duties. "I could even go to the village with you. Perhaps Dapurazo would like to go too. I think he's a little bored out here in the country."

Mut-tuy's face brightened.

"Let's go right now," Neferet said eagerly. "It'll be light for a long time yet."

"Let me tell your mother where we'll be and see if our friend from Keftiu wants to join us."

Nub-nefer was supervising the alternate-shift kitchen girls. With the entire family—including her eldest son Aha—present, preparing meals had taken on the complexity of provisioning a battalion of soldiers, and her usual staff was off duty for the holiday.

"How is my beautiful quartermaster?" Hani kissed the back of his wife's neck as she leaned over the oven. "Neferet and her gang have just arrived, and we're going to the village briefly. It turns out our corpse isn't who we thought he was."

Nub-nefer rose, her face glowing with heat. "How nice. Are they going to stay for the entire holidays?"

"She hasn't said. I'm sure we'll get the whole story at dinner."

"Which will be at sundown. Try not to be too late, my

love." She returned to her task, and Hani clumped up the outside steps to the roof terrace. There he found Maya and Dapurazo engrossed in a game of Hounds and Jackals while Mery-ra looked on, making urgent noises as he spotted a move.

"Gentlemen, the girls' case has just become less clear. We need to reidentify their corpse. Anyone care to make a little trip to the village?"

The players and their coach looked up, interested.

"That would be a nice diversion," Dapurazo said with genuine relief lighting his face.

Hani's father and Maya chimed in with their own agreement, and the four men paraded down the stairs and into the front yard of the farm, sending the geese scattering. There, they joined the three young women and their mastiff, and in a rather formidable block, the whole group set off together across the fields toward the village.

"So, what are we doing exactly, son?" asked Mery-ra as he toddled along at Hani's side.

Neferet explained how they'd learned that the corpse was no longer the missing Tjay. "We need to find out who it is. It could be *anybody*."

"We probably ought to ask around at random if anyone else is unaccounted for," Hani said.

And Neferet added, "Or if anybody saw anything suspicious. The body must have been dumped in the River around here. Otherwise, it would just have been chance that it washed up in that spot in the marshes."

It struck Hani how casually they all referred to the dead man as "the body." The man had a soul too. He'd once been alive. He'd had loved ones, who were probably frantic now, seeking word of his whereabouts. It had, after all, been more than a week since someone had struck the fatal blow. Hani realized that it was, in fact, important to him to give the man back his name, without which the poor soul's happy sojourn in the Field of Reeds was jeopardized.

"We're going to be a little intimidating to the villagers, marching up on them in such large number," Maya said, eyeing Brute. "Maybe we should split up."

"Good idea. Women in one direction, men in the other," Hani said. They'd entered the palm-shaded outskirts of the little community, and Hani pointed up first one side of the main path, then the other to indicate their respective territories.

"No!" cried Mut-tuy in anguish. When the others stared at her, she dropped her head, and her face grew scarlet.

Neferet and Bener-ib exchanged a disabused look, and Hani suppressed a grin. He hadn't missed the mooncalf gaze of the girl lingering on the man from Keftiu, who was good-looking in a pale northern way. "Or we could divide up so that each group had some men and some women. Perhaps that would make it easier for female witnesses to express themselves."

"Papa," said Neferet wearily, "women aren't afraid to talk to men."

Hani could well imagine that some simple village women might find their tongues tied in the inquisitive presence of upper-class men. Still, he didn't want to be the leader of their group. That would commit him to pursuing the investigation to its end. He preferred to defer to his daughter.

"As you like, then," he said with an easygoing smile.

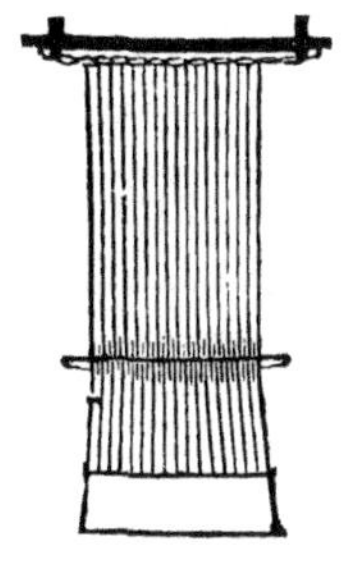

CHAPTER 8

THE MEN WENT UP ONE side of the village and the women the other. Adults were setting out picnic suppers under the trees, while the children gamboled underfoot, screaming loudly in play and hollering with the joyous laughter of a holiday from work. People broke off and stared as the four men approached. Hani had to admit they made an eye-catching array—two uncommonly broad fellows, one middle-aged and one old; a dwarf; and a long-haired foreigner in a bright-carmine kilt.

"The lord of the horizon give you a joyous festival," he called in a friendly voice. "We're looking for some information. Can you help us?"

He recognized one of the household workers from the farm—a sturdy youth named Huy—and two of the off-duty kitchen girls, who were helping an older woman who must have been their mother.

"Lord Hani," said Huy, bowing respectfully. "Please join us for our supper."

"That's generous of you, my friend, but we have our

own supper cooking and instructions from the mistress of the house not to be late. We're trying to identify a corpse that washed up near the farm a week or so ago. Has anybody lost a relative or friend? He's about thirty, slim, curly-haired, with a big scar on his wrist."

The villagers looked back and forth at one another, shaking their heads and murmuring. An elderly man said, "It ain't Tjay? I heard it was Tjay."

"Kem-sit'll know," someone else said.

A third added, "Hotep the laundryman died, and nobody's found the body."

Hani thought it was an unlikely identification, given the unhardened hands and formal dress of the deceased, but he asked, "Are you sure he's dead, then?"

"Oh, aye," the man assured him with ghoulish enthusiasm. "I seen him get dragged under by a hippopotamus. Right here near the village. It was a rare old sight. No way we coulda saved him."

But their corpse had definitely not been mauled by a hippopotamus. His killer had been of the two-legged variety. Otherwise, nobody seemed to be aware of any young men going missing.

"Sorry to disturb your festivities, then, friends. If you think of anyone, or if you happened to have seen anything that might have been a crime going on in the marshes, be so good as to let me know. Huy or one of these girls can transmit the message." Hani and his fellows reluctantly turned away and, accompanied by the tasty smells of fresh bread and grilling fish, drifted back to the road.

"No luck," Maya murmured in disappointment.

"Should we, in fact, check again with Kem-sit? If any family has a missing person, they would have told her."

They headed inland into the shady grove, where guinea hens gobbled and the perpetually tethered donkey eyed them. Three little girls chanted the song to some game in the trampled earth yard before the door. They fell silent as the men approached, then they ran away, giggling.

Even before Hani could knock, the mayor leaned down over the parapet of her roof terrace and called, "Who's there?"

"It's Lord Hani and his people," said another feminine voice. Ta-em-resefu stepped out from among the trees, a load of dry brush in her arms despite her good festival clothes. She approached, looking wary. "Can we help you, my lord?"

Hani was touched by the sorrow in her face. If the thought of her husband's death had left her unmoved, the thought of his being alive seemed to have plunged her into real grief. Her lids were red and swollen. But even in the absence of kohl, she was still an undeniably attractive young woman with big gazelle eyes. He noticed Dapurazo's own eyes fastened on her face, his features twisted empathetically into a chagrin like her own.

Hani said in a kindly voice, "We thought Kem-sit might have heard something about the possible identity of the corpse, mistress. Since it isn't… who we thought it was."

"I-I don't know, Lord Hani. You can ask her."

Kem-sit herself appeared in the doorway. She, too, was stiff and uneasy looking. Something about their manner struck Hani as strange. He repeated his question to the mayor, who listened, eyes averted.

"Just the laundryman who was dragged under by hippos," she finally said. "A village this small, we don't have all that many unexplained deaths in a week."

"Then he must have been a man of Waset," said Mery-ra. "But special as the citizens of our fair city think they are, he couldn't have floated upstream, could he? Maybe somebody brought his body into the countryside to get rid of it discreetly. We're hoping at least to find a witness."

"Lord Mery-ra," said Kem-sit earnestly, "you know how we appreciate your family and all you done for us. If we knew anything, we'd tell you. But we don't. If it's not Tjay, all we got is suspicions. Fears. You'd be better off asking around in Waset, you know what I mean? Maybe people you know'd be a good place to start." She fixed Hani and his father with a piercing stare as if to will them to obey.

Stranger and stranger, Hani thought, puzzled. But it was clear the women intended to say no more. "Then we leave you, mistresses. A blessed festival to you." He wheeled to go, and the others followed, but suddenly, Dapurazo turned back.

"I hope this won't mean that you're not free to come teach my workers. I don't know what rights married women have here." The man of Keftiu looked questioningly from one woman's face to the other, his gaze lingering on Ta-em-resefu.

But no one could answer him with legal details.

"Better ask Khnum-em-heb," said Kem-sit pointedly. And then she said it again: "Ask Khnum-em-heb."

"Well, that didn't turn up much," said Neferet in disgust

when the two groups had rendezvoused. "Everybody seemed disappointed that it wasn't Tjay who was found dead, but nobody had any ideas about who it might have been otherwise. What name is the *sem*-priest going to use at his funeral?"

Papa said pensively, "There was something more than a little strange about those weavers' behavior. Didn't you think so, Father? I felt like Kem-sit was trying to tell us something without saying it openly, although I can't imagine why."

They'd reached the edge of the village, and the drowned fields stretched out around them, glimmering with puddles. Beyond, the sun was sinking behind the jagged purple edge of the Mountains of the West. Mama would be serving dinner any minute.

"She wants you to talk to Khnum-em-heb. What could he know if the corpse isn't his bookkeeper after all?" Maya shook his head.

Neferet shared his bafflement. *From a solved case to an absolute enigma. We no longer even know who was killed, let alone who killed him.*

By the next day, the concentration of family members at the farm had become a bit oppressive. At least Aha and his brood had left, aiming to spend the bulk of the long vacation at his wife's familial country place—by far more elegant than that of Mama and Papa, which, at the moment, was a bit like a makeshift barracks. The two *sunet*s were prepared to take their whole troop back to Waset, but the children begged to stay, so it was decided Nurse would keep them for the remaining week of holidays, while Neferet and Bener-ib returned. They wanted to see if anyone had turned up at the dispensary, looking for care, and to reassure the three old dogs that they hadn't been forgotten.

Once back, they were greeted with much joyous barking and wagging of tails. Even the aloof Cheetah deigned to wind himself around their legs in greeting.

"Lady Neferet, there were four patients who came to the gate in your absence," the guard said. "Nobody indicated it was an emergency. There was also a fellow named Khnum-em-heb. He said to ask you if the foreign man had made a final decision yet. Otherwise, things have been quiet. No attacks." He grinned. He was a stocky man in early middle age who had lost his front teeth defending Lord Ptah-mes during the dark period of rioting in the reign of Nefer-khepru-ra.

"Thank you, Ka-sa. Why don't you take the rest of the day off to celebrate with your family? We'll be here during the day. Whoever's assigned to the night shift can come as usual."

He took his leave gratefully, and the two *sunet*s and their apprentice entered the house. It smelled stale already. Bener-ib propped open the door with a rock, and the others collapsed onto the stools, happy to be out of the sun and wind. Cheetah had left them half a rat as if to demonstrate how valuable his presence had been.

"I suppose we need to visit Khnum-em-heb, but I don't really know what to tell him about Dapurazo," Neferet said. "On the other hand, Papa seemed to think Kem-sit wanted us to talk to him regarding the dead man. What could he know?"

"Maybe another of his employees has disappeared," Mut-tuy said.

Bener-ib was staring pensively into her lap. "I hope someone thinks to tell Tjay's sister that he isn't dead after all. She'll be so happy."

Only Ibet would care about that strange woman, thought Neferet, her heart swelling with admiration. She squeezed the little *sunet*'s hand. "I guess we should pay Khnum-em-heb a visit, then. Once I get home, I don't think I'll want to budge again. Who's for coming along?"

"Someone should stay in case any of those patients come back," said Bener-ib. "I can do that."

Neferet shot her a grateful look. She had just saved them from an argument with Mut-tuy. Bener-ib opened the kitchen door to air the stuffy place and saw Neferet and their apprentice out the gate, Brute at their heels.

"We'll be back well before lunch," Neferet called over her shoulder as they set off down the lane.

Somehow, she found the weaver's workshop. They were admitted by the old servant and led across the empty work court to the master's modest house, where Brute threw himself down in the shade beside the door.

He lives pretty simply for a rich man, Neferet thought in approval as they entered the vestibule. He'd probably occupied the same home since he'd been a lowly weaver.

A moment later, Khnum-em-heb appeared from within the salon and greeted them. His big, hearty smile was in place, but Neferet could see that he was troubled by something.

She said cheerfully, hoping it would resolve his anxiety, "I'm sorry I can't give you a definitive answer about the fabric deal, master, but for sure, Dapurazo is still interested. And here's some good news for you—Tjay isn't dead after all. Although he has run off, so it's pretty much the same thing from your perspective, I guess."

"Excellent, excellent," he said, his eyes darting unhappily around the shadowy room.

Neferet, never one to observe unnecessary subtlety, asked, "Is something wrong?"

"I, I don't know, my lady." He hesitated. Then, seeming to make a decision, he drew the two young women into the salon. "You're doctors. You must hear all sorts of things." His voice dropped. "Something may have happened to my son. Or maybe not. But we don't know where he is."

"I thought you sent him to Men-nefer."

"I did, but he never got there. It's been almost two weeks." As if just remembering his manners, he urged his visitors to a pair of stools and dropped heavily onto one as well. His pretense at good cheer had given way to an unapologetically anxious expression. "I found that my boat never left port—the crew told me Hapu-seneb never embarked."

Neferet remembered Khnum-em-heb's comment about his yacht. "You thought he must have taken a public ferry."

"That's what I assumed, but I started getting worried, so I sent a fast courier to the capital to see if he ever showed up. The man just got back this morning. Hapu-seneb never went to the merchant he was supposed to contact. Khonsu the Traveler, where is he?"

Neferet's heart sank. There were several possibilities, and none of them was good. The worst, of course, was very bad indeed. She grimaced but then scrambled for a bit of optimism.

"Any chance he just ran away too? To be a poet or

archivist or whatever it was he wanted to be?" *But would he have left Ta-em-resefu? Unless he planned to sneak back for her once he had dropped out of his father's sight...*

Neferet had to admit she wasn't much convinced by her own argument. Neither was Khnum-em-heb. He shrugged as if the gesture was painful.

"Lady Neferet," he said humbly, "you said you'd investigated things before. I know you have patients to tend and all that, but if you could just keep an ear open? Perhaps some little rumor might come to you. His mother and I would be so grateful."

"Of course," she said, grasping his big hands in sincere compassion. "And my father will sniff around too. He's solved cases for the king. We'll find out what's happened. Hapu-seneb's probably fine somewhere."

Khnum-em-heb had walked them to the door as they spoke. As the girls passed over the sill, Brute rose from his spot and stood in his enormous brindled glory, calmly panting. The weaver smiled uneasily.

"My son is afraid of such dogs. When he was a little fellow, a big dog like that grabbed him by the arm and dragged him across the court. It scared him half to death and left his arm all bloody besides. Could have killed him. My only son..."

Suddenly, something clicked into place in Neferet's thoughts. The sad and obvious thing. "Did it leave a scar?" she asked, hoping not to hear what she suspected. "On his wrist?"

Khnum-em-heb caught Neferet's eye, and she could see the fear in his pupils. "Yes," he said in a scratchy voice as if it were failing him. "Why?"

Neferet wasn't sure how to say what she needed to. *If only Ibet were here—she's always so tactful and gentle in giving bad news.* "I'm afraid the dead man we thought was Tjay had a big scar on his wrist," she said hesitantly.

"Where's the body?" he roared. "I want to see it."

"It's in the hands of the servants of Inpu." Nobody would want to see their loved one after the embalming process had begun.

Khnum-em-heb let out a howl of anguish, clutching at his hair. "No! It can't be him!"

Neferet said nothing, but as she looked at the weaver, it struck her how much he and the Osir resembled each other under the difference in age and weight—the unruly curls, the amiable round-arched black brows, the dent in the chin and nose as if a straight edge had been pressed up the middle of his face. *Yes, it's Hapu-seneb. All this time, we didn't even think about that. He wasn't the killer—he was the victim.* And she wondered all at once if Ta-em-resefu hadn't suspected that as soon as Neferet had told her about the scar.

A servant came running from within the house.

"Get the mistress of the house," Khnum-em-heb gasped between sobs.

In a moment, a woman who strangely resembled her husband emerged from the back of the house, her face frozen with trepidation. "What is it, my dear?"

Khnum-em-heb folded her in his arms and seemed to collapse upon her. For a while, he couldn't speak, but his disarray must have made her suspicious of the worst. She gaped first at him then at Neferet. "Is this about… about Hapu-seneb? What's happened?"

Neferet nodded sadly. "He was found floating in the River nearly two weeks ago, mistress. We thought he was somebody else."

The bereaved parents wailed together for a long time. Finally, Khnum-em-heb settled his hysterically weeping wife on a stool and said to Neferet in a grimly determined voice, "Tell us everything, my lady. How did he die?"

She explained about the violent blow on the head and how the Osir must have been killed in the vicinity of the village or been taken there, since he couldn't have drifted upstream from the city. The weaver fastened bloodshot eyes on her through the whole recital, although she couldn't have said how many of her words actually penetrated his grief-stricken thoughts. He was evidently a man of large emotions, and his thirst for vengeance seemed to be building like a sandstorm on the horizon. Mut-tuy followed them both with a blazing round-eyed stare.

"You have to find who did this, Lady Neferet. I'll help you in any way I can. We must find him and see that he's punished. I want to know why my son died—do you understand? Anything you can discover." He turned to comfort his wife and left the two girls to find their way out on their own.

Neferet and Bener-ib dined with Lord Ptah-mes that evening for the first time in a good many weeks. Neferet's marriage with the Master of the Double House of Silver and Gold was unconventional, to say the least, although it suited them both. Ptah-mes was Papa's friend and former superior—one of the richest, most blue-blooded men in the Two Lands. When his first wife had died violently some years ago, he'd found himself unable to face the eager women who flocked to court such a handsome and eligible target. Neferet, then an adolescent, had wanted a white marriage to provide her and the lady of her heart with respectability, so they had mutually agreed to the union. It had added fuel to the fire of animosity between him and his children, who were older than Neferet, but all that was resolved now.

"How is your father, my dear?" Ptah-mes asked in his impeccably courteous way as the three sipped their sweet herbed beer. "With everyone dispersed for the holidays, I haven't seen as much of him as usual."

"Oh, he's well, thanks. He's helping us with our latest murder," Neferet said casually.

Ptah-mes's arched eyebrows rose slightly—the extent to which he was ever likely to show astonishment. "Have you murdered someone again?" he asked in his bone-dry tone.

"No, no." The girl laughed, tickled. He could be so funny, although it was easy to miss. "We're *investigating* a murder. A man washed up in the marshes near the farm. At first, we thought it was a bookkeeper named Tjay, but it turns out he's still alive. Instead, it's probably another bookkeeper named Hapu-seneb. He's the son of Tjay's boss, and he was having an affair with Tjay's wife."

"There's a classic motive for you. So, you think Tjay is the killer?"

"We think so," Bener-ib said shyly. "But he's disappeared."

"His wife only saw him by accident here in the city. We need to reconstruct how he committed the crime. It was probably done in the village or outside Waset. At least, I hope so."

Neferet gave Bener-ib a significant wag of the eyebrows. They both knew what it would mean if the crime had been committed within the jurisdiction of the *medjay*, the city police. *Mahu.*

Lord Ptah-mes understood too. "Let's hope our friend Mahu doesn't get involved."

He had as icy a relationship with the corrupt police chief as Papa did, having defied—and publicly humiliated—him several times. Given his rank, Lord Ptah-mes didn't really have to be afraid legally of anyone except the king, but Mahu wasn't too scrupulous when it came to making those who stood up to him pay—within or without the law.

A servant bowed in the doorway to signal the service of dinner. Several others brought in an array of beautifully presented dishes and set them on the small table beside the diners. A naked little boy with a water lily over his ear offered them bowls of warm, perfumed water for their fingers. The whole ceremony was so far removed from anything Neferet was likely to encounter on an ordinary night at her parents' house that she might as well have been a desert-dwelling Meshwesh. But she was sure Lord Ptah-mes didn't even give it a thought. He simply took it for granted, just as he took the priceless objects that furnished his ancestral home for granted without any particular pride or even—she suspected—enjoyment. He was curiously austere.

The three fell silent as they served themselves and began to eat.

"How is your dispensary doing?" Ptah-mes asked after

a while. He wiped his fingers on the fine linen towel beside his dish. "Patients coming now?"

"Oh, yes. Even when we've been gone at the farm, several people have shown up, according to the guard. Ibet waited there all morning in case any of them came back. She's the best physician ever." Neferet shot her a fond look and a wink.

"She is certainly very devoted," murmured Ptah-mes with a courtly nod at the smaller woman.

Bener-ib reddened. "Nef'et would've done the same."

They finished the meal in the same awkward silence, broken now and then by her husband's polite attempts at conversation. Neferet was usually not at a loss for words and could chatter on endlessly about her activities, but that night, her thoughts were wrapped up in the surprise turn their case had taken—and the shock and grief of the dead man's bereaved parents. It was almost enough to make her behave more prudently. The idea of causing such pain to her own beloved mother and father was soul crushing.

After dinner, as was his habit, Lord Ptah-mes withdrew to the garden pavilion to enjoy the relative cool of the evening. Neferet and Bener-ib lingered in the salon, playing with Brute, who lay stretched out on the cool gypsum floor, his floppy jowls trailing. At first, they paid no attention when a knock sounded in the vestibule and the gatekeeper murmured something to the steward. Then a more familiar deep voice, warm with good humor, spoke, and Neferet jumped to her feet almost as quickly as Brute.

"It's Papa! What's he doing in the city?"

The steward entered the salon with the guest at his heels, and Neferet ran to them and threw herself on her father with delight. "Papa!" Behind him, she saw Maya and the man of Keftiu. "Maya. Lord Dapurazo. What brings you three back?"

"I had some dispatches to check, my duckling. And Maya wanted to be sure his garden was getting watered. Dapurazo, here, needed to talk to Khnum-em-heb about a contract. So we took a late ferry. We'll spend the night and morning here and head back after lunch tomorrow."

That means they were bored to tears with all the children running around at the farm, Neferet thought with a silent snicker. She would have said it out loud, but she didn't want to embarrass their foreign guest. *See? Ibet is a good influence on me. I'm getting downright diplomatic.*

"Are you here to visit us or Lord Ptah-mes?" she asked, still hanging onto Papa's hands.

"Both. We had a question to ask your husband about customs on imports and exports."

"And we have some news for you—we know who the dead man is! He's Khnum-em-heb's son, who was supposedly in Men-nefer, but it turns out he never showed up, and why? Because somebody bonked him on the nut and threw the corpse in the River. And that somebody has to be Tjay. He must have found out that Hapu-seneb was having an affair with his wife. And he was already jealous because Hapu-seneb was Khnum-em-heb's son and had all the privileges that Tjay thought he deserved because he worked harder. So—"

"Wait, my girl!" Papa threw up his hands in surrender and laughed. "What part of this is fact, and what part is speculation?"

But Dapurazo looked discomfited. "Khnum-em-heb's

son just died? He's not going to be in a mood to talk business."

"I don't know," Maya said dryly. "He strikes me as a man who's never not in a mood for business."

The steward, who had been standing in silent attention behind the visitors, cleared his throat discreetly. "I believe the master is in the garden, Lord Hani. Unless you'd prefer to speak here with the mistress of the house..."

"We'll all go outside," Neferet said cheerfully. "It's hot in here anyway. And Brute wants to sleep, don't you, boy? It's only because he's such a gentleman that he didn't tell us to go away."

They trooped outside into the twilit garden. Lightning bugs flashed here and there in the liquid half dark, and a nightingale poured out its pulsing song from high in a plane tree. Lord Ptah-mes was sitting in the unlit kiosk, a ewer of wine untouched on the table before him. He looked up as the footsteps of the visitors crunched on the gravel in approach.

"Guess who's here, Lord Ptah-mes!" Neferet called.

Her husband rose to his feet. "Hani, my friend," he said with obvious pleasure in his voice. What brings you back to the City of the Scepter? I thought you were going to spend the holidays at your farm."

Hani went once more through the litany of reasons each of the men had wanted to return. At Ptah-mes's urging, they all seated themselves under the shelter of the kiosk, with Neferet and Bener-ib on the steps. Ptah-mes told the steward to fetch more cups and a servant with a fan to keep away the mosquitoes, which had begun to feast at their favorite hour of the day. It was always like that after the Inundation, when all the irrigation runnels were full.

Papa took advantage of the wait to introduce Dapurazo.

"Welcome, my lord," said Ptah-mes with grave courtesy. "Do I understand that you are an official emissary of your king?"

"That's the case, my lord. Although I am also a merchant in my own right. As you no doubt know, for the last hundred years or so, the kings on our island have been men of Ahhiyawa, but we whose lineage is indigenous to Keftiu have proved loyal in their service."

"Your country is occupied by foreigners?" Neferet cried in surprise. "That sounds awful."

Bener-ib poked her.

But Dapurazo didn't seem offended. His white smile was barely visible in the darkness. "After three generations, not so much, my lady. Life goes on peacefully, and men of my age serve the Ahhiyawan kings as we would serve kings of our own dynasty. We call them *wanax* instead of *kiro*, but nothing else has changed, frankly."

The other men nodded thoughtfully. Papa was probably thinking about how close Kemet had come to having a Hittite ruler.

"Neferet just told us that the weaver Khnum-em-heb has lost his son," Papa said. "We were hoping to conclude a contract with him for a load of his gauze and also to engage some of his women weavers to teach Dapurazo's countrymen how to make that magnificent textile. Now I'm not sure what to do. He'll have other things on his mind."

"We can pay our respects," Maya said, "and sound

him out. He must still need to carry on the business, even though his foreman has flown into the West."

Neferet hastened to correct him. "*He* hasn't flown, Maya. It's the son who's dead. Tjay just ran away because he's guilty of murder. Of course, Tjay might as well be dead for all the good it does Hapu-seneb's father. Khnum-em-heb really wants us to lay hands on the murderer, too, Papa."

"I don't doubt that," Papa said with feeling.

A pensive silence descended. The men sipped their wine. The crickets pulsed quietly. The servant rhythmically raised and lowered his fan of trimmed palmetto frond, leaving a wake of tepid air on the faces of the girls seated on the step, but it didn't suffice to discourage the mosquito that whined past Neferet's ear.

"I was in Keftiu many years ago," Lord Ptah-mes said finally. "Which part are you from?"

"I was born in a port city called Dawo, my lord, on the southwest coast of the island. But I grew up in my family's house in the royal district of Paisto nearby. The sea has always attracted me. I guess that must be true for the sons of merchants, mustn't it?" Dapurazo lifted his cup to his lips.

"I've never even seen the Great Green," Neferet said regretfully.

"I was born on the coast too." Bener-ib's wistful tone was as close to homesick as Neferet had ever heard from the girl. Neferet had rather thought Ibet never wanted to go back to Sau, the scene of so much suffering. But maybe they ought to take a trip there one of these days.

Eventually, the men fell to discussing imports and customs fees and packing protocols. Neferet found her attention drifting. She was still chewing over the spectacle of Khnum-em-heb and his wife's grief. Life wasn't altogether the happy place she'd inhabited for twenty-four years. Every time a corpse floated to shore, no amount of excitement and curiosity on her part could wipe away the fact of devastated family members left behind. Every time she had to tell a patient, "I cannot treat this case," someone went home, weeping hopelessly. It was too painful.

"Come on, Ibet. Let's go," she whispered. She climbed to her feet and drew the other young woman after her.

The next morning, when the two doctors, accompanied by their mastiff, reached the gate of the dispensary, Kem-sit was standing impatiently in the street. Her face was grim.

"Thank the gods you're here. I looked for you at the farm, and your mother told me you'd come back to the city, but I didn't know where you lived." She grabbed Neferet's arm with fingers of bronze and said under her breath, "Someone tried to kill Ta-em-resefu."

CHAPTER 9

Neferet and Bener-ib exchanged a look of horror. "Is... is she all right?"

"He drew blood, but she screamed and got away before he could kill her. I don't think she's too badly hurt. The children's traumatized."

Neferet pushed open the gate and hustled the others inside. The guard looked up from his seat on his haunches but, seeing who had entered, returned to his whittling. The three old dogs thronged the women joyously, although no one paid them any attention.

"It was Tjay, I assume?" Neferet asked.

"She didn't see him—she was in bed asleep when he attacked—but who else could it've been?" Kem-sit's teeth were clenched. "That jackal turd. After we seen him in the street, I was sure somethin' like this was going to happen. Ta-em-resefu said she didn't think he'd dare show up in the village, but I at least convinced her to come stay at my house with the little ones. Guess I was right and she was wrong. Only, even at my house, she wasn't safe."

"Mut, the mother of us all," Neferet murmured, the stubble standing on end on her shaven scalp. "This is getting serious."

"Did you talk to Khnum-em-heb?" the weaver suddenly asked.

"Yes," Bener-ib said. "It was his son who was killed. You knew that, didn't you?"

Kem-sit nodded, her lined face grave. "Soon's you said about the scar on his wrist. Course, we weren't sure. Nothing but suspicions at that point—lots of people have scars—so we didn't want to say nothing. It woulda seemed like puttin' a curse on him. But Khnum-em-heb confirmed it, did he?"

Neferet nodded glumly, remembering once more the devastated parents of the victim. "Hapu-seneb never showed up in Men-nefer, where everybody thought he was. He was supposed to have taken his father's boat to the Lower Kingdom just about the time we found the corpse. Of course, he never embarked."

"Let me catch that hyena-souled wretch of a Tjay, and I'll rip his head off. He's ruined too many lives ever since he was a boy. Nothing but grief for his father. In fact, I hold him responsible for Pa-shedu's death. He provoked him into a terrible argument. Pa-shedu was all red-faced, with veins standing out on his temples, and that very evening, he collapsed and died. He was a good man. Always fair. Merciful. A hundred times the man Tjay ever was, yet that dog turd dared hold him in contempt just because he couldn't read and write. The boy was a piece of shit from the start. His mother saw to that."

"I guess we'll have to tell his sister it wasn't him in

the River after all. She, at least, will be happy he's alive." Bener-ib, as usual, tried to find some good in the situation.

"Her." Kem-sit sniffed. "Usret's a good girl, but she worships the very footsteps of that worthless, arrogant brother of hers. I can't imagine why—even when they was little, he always treated her like a dog."

Brute looked up as if to ask what was wrong with being a dog.

And that gave Neferet an idea. "What if we put Brute on his trail? We can track him down."

"But how, Nef'et?" asked Bener-ib. "Do we just start making circles at the embarcadero, where he might have gotten out of a boat? What if he didn't come back to Waset?"

Neferet stuck out her lip and frowned, disappointed. "True. I had thought to start at Kem-sit's house, but once he got onto the water, the trail would stop." She ran her fingers through Brute's close fur without even thinking about her action. Her thoughts were racing ahead. "We need to go back to the village. Is Ta-em-resefu safe while you're here?"

Kem-sit nodded. "She's at her brother's house. I told her not to stay alone."

"You're in danger too, Kem-sit," Bener-ib said, her brow pleated with concern.

But the mayor of the village thrust out her jaw in defiance. "Let the bastard try to do anything to me."

Neferet called out to the guard to tell him where they were going. That way, Papa would know if he came looking for them. Then she filled the dogs' water while Bener-ib gathered a basket full of medical supplies, and the three women piled hastily out the gate, Brute at their heels.

Neferet saw Papa's red-and-green yacht bobbing playfully at anchor along the quay, but she hailed a ferry instead. The poor ferrymen never had a day off—luckily for her. She rewarded the youth generously when they finally stepped out of the boat and scrambled up the bank into the village. Before them stood the tumbledown house of Usret and her bald companion. He was at work on another reed boat in the littered yard, with guinea hens and a couple of nosy goats milling about underfoot. The women waved as they passed him.

"Should we stop and tell her that Tjay is alive?" Bener-ib murmured into Neferet's ear.

But Neferet didn't want to have to deal with the woman. "We need to see to Ta-em-resefu first. She may need medical attention. Kem-sit can tell her later."

They'd set off inland when a tall, skinny figure emerged from the dust and shadow on the main path at the top of the slope. Head down, oblivious to their surroundings, the person was trekking methodically toward the mayor's house. Brute's tail gave a wag of recognition.

"What in the name of seven demons!" said Neferet, agog with surprise and annoyance. "It's Mut-tuy. What's she doing here?"

"That girl who's always with you?" Kem-sit asked.

"Yes, our apprentice. We left her at the farm with the other children when we went back to Waset."

Bener-ib bit her lip and gave Neferet a knowing look. Somebody hadn't been pleased to be left behind. Somebody had defiantly ignored the order to wait at the farm.

"Mut-tuy!" Neferet shouted in a voice like the blast of the silver trumpets that announced the appearance of the king. The girl stopped sharply then changed path, striding toward them with a murderous look on her face. As soon as Mut-tuy had drawn up to them, her mouth open and words half out of it, Neferet said hastily and firmly, "We'll talk about this shocking disobedience later. Right now, we're going to see Ta-em-resefu, who was almost killed last night."

"If you think I don't—" the girl began furiously, her face glowing like a brazier.

Neferet cut her off with a peremptory stare. "Later."

The sun was moving up the sky as Kem-sit led the *sunet*s and their steaming apprentice to a neat two-story house of modest dimensions, screened from the river by a line of dense fig trees. A woman with her hair knotted back in a scarf was beating a rug that hung over a pile of brush. She looked up as the three approached.

"Kem-sit, you're back already. Ta-em-resefu's up on the terrace with the children."

"How's she doing?" Kem-sit asked in a low voice.

"She'd stopped crying when I saw her last. But the little ones are a mess."

As she led the younger women up the outside stairs, the mayor explained, "That's her sister-in-law. Tjay hardly ever let her associate with her brothers' families, but they've welcomed her in."

They found the weaver sitting cross-legged on the ground, leaning wanly against the parapet, her three naked daughters clinging to her. Her shoulder was clumsily wrapped with blood-smeared cloths. She looked up fearfully, then her face relaxed.

"Kem-sit, thank the gods you're back safe. Lady

Neferet. Lady Bener-ib. Thank you for coming." Her voice was shaky and threatened to break, but she forced a smile. She said to the little girls, "Isn't it nice that they came?"

The girls had clearly wept until their whole faces were swollen and red. *This is heartbreaking*, Neferet told herself, anger rising like steam from her face. *To terrorize his own children that way.*

Bener-ib had already squatted at the weaver's side and began unwrapping the makeshift bandages. The woman wasn't dressed in a proper shift—no doubt because she couldn't lift her arm to pull one over her head—but wrapped in a length of cloth that was tucked tightly above the breasts. She loosened it and lowered the panel. Tjay had stabbed his wife in the back of her shoulder and administered an additional slice or two as well. Neferet pictured her asleep on her side and slightly rolled toward the front when the blow fell. She must have awakened immediately and struggled.

"What happened?" Bener-ib asked in compassion, drawing a pad of lint wrapped in a cloth from the wicker chest of supplies.

"I'll go see if they can't heat us some water." Kem-sit clopped down the stairs.

Ta-em-resefu, her face scrunched in pain and her eyes black ringed, looked up at the two doctors. "Kem-sit had made me come spend the night at her house. I was asleep up on her terrace with her and the girls, me nearest to the outside stairs. Kem-sit told me later she had gone down into the yard to pee, but the rest of us were all still asleep. Suddenly, I woke up with a terrible burning pain in my back. I started to jump up and could feel blood running down my side. I realized someone had stabbed me and was still holding me. He tried to get me again, but I rolled away and started screaming. He fled. The children woke up, too, and were screaming in fear. They've already been scared by their father's disappearance and everything—and now this." Her tears started to flow again, and she drew the little girls to her with her good arm. The oldest one couldn't have been any more than six.

"Luckily, he hit you on the shoulder blade and the knife slid. It could have pierced a lung otherwise," Bener-ib said gravely. "The other blows aren't deep since you moved away as soon as you felt yourself struck."

Good thing the turd didn't know how to use a knife, Neferet added to herself, her teeth clenched. *This man is a pitiful hyena prick.*

Kem-sit reemerged with a steaming basin. "I tried to clean her up and bandage the wounds. But you can do a better job." She carefully set the basin on the packed-clay floor of the terrace between the two *sunet*s, along with a stack of clean, folded rags. Then she squatted on her haunches at Neferet's side.

"Did any of you actually get a glimpse of Tjay? If we take him to court, we'll need witnesses and all that." Neferet squeezed out her padded cloth and began delicately to clean the lacerated flesh. Kem-sit had, in fact, done a good job of removing the blood, which must have flowed copiously. From their basket, Bener-ib passed her a pot of unguent, and Neferet smeared it on with gentle fingers.

The two weavers looked at one another, and Ta-em-resefu said apologetically, "He was behind me, and it was dark except for the moon. But who else would have done such a thing other than Tjay? He wanted people to think he was dead, and I'd seen him alive."

"It was Papa," said the oldest of the three little ones in shy agreement. "It was Papa, and he was dressed like a girl."

All eyes turned to her. She looked very young and very fragile, clinging to her sisters like a baby monkey, with her Horus lock dangling and her big, frightened eyes.

Shame on that man for scaring these little creatures so. I want him to roast in the Lake of Fire.

Then the child's words sank in.

"He was dressed like a *girl*, you say? You mean he had on a dress?" Neferet asked.

The little one nodded, but she no longer seemed so sure.

"It was dark, my girl. Are you certain you recognized him?"

She nodded again, looking to her mother for corroboration.

"I saw him, then," said Mut-tuy triumphantly. "Sneaking around between the houses."

Neferet was dying to demand what a thirteen-year-old thought to be asleep at the farm with the other children was doing prowling the streets of the village in the wee hours, but that would have to wait.

Kem-sit said, "That makes sense, don't it? Anybody who saw him walking around in the middle of the night would be a lot less likely to feel uneasy if they thought he was a woman."

"And he didn't want anyone to know he was still alive," Bener-ib added. "Anyone in the village might have recognized him otherwise."

Neferet mulled this over. "If Tjay went to all the trouble to disguise himself, he certainly had premeditated murder on his mind. He must have taken a ferry up from the city before dark then concealed himself somewhere until everyone was asleep. He probably would have looked for his wife at their own home first, then, not finding her, sought her at the next-likeliest address—that of her mother-in-law. If we ever catch him, he's done for. He may claim an act of passion for killing Ta-em-resefu's lover, but not for this." She bared her teeth in a murderous grin, a flame of victory burning in her heart. *We've got him.*

Neferet wrapped Ta-em-resefu's shoulder as neatly as the priests of Inpu could have done and tied up the ends of the bandage. "I'm afraid you won't be able to weave for a while, my girl."

"Will she be safe in the village now? Tjay knows every house where she's likely to seek refuge." Bener-ib looked in concern from face to face.

Ta-em-resefu hugged her children to her, her expression fearful. "All my relatives are here. Where else can we go?"

"I know Mama would be willing to hide you up at our farm," Neferet said kindly. "There are a lot of people there now because of the holidays. But that's better. It won't be at all obvious that we have a few more guests. You'll blend right in."

"Do it," Kem-sit urged her. "You won't be safe here anymore."

"Th-Thank you, Lady Neferet. I don't know what else to do."

"And you girls will have lots of other children to play

with," Neferet said to the little daughters with a complicit smile. "It will be more fun."

They decided not to make the injured woman walk. Instead, Neferet found their field foreman at his house and arranged that he should conceal the guests in his donkey cart, which they then covered with a thin layer of straw. That way, if Tjay were still in the vicinity, he would have no idea that his intended prey had gotten away.

As they plodded off in the wake of the cart, Neferet squeezed Kem-sit's hand and said under her breath, "Are you sure you're safe? You saw Tjay too."

"I'll be all right. Usret comes by more or less every day. I'll tell her to notify you if she finds me dead on the floor." The woman's weathered face cracked in a grin. "The gods go with you and bless you for all your help, my lady."

They waved goodbye at the edge of the settlement and, accompanied by the creak of the cart and the rhythmic clop-clop of the donkey's hooves, set out across the sun-slathered fields. Kem-sit turned back, and Neferet's last view of her was a slash of white disappearing into the shadow of the trees.

"I saw Tjay sneaking around," said Mut-tuy breathlessly as if she'd held herself in for hours. "And I heard the scream when he attacked Ta-em-resefu."

"Did you see him come out afterward?" Bener-ib asked.

"Yes! He ran down toward the River. He probably had a boat waiting."

Neferet gave her an obsidian-hard stare, and the girl added defensively, "There was a moon last night."

"That's not what I was looking at you for. Mut-tuy, you had no business being out of the house in the middle of the night. And walking down to the village alone? Mut, the mother of us all." Neferet gave a huff of disbelief.

"There was a moon."

"I'm not worried about you stubbing your toe, girl. We have a murderer running loose around here, you know." She shook her head, simmering. "What were you thinking?"

Here, obviously, was the opening Mut-tuy had waited for. She said in a loud, angry voice, "Well, if you'd taken me with you back to Waset instead of leaving me with those children… there was nothing to do all by myself at the farm."

"I believe the usual activity at night is sleeping."

"There were things to investigate. And look—I actually witnessed a crime."

You're wasting your breath, Neferet told herself, letting a good squirt of that breath out her nose. *The Queen of Stubbornness will never fail to have an argument.* A little pang of guilt washed over her at the thought of her own legendary childhood stubbornness. *I must have put Mama and Papa through a lot.* But her parents had always been patient. A bit sarcastic sometimes, but never angry.

"All right. Tell us what you saw last night," she said wearily.

The girl grew animated, her eyes round, "Somebody I thought was a woman was sneaking through the village from house to house. He was wearing a dress, but that's all I could see—you know how white glows in moonlight."

"Are you sure it wasn't a real woman?" Bener-ib asked thoughtfully.

"He wasn't shaped like a woman—no hips, no… no shape. And he didn't run like a woman much either. More like a man trying to run like a woman, you know? I first saw him down at the other end, where that big house is, then he went to Kem-sit's. Then I heard an awful scream and lots of other voices screaming. Then the 'woman' came shooting down the steps and off into the trees. I followed him and saw him heading down toward the River. By then, other people were starting to come out of their houses and run toward Kem-sit's, and the servants were running up the stairs and everything, so I headed home as fast as I could go."

"I should hope so. It would have been easy to mistake you for the attempted murderer. Somebody might have shot you with an arrow or thrown a rock at you."

"What were you doing in the village, anyway, Mut-tuy?" Bener-ib asked. "What did you hope to accomplish? You didn't expect to see a crime, surely."

"Oh yes, I did. If I were pretending to be dead and two people who knew me had seen me, I'd try to shut them up. Tjay knew very well where he could find his wife."

"Kem-sit will be the next attempt," said Bener-ib in a hollow voice, and Mut-tuy bobbed her head in savage agreement.

CHAPTER 10

"LET'S LET OUR WITNESSES OUT from under the straw." Neferet bade the foreman to stop the donkey. She started pulling the straw out of the cart until Ta-em-resefu and the three girls emerged, red-faced and gasping. "Everybody all right under there?"

"I'm thirsty, Mama," the smallest child said plaintively.

"We're almost home, and then you can have a big cup of tamarind drink. My mama puts it in the well to keep it cold," Neferet promised. "I'm sorry about that hot, uncomfortable ride, Ta-em-resefu. But if Tjay is still somewhere around the village, he might have seen you and figured out where you were going."

The weaver smiled faintly. "We're only grateful, Lady Neferet."

They entered the yard of the farmhouse, where she helped the wounded woman and her children out of the cart. "Thanks for the loan of your donkey," Neferet said to the foreman. Like everyone in the village, he knew about Tjay and seemed happy to have helped the supervisor's wife escape him. "I'm sure the steward will give you something for your pains, and there's cold water before you start back."

The rustling palms cast a shade that was deeply welcome after the late-morning glare in the fields. A pair of swallows zigzagged overhead as the cavalcade approached the house. Mama, Sati, and Pa-kiki's wife, Mut-nodjmet, were sitting under the grape arbor around the corner, stuffing vine leaves, but they rose and came to greet the new arrivals. Baket-iset called out salutations from her couch.

"Hello, girls. Who are these lovely children?" Mama said with a smile.

"This is Ta-em-resefu, from the village, and her three daughters. They're going to stay with us for a bit if that's all right. Her husband is trying to kill her," Neferet added in a stage whisper.

Mama's eyes widened, and she took in the bandaged shoulder. "Of course you can stay with us. Sati, my love, could you get a few more loaves of bread out of the pantry? I assume you haven't eaten yet, Ta-em-resefu."

"No, my lady," said the weaver shyly. "We're so sorry to inconvenience you."

"No inconvenience at all, my dear." Mama took her elbow and led her gently into the house.

"Pa-kiki and I and the children are going back to Waset this afternoon anyway," said Mut-nodjmet over her shoulder as she followed them. "He has things to see to at the garrison, and the older boys have been away from their classroom long enough."

"There. That works out fine." Neferet thanked the gods for her calm and compassionate mother, who was never flustered by any social emergency. This was the perfect solution.

It must have been awkward for the wounded woman to see around her, as servants, several of her neighbors from the village—a reminder of the difference in social class between her and her hosts—but Mama and Papa had always treated their employees with so much respect and affection that they were more like members of the clan. Many of the families had served the household for generations. The servants spread blankets for a picnic for the children, while some of the grown-ups, including Pa-kiki and Grandfather, chose to sit on stools. Neferet and Bener-ib took their place with the orphans and their nursemaid, a jolly, buxom young woman who seemed unfazed by any behavior. Sati was her sunny self, full of stories about the children that helped put their guest at ease. Although the three little girls were timid at first, the cousins soon welcomed them into their circle as treasured playmates. In all, it was just the sort of simple, congenial meal with plenty of laughter that made holidays at the farm so wonderful.

They'd almost finished when Papa, Maya, and Dapurazo came hiking up from the boathouse. Papa greeted Ta-em-resefu in surprise.

"Tjay tried to kill her," Neferet said over the children's heads. We'll tell you all about it after lunch."

There was a flurry of activity as the meal ended, with Pa-kiki and his brood packing up to head back to the city. The rest of the children were hustled off to a nap, and everyone solicitously urged the wounded woman to rest as well. Mama led her off to the room she and her daughters occupied, and Papa drew his stool closer to the girls.

"Tell me what's going on, duckling."

She explained in eager detail what had happened the previous night, and Mut-tuy filled in proudly with her observations. Neferet could see Papa itching to ask how the adolescent happened to have seen the fleeing criminal in his disguise, but he bit back any questions.

"We went to visit Khnum-em-heb," Papa said. "He's grief-stricken and furious but still thinking clearly when it comes to business."

"He signed the contract," Dapurazo finished. "If Ta-em-resefu is willing to come to Keftiu, this could take her out of harm's way for a while."

"Sounds to me like that lady mayor's the one in danger now." Grandfather scratched his close-cropped gray hair.

Neferet shrugged. "She said Usret checks in on her every day. Although unless Usret sleeps there, too, it may not help much. Maybe Kem-sit should live with her stepdaughter for the time being. Until we catch Tjay."

"That didn't seem to protect Ta-em-resefu. The roof terrace of any house with an exterior staircase is too risky. She should sleep indoors with a guard. Or a dog," Papa added, rubbing Brute's big, furrowed head.

"Maybe she should stay here too," Mut-tuy said.

But Neferet shook her head. "She wouldn't do it. She probably feels she has responsibilities to the village as its mayor. Besides," she added mischievously, "she's stubborn. And stubborn people often end up doing very foolish things to make their point."

Mut-tuy let fly a withering glare, but Bener-ib said in her practical way, "Maybe we should lend her Brute."

"Now that, my girl, is a marvelous idea! Let's walk him

down right now. She may or may not be taking a siesta, but this could save her life."

"I'll go with you," Papa said. "It doesn't seem to be too safe around here all of a sudden."

Although it was getting into the hottest part of the day, the three young women and Papa stood up and prepared to leave. Dapurazo and Maya seemed less enthusiastic.

"Stay here. We don't need six people to transfer Brute to the mayor's household," Papa said with a grin. "Someone tell Nub-nefer where we've gone, though. Father, I believe that means you."

Grandfather slapped his son amicably on the back. "I think this doddering oldster can manage to carry out that mission. Maya will remind me if I forget what I'm supposed to do."

Everyone laughed. Grandfather's memory was perfectly good.

They set out once again on the path through the fields. Neferet had thought to snag a towel on her way out, and now she fixed it around her head like a scarf, with the knot jauntily over one shoulder. "I'm starting to feel like a fried egg," she explained.

Hani hadn't been back to the village for some days, and perhaps it was his imagination, but the shadowy recesses beneath the trees seemed less welcoming than they had before. The tethered donkey watched them with suspicion. During the siesta hour, no childish games disturbed the cicada-drowned silence, and a sense of waiting hung in the air. Waiting… for another attempt at murder?

Their footsteps, crunching on the dry leaves and sticks that littered the village between paths, struck Hani as unnaturally loud. So was the knock he pounded on the frame of Kem-sit's door. Almost immediately, she appeared in the opening.

"Lord Hani. Lady Neferet." She nodded to include the others. "What brings you here?"

"We thought you might need Brute more than we do for a while." Neferet patted the dog affectionately on the head. "He's the best guardian ever. He saved our lives once."

Kem-sit looked skeptically at the animal panting and drooling peaceably at the young doctor's side. "I don't think that's necessary. I don't know how I'd feed somethin' that big anyway." She finally reached out and caressed his ears.

In the doorway, Usret pushed aside the fly mat and stuck her head out. "Oh, you have company."

"You remember Lady Neferet. This is her father, Lord Hani, the local landowner. They thought I might want to borrow their guard dog."

The younger woman bobbed a small bow, her eyes fixed on Brute and her expression uneasy. She was the thinnest person Hani had ever seen who wasn't in bed, dying. She seemed, however, spry enough, like some sort of long-limbed insect.

"That dog's not safe," Usret said. "He's more likely to bite you than protect you, Kem-sit."

Hani felt his hackles rise. No one spoke ill of animals in his presence. But some people were simply afraid of them, and it was true that Brute had a formidable presence. "I guess Kem-sit has told you the good news that the dead man we found wasn't your brother, mistress."

"Why, yes." Usret broke into a huge smile that didn't seem to touch her eyes. "She gave me back my reason to live."

The mayor said dryly, "I also told her what Tjay attempted on his wife last night."

The two women exchanged a glance, and Usret's smile melted off into an expression of wide-eyed disbelief. She said with great animation, "I just can't accept that, Lord Hani. I know that's what the little girls thought they saw, but Tjay would never, ever do something like that. He's a gentle soul."

Kem-sit appeared to restrain herself with difficulty but said nothing.

"You never knew him, any of you, or you'd realize that none of this could be his doing. He's a scholar, a literate man." Usret hastened to add with ostentatious humility, "I mean, I don't mean to contradict you, you understand."

Hani thought that he'd known a good many literate men who were thoroughgoing scoundrels. And as for Tjay's being a scholar, Hani wasn't sure bookkeeping—or lording it over intimidated women weavers—counted as scholarship. Tjay sounded very much like the sort of person Hani didn't like at all, and this sister who defended the rascal rubbed him the wrong way. He wondered how she excused his habitual treatment of Ta-em-resefu. *Although love often does blind one*, he thought in the interests of *ma'at*.

"Don't worry, mistress. If he's guilty, there'll be proof. If not, he'll be cleared. No one wants to punish the wrong man. It's Kem-sit and her council who will judge this case, and you know she's a fair person." He smiled at Usret comfortingly.

"It's so good of you to reassure me." Usret smiled again with a melting tilt of the head, staring hard into Hani's eyes in a way that made him itchy. Her emotions seemed both intense and strangely detached.

An odd woman, he told himself. *I don't feel like I have a grasp on her.*

"You're sure you don't want Brute to guard you?" Neferet asked Kem-sit as if to change the subject.

"No, but I thank you for the thought, Lady Neferet. You've all been real generous." She turned to Usret. "They're the ones who are puttin' up Ta-em-resefu and the girls."

"So very generous," her stepdaughter echoed earnestly.

"Well, we take our leave, then, mistresses. Watch out for yourselves. If you need anything, we're at your service."

They turned to leave, but Usret said to their backs, "Tjay would never have dressed up as a woman, Lord Hani. He has too much dignity."

Hani faced her again briefly and said in an amiable voice, "That may well be true, mistress. And if so, Ma'at will make known her truth."

They set off through the settlement. Here and there, a villager, watching their departure, lifted a hand in greeting. *Everybody here probably knows exactly what's going on.* But that was good. The more eyes peeled, the more likely they were to see something.

The little party had almost entered the uninhabited fields when they heard someone hailing them from behind. Hani spun and saw a man running after them from the shadow of the trees, waving his arms. Hani put out a hand to stop his daughter.

"What can we do for you?" he called.

The man jogged up to them, panting. He was youngish, dressed only in a loincloth, and toasted as brown as a carob pod by the sun. "You're Lord Hani, right?" he gasped. "They all said you wanted to know anything unusual, so here it is. I'm a fisherman, and I wanted to tell you I seen something odd about a week ago. I was comin' home around twilight or even after—my net had got stuck in the reeds, and it'd took a long time to get it loose. Everybody else'd gone on. It was pretty dark down in the marshes, you know? I saw a crocodile slippin' around, so I finally pulled my boat up on a sandbar and was gonna walk the rest of the way back to the village. Didn't have much in my creel, but them crocs smell the fish, and they can be on you in a minute, you know? Not a good idea to be on the water after dark."

Hani assured the man he knew. *Get to the heart of your story, my friend*, he thought impatiently.

The fisherman, his eyes wide, was enjoying being the object of everyone's attention. "But then I heard rustlin', like somethin' big comin' through the rushes. I froze, like, thinking it was a croc for sure, and then I saw two people in the reeds. One was pullin' the other one, who was like dead or knocked out. Then they shoved him into the River an' went away. I hotfooted it outa there."

Hani's heart stepped up its pace. *Could this fellow be an eyewitness?* "You didn't notify anyone?" he asked, trying not to sound judgmental. "Even when everybody knew there'd been a murder?"

"I been gone, my lord," the fisherman said defensively. "I been up to Seyawt to see my sister. She's been sick. Anybody'll tell you. An' then she died, an' I hadn't given no more thought to that stuff in the marshes till today, when I come back. Everybody's been sayin', 'Tell 'em! Tell 'em!'"

"Were they two men, or was either of them dressed like a woman?" Neferet asked, her voice quivering with eagerness. "Did you recognize any of the villagers?"

The fisherman started to look uneasy. He probably hadn't counted on questions. "I, I don't know, my lady. It was dark, and they wasn't a lot of moon a week ago. I just saw white clothes. Long, I'd say. Coulda been a man or a woman but not dressed like me, you know? Long clothes. Both of 'em."

"Two scribes." Neferet fixed Hani with a look of triumph.

"Could be," said the fisherman. "They's only one scribe in our village, but I couldn't swear either one was him. It was dark, and they was reeds between us."

Hani pulled off the faience ring he was wearing and slipped it to the man. "Thank you for your information. It's very useful. You did right to tell us."

"Thanks, Lord Hani." The fellow examined the ring delightedly. It would buy him a week's good dinners. He bobbed a hasty bow.

"If you think of anything else, be sure to tell Kem-sit. She knows where we live."

"Yes, my lord. Thank you, my lord." The fisherman turned and jogged back toward the settlement, leaving Hani and the young women staring after him.

"I feel like his witness is important," said Hani after a moment's digestion. "But I'm not sure that he really added anything to what we know."

Neferet narrowed her eyes in thought. "You know what

strikes me? The dead man had on no jewelry, no amulets—nothing at all that could have identified him. Do you suppose they fell off in the reeds or where he was killed? Because I'm not sure that a self-absorbed jackal like Tjay would have thought to take them off him."

"Maybe the fisherman took them," Mut-tuy said avidly. "I mean, he must have approached the victim—what if the injured man was still alive? He might've drowned. Wouldn't you have run to help?"

She's sharp, Hani observed. "Maybe not if you were afraid there was a crocodile lurking around and wanted badly to get away from the water. Although it would have been the right thing to do. It's also possible that the reed cutters who found him took them."

Neferet put her hands on her hips. "But this at least means he was killed here, near to the village, doesn't it? The person who shoved Hapu-seneb into the River approached by land. He didn't dump him from a boat."

"That seems to be the case."

Neferet nodded. "So it's just as we thought. Tjay lured Hapu-seneb to the village—"

"Or caught him red-handed with Tjay's wife!" the adolescent said.

"And probably killed him right there and then dragged him into the reeds to dispose of him."

"How far away from the village is this sandbar where everything took place?" Bener-ib had finally said something, and as usual, it was well worth considering. "Because it would be hard to drag a limp body any distance. It would have made noise, and somebody in the village would have seen or heard."

"That's true," Neferet said. "We need to ask the fisherman. Maybe Tjay carried Hapu-seneb over his shoulder. The dead man seemed like a lightly built person."

"Even harder over marshy ground. The bearer's footsteps would have sunk into the wet sand under that doubled weight. Bener-ib has made a good point." Hani tipped the little *sunet* an admiring nod.

"Why does it matter to reconstruct the place of the murder, though?" Mut-tuy asked.

Hani said, "When we take Tjay to court before the village council, he'll use anything he can to make it sound like he couldn't have committed the murder. We have to be able to describe the crime convincingly. For example, someone needs to ask Ta-em-resefu exactly how that last evening of her husband's presence played out. Would he have been able to leave the house without her knowing? How long was he gone? How was it no one saw him at sundown in a village that small, with everyone outdoors all the time? That sort of thing."

Neferet gave him a big hug. "Papa, you clearly know what you're doing. It's a joy to behold a master craftsman at work."

Hani threw back his head and laughed, warmed despite himself by the admiration of his little duckling. "I wouldn't go that far. It's just a matter of trying to foresee all objections."

"I say we three"—Neferet was already straining back toward the village they had left— "should go back and interrogate that fisherman again and see if anybody else can add anything to our information. And then we need to talk to Ta-em-resefu when we get back to the farm. Unless you do that part, Papa Duck."

"Very well," he said. "I can do that. But you girls be careful. It's getting late. Be back before dark, understand? Things are dangerous around here until Tjay is found and locked up."

The trio of eager investigators took off, running back toward the village. Hani watched them go, his heart clenched with trepidation. He'd sworn to himself he wouldn't give them orders like little girls, but perhaps he was getting too close to encouraging them in their innocent pursuit of a killer. *Great Hidden One, protect them*, he prayed. *Mut, the mother of us all, watch over them. They're trying to serve your daughter, Ma'at.*

CHAPTER 11

"YOU LEFT THE GIRLS IN the village?" Nub-nefer cried. "Hani, my love, I thought you were going to look out for them."

Hani squirmed. He feared he'd made a mistake in his determination to trust the maturity of his daughter and her friends. "That was my intention, my dove. I thought they'd be safe in broad daylight."

"Well, let's hope they have the sense to come back before it's no longer daylight."

The two of them stood inside the vestibule, in the semidarkness. The rest of the family was outside under the grapevine—he could hear the laughter and chatter of his daughters and the chanting of the children, who were involved in some raucous game.

It pained Hani to have been the instrument of his wife's disquietude. "I can rejoin them if you think that would be a good idea."

"If it starts to get late and they're still not back. But I suppose we have to give them room to prove themselves."

She put her arms around him and laid her head on his chest. Her voice echoed straight into Hani's heart. "Neferet has given us more anxiety than all the others put together. She's good-hearted and smart, but she doesn't have a healthy dose of fear about things. And Mut-tuy is worse, although who can blame her? She's just a child. Neferet should be setting an example."

"I continue to hope," said Hani with a strained smile. "Between the good influence of Bener-ib and Baket's oracular assurance that the duckling will be all right, I have to be optimistic."

Nub-nefer drew back and stared her husband fiercely in the eye. "When I see how terrorized those little girls are and how cowed poor Ta-em-resefu has grown over the years, it makes me realize what a terrible person our girls are up against. You have to apprehend him, Hani. Don't leave these poor people alone and vulnerable."

"I know," he said uneasily. "I won't. I have some questions to ask Ta-em-resefu, then I'll head back to the village." He sighed. "I'd just as soon leave poor Dapurazo out of it. He's only here for business on behalf of his king, but he seems to have gotten emotionally involved. He has the same kind of curiosity that Neferet has."

"He's a nice man," Nub-nefer said. "He blends quite well into what must seem like the very foreign environment of our family."

Hani bent to kiss the top of his wife's hair. "Shows his good taste."

"Is he married, do you know?"

Hani laughed. "Who are you trying to match him with? No, actually, I believe he's a widower."

"I just wondered if he had children of his own. He's very at home around them."

"He's never mentioned any."

Unsurprisingly, Ta-em-resefu and her daughters were outside with Mery-ra, Maya, Dapurazo, Baket-iset, Sati, and the latter's children. Tepy, at ten, was a regular little father of the family. He'd organized his siblings and the orphans into teams and was putting them through game after game. The resultant chaos provided the adults with an amusing spectacle. But the weaver's three little girls clung timidly to their mother until they were gently disengaged and urged to join the other children.

"Ta-em-resefu, my dear, do you mind if I ask you some questions? We'd like to know about the night before your husband disappeared." Hani crossed his ankles and sank to the ground at the young woman's side.

"Do you want us to leave, Lord Hani?" asked Dapurazo, who was seated at the weaver's other side.

"No, no. None of this is a state secret." Hani gave the man of Keftiu a wink then turned back to Ta-em-resefu.

"Whatever you want to know, my lord."

Mery-ra and Maya scooted closer, and the men all leaned in. Anyone passing might have thought they were shooting knucklebones.

"When did you see him last?"

"About two days before, before… the body showed up." She struggled to contain the tears that welled up in her eyes. "As usual, he was angry with me. He rarely flew into a rage, but he could become very cutting. He had me in tears. I was so emotionally exhausted that I fell asleep as soon as I dropped into bed."

"Did he go to bed with you?"

"Not as far as I know. He left the house before I even lay down, with a big slam of the door, as he often did. He was always threatening to leave me. I think he wanted me to worry each time that this time, he wouldn't come back." She gave a hiccup of dark humor. "And it was finally true."

"Was he aware of your relationship with Hapu-seneb?" Hani asked. Tjay's promise to leave might not have been such a threat to a woman who dreamed of being free to remarry.

Ta-em-resefu shook her head slowly. "I don't believe he was. He never said anything, and I'm sure he would have. He was extremely jealous, always thinking I'd looked at some man. Once, he even got mad because he found Khnum-em-heb at the house. His master! He had just come to look for Tjay. No, if Tjay had known, he would've beat me black and blue. Probably killed me."

There goes Tjay's motive for killing Hapu-seneb, Hani thought in surprise. "What did the two of you quarrel about that night?"

"I wanted to weave again, but he refused to let me. He said it was low class, and people would think he couldn't support his family."

"Do you have any idea where he went when he stormed out of the house like that? Is there a beer house in the village?" Mery-ra asked.

"No, there isn't, Lord Mery-ra. At least sometimes, he went to his sister's. She would tell me the next day."

Hani tried to picture Usret, such a loyal supporter of her brother, tattling on him to his wife. Perhaps his visits were a source of pride, and Usret would want to flaunt them. "What's your relationship with her? Did you see her much?"

"I wouldn't say we're really close—she's an odd sort. But I see her a lot. She's over at Kem-sit's all the time. She was young enough when Kem-sit married Pa-shedu that I guess she thinks of her as her mother. She tries to make me see Tjay's side of arguments. But I can't say she doesn't seem sympathetic to me too. She's actually a nice person. I don't know why I don't feel more at ease with her."

Hani understood her ambivalence. "Let's say that after he left your house, Tjay headed down to his sister's. Would people in the village have seen him? It's a small place. I can imagine not much is private there."

"That's true, but it was after dark. Most people would have been eating inside or even have been in bed. There was a moon, but I still think it would've been mere chance if someone saw him. The mosquitoes are too terrible at night to stay outdoors, even if it's hot."

Hani leaned toward the woman and said quietly, "Ta-em-resefu, a fisherman saw two people in long clothing down in the marshes that night. One dragged the other one to the water's edge and threw him in. What was Tjay wearing when he left your house?"

The weaver's eyes grew wide with anguish. Perhaps she was picturing her lover's last moments. Dabbing at her nose with the back of her hand, she said in a halting voice, "His usual clothes, Lord Hani. A shirt down to midcalf and a kilt on top of that. He had a nice faience *weshket* collar that he always wore because he thought it looked high class, but he'd taken it off for the evening. No jewelry. A wig with long lappets."

"Is that what he was wearing when you saw him in Waset?" asked Maya.

"I, I don't even remember, my lord. What I noticed was his face." The tears had started to flow again, dribbling unwiped down her cheeks.

Hani sat back, pondering. "Usret's house is near the water's edge. Maybe he didn't go to his sister's after all but continued down along the riverbank. Did she say anything the following morning?"

Ta-em-resefu's eyebrows grew tense, as if she were trying hard to recall the memory. "I don't think I saw her the next morning, Lord Hani. Which wouldn't have been unusual, because neither her nor me always came to Kem-sit's at the same time of day. It was just whenever I could get away, and I suppose it was the same in her case."

Mery-ra caught Hani's eye. "He might well have gone into the marshes, son. But why? Did he have a rendezvous with Hapu-seneb for some reason? Might his sister have told him the man was alone among the reeds?"

"Maybe, but the question is still why," Maya said. "Why was Hapu-seneb even in the village at night? He lived in Waset."

"Perhaps he came to see Ta-em-resefu. For a man who loved her, her presence must have been a powerful attraction, even enough for him to risk his life." Dapurazo gazed at the weaver moonily.

Hani asked her, "Were you expecting him?"

"No. But I guess I was hoping. Sometimes, he would show up unexpectedly when Tjay had left."

"That must mean he was watching your house," Mery-ra said with a knowing nod. "He must have come often to the village. Any reason he might have gone into the marshes?"

Maya looked eagerly from Hani to his father. "Could he have expected to meet Ta-em-resefu there?"

"In the marshes?" She looked confused.

But Hani had a sudden suspicion. "What if he was planning to run away with you that night—to take you up to Men-nefer, where he'd been sent, and disappear with you there?"

"We had talked about it in a general way. But he never said anything about that night. How was I supposed to know?"

"You aren't literate, so he couldn't have written you a note. He must have sent someone with a message. Someone who never arrived." A thrill, as of the truth hanging just outside his grasp, twinkled its way up Hani's spine.

The next step was for someone to pronounce the name of the messenger. But nobody knew it. Ta-em-resefu stared expectantly from face to face, twisting her hands in her lap.

"Can you think of anybody you both knew?" Hani prompted.

"Tjay. Kem-sit. Maybe the other people who wove for his father."

"He might just have seen somebody walking around the village that evening and called out to them, figuring everyone knows everyone else. It might even have been a youngster who forgot or was called inside or didn't take him seriously," Mery-ra suggested.

Ta-em-resefu was puckering up again. The terrible irony of such a scenario must have wounded her worse than the knife that had pierced her shoulder.

"Think, my girl. Who in the village had any kind of link with Hapu-seneb?"

She bowed silently over her hands in thought, gnawing her lip, then looked up at Hani. "Other than the weavers… nobody. But even there, it's not like he was involved so much with the business. We'd just catch sight of him with his father now and then. It was Tjay who went around and collected the piecework and paid people. I don't think most people in the village would even know who Hapu-seneb was if they saw him."

Hani heaved himself awkwardly to his feet, and the others followed. "I'm going to take this information to Neferet and the girls in the village. Then we can split up and ask around. If our theory is correct, Hapu-seneb spoke to somebody that night—somebody who didn't reach you with a message. But somehow, Tjay got wind of it."

"I'll go with you, my lord," said Maya in a determined tone.

Dapurazo looked apologetic. "Do you mind if I stay here, Lord Hani? Perhaps I can coax some more memories out of our victim." He smiled beguilingly at Ta-em-resefu.

Mery-ra leaned toward his son and said in a stage whisper, "Sounds like they may need a chaperone."

Hani grinned. "Then come on, Maya. It's getting late. We need to do what we have to and bring the girls back before dark."

Neferet mopped her forehead and adjusted the towel on her head. The afternoon heat sat on her shoulders like a sack of lead, and humidity rose in a visible blur from the waters of the River in a way that it didn't even reach as far inland as the farm. They'd tracked the fisherman up and down, but he had apparently returned to the marshes, and Kem-sit had been involved with the men and women of her council, so they hadn't been able to talk to her, either. It had been a fruitless, unpleasant afternoon, and Neferet's temper was worn to the warp threads. Bener-ib trudged doggedly at her side, sweat running down her face from under her heavy hair, and Mut-tuy snapped at anyone who said a word. Only Brute seemed patient, but his tail hung lower and lower.

"Let's try Kem-sit's again. We've got to find some water. She must have a well."

They dragged back along the dusty path into the welcome shade of the trees that skirted the mayor's house. No voices came from the roof terrace, and Neferet dared to hope that the meeting had ended. The tethered donkey watched them pass, its switching tail the only sign of life. The cicadas' razzing was a curtain of sound so thick it required effort to wade through.

Neferet banged on the frame of the open door. "Kem-sit? It's me."

The mayor appeared a moment later with a big wooden spoon in her hand and an apron around her waist. "Lady Neferet. What can I do for you?"

"Could we have a drink of water?" the young woman pleaded unashamedly. "I swear by Mama's *ka*, I've never been so hot in my life."

"It's a bad one. Feels like something's coming." Kem-sit invited the three inside. The airless salon was no more pleasant than the exterior, but the jug of water the mayor brought them a moment later, sparkling with condensation, made Neferet's parched mouth salivate.

Kem-sit poured each of them a big cupful, and the young women drank greedily. Neferet set out the last of hers on the floor for Brute, who lapped it with noisy gusto.

"How's the investigation going?" Kem-sit asked.

"At the moment, we aren't making much progress. I hope Papa has found out something. He was going to ask Ta-em-resefu about the last evening before Tjay disappeared." Neferet pulled the cloth off her head and waved it in front of her face like a fan. A tepid breeze rewarded her.

"Let's go up on the roof terrace," Kem-sit said. "It'll be cooler up there now that there's shade."

She led the way out into the yard, scattering the geese with a flap of the apron. They mounted the steep masonry stairs and settled on the terrace, where the trees had begun to protect the area with their rustling late-afternoon shadows. Overhead, the sky had taken on a strange yellowish-brown color.

"This morning, a fisherman told us he had seen two men in long clothes out in the marshes the night Hapu-seneb was probably murdered."

"Or women—he couldn't tell," Bener-ib inserted.

"Or a man and a woman." Mut-tuy had to get her opinion in.

"Right," said Neferet. She shot Mut-tuy a look. *Let me finish, or we'll be here all night.* "Or a man and a man dressed as a woman. He couldn't tell, all right? It was dark, and he was afraid because there was a crocodile around. He wanted to get off the water. But he saw one of these people push the other one into the River. We wanted to talk to him again and get more information from him. Like, where is the sandbar all this took place on? Is it close to the village? Because it wouldn't be easy to drag a dead body very far. But we've spent the whole afternoon looking, and we can't find him."

Kem-sit nodded. "That's Int-ef. He just got back today from his sister's funeral, and I told him he needed to talk to you. He's probably back on the water by now."

"Do you know at what spot in the marshes he saw this take place?" Neferet asked eagerly.

"Not for sure. But I know where the sandbar is. If somebody dragged a body, it would've crushed down the reeds. You could probably find the exact spot pretty easily."

Excitement hit Neferet like a bucket of cold well water upended over her head. She sprang to her feet. "Come on, people. Let's find this place!"

"Lady Neferet," said Kem-sit hastily, scrambling after her as Neferet headed for the door. "There's something I didn't get to tell you. Remember when you was here this morning and Usret said Tjay would never have dressed as a woman?"

"Yes?"

"I hadn't said—"

"Oh, are you leaving?"

The words made the four women turn. Usret stood at the top of the stairs, a basket in her arms, covered with a towel. "I made sesame treats, Kem-sit. But if you're all going out..."

Kem-sit looked startled, but she regrouped quickly. "Thank you, my girl. Perhaps Lady Neferet and her friends would like some before they leave."

"I wouldn't say no," Neferet said. Usret peeled back the towel and offered the basket, and Neferet helped herself to a pair of honey-saturated cakes. "These look really good. Thanks."

They stood around, scoffing down the treats, which were, in fact, delicious. Usret might look half starved, but it wasn't because she couldn't cook. "What brings you to the village?" she asked with her smile both vague and penetrating.

Neferet explained briefly about the fisherman's testimony.

Usret listened, seemingly fascinated. "I can take you there. I know where that sandbar is. Everybody does."

Bener-ib eyed the sky, which had grown darker. "Is it far? Looks like it may rain."

Just our luck, thought Neferet, annoyed. *The one day all summer that it rains is the day we want to go out into the marshes.*

"No, it's not far. Do you think it's all right, Kem-sit?" Usret looked to her stepmother with girlish deference.

"Hurry, then. It's gettin' toward evening anyway."

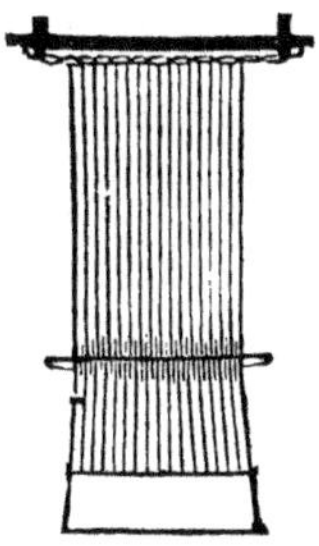

CHAPTER 12

THE THREE WOMEN AND A girl thudded down the stairs. At the bottom, Brute stood waiting. He sniffed Usret with the earnestness of a customs officer, his tail slowing gradually, while Usret looked petrified.

Only when the mastiff had completed his examination did she dare go on, murmuring, "That dog is dangerous."

No, but he can sense which people are trustworthy, Neferet thought. Only she wasn't sure what the verdict had been on Usret. There had been no growls, but neither had the welcome been warm. Perhaps even Brute was confused by the woman's odd affect. Neferet herself was pondering Kem-sit's incomplete message—"I hadn't said"—before Usret had interrupted them.

The three *sunet*s followed Usret's quick steps through the village. She moved oddly, like a stick figure, all angular movements. Now and again, a fellow villager waved, and she responded with effusive friendliness. The air had grown heavier and heavier.

Neferet was almost ready to say, "You know, it's late, and

we're about to have a storm. Let's just wait until tomorrow," but the houses and trees of the village had fallen behind them, and the tall, luminous fronds of the papyrus and reeds began to stretch overhead. The solidity of the bank sank into mire, where only a narrow trail of firm ground meandered between the lapping dark bog waters. A distant rumble of thunder rattled the cattails. Behind them, the reeds had closed solid, hiding the habitations, which had to be less than half an *iteru* in distance. Yet the four women might just as well have been on the Primal Mound before the creation of the world. From somewhere in the River, a heavy splash sounded.

Bener-ib let out a squeak. "I want to go back, Nef'et. Let's go back."

Neferet was uneasy as well. Her flesh crept with the thought of a murderous crocodile cruising the waters just a cubit or two from her feet. "Go back, then, my girl, and Mut-tuy too. When Papa comes, you can tell him where we've gone."

"But I want—" Mut-tuy began.

"Please, Nef'et. You come back too. This isn't a good time to be out in the marshes." Bener-ib's face was drawn with anxiety. If her eyes had possessed hands, like things sometimes did in pictures of the afterlife, they would have been clinging to Neferet's dress, trying to drag her back.

"But, Ibet, my girl…" Neferet felt helpless. Half of her wanted desperately to turn back, and the other half would have done anything not to hurt Bener-ib.

But that half also didn't want to look like a cowardly little girl. Usret didn't seem afraid of the weather. Surely, it wasn't so perilous.

Neferet lowered her voice and said in an almost whisper, "Ibet, I swear nothing will happen to me. If things look too dangerous, I'll come back. We said we'd always be together, right? I won't let anything happen."

Bener-ib stared at her with anguished intensity. Then she lowered her gaze, but not before Neferet saw tears sparkling on her cheeks. "Just be careful. Don't take any chances. I-I couldn't bear to lose you." She stretched up and deposited a quick kiss on Neferet's lips.

Neferet's heart was pounding. She was afraid she'd tempted the gods by insisting everything would be all right. Besides, her conscience was as raw as if she'd dragged its nails over a piece of slate. If they parted right now, Bener-ib would be in as much danger as Neferet would.

Neferet tried to sound composed and fearless, but her voice trembled. "Mut-tuy, go back with Ibet, and take Brute with you."

She pictured the two young women standing in full view, all alone in the twilight, waiting for Papa—easy prey for a worse sort of predator than the four-legged kind. Perhaps it was the impending storm darkening the sky that gave her such a sense of foreboding, but suddenly, their whole situation seemed terribly dangerous.

"Do it," Neferet said. "It's important. One of you may have to go for help."

She could see by the fear on Bener-ib's face—and even Mut-tuy's—that she'd succeeded in infecting them.

"Be careful, Nef'et," murmured Bener-ib, grabbing her quickly and fervently by the hands.

Then Bener-ib and the adolescent took off running, following the trail of broken reeds they'd left on the way in.

After a questioning look, Brute loped off in their wake. A good soldier didn't challenge orders.

"That Mut-tuy is so stubborn," Neferet said, more to tamp down her fear than because she felt any inclination to make small talk. The hair on the back of her neck was practically buzzing.

A shocking noise, like an explosion, sounded from just beside her. She jumped, nearly crying out, but then realized it was a frog.

"You're lucky to have friends who care so much about you." Usret turned and set out once more. It was nearly dark under the tall papyrus. "There used to be somebody who loved me. But that didn't work out."

"You're married, aren't you? Surely, your husband cares for you."

"I guess."

Neferet was aware that she was expected to show interest. The marsh was a place where she felt like human voices were a profanation, but she asked dutifully, "Do you have children?"

"No. Only my brother. And Kem-sit."

"She cares about you, I'm sure."

"I'm not. You know, Lady Neferet, I try to be a person people like, but I'm not convinced I succeed."

It was such an odd thing to say that Neferet's sense of ill increased. "But you're very likable. Kem-sit and Ta-em-resefu have both said how nice you are."

"That says more about them than about me." Usret stopped and turned to Neferet. A heavy growl of thunder punctuated the gesture. She was staring, and her head tilted like a bird's, trying to understand. "Kem-sit said you're a doctor. Is there something wrong with me?"

Somehow, the question sent un uneasy ripple up Neferet's spine. The setting, the hour, the conversation—it was all so nightmarish, with the fractured logic of a bad dream—that she wouldn't have been surprised had Usret floated away at that point and a frog spoken human words. The River at their side gave another ominous gurgle.

"Because you don't think people like you? No, no. You simply lack self-confidence." Neferet forced a big smile. "Just keep being the good person you are. How far is that sandbar, do you think?"

All at once, and for no obvious reason except that her thoughts had finally absorbed it despite their distractions, the meaning of the warning Kem-sit had tried to send jumped out at Neferet. Usret had mentioned the fact that Tjay was disguised as a woman, but Kem-sit hadn't told her about that. Usret must have been communicating directly with her brother. She had to be in cahoots with the murderer.

The weaver turned once more and began to walk. "Not far."

But the going had become much more difficult. This was by no means a much-used path, and even Usret, who was about as narrow as an adult human could be, had to push aside the reeds with both hands to advance. Meanwhile, a few heavy drops had fallen. The sky overhead, where it was visible, was a bruised indigo.

Neferet's heart was walloping her ribs like a trapped bird. "You know," she said in a falsely cheerful voice, "it's getting really dark. I'm afraid we're going to have trouble finding our way home. Perhaps we'd better come back by daylight."

"Do you think? The sandbar is very close."

She could no longer remember why it was important to find the sandbar. *Ah, yes. Hapu-seneb was perhaps killed near there.* A chill wind lashed in off the water, sending the reeds clacking loudly one against another, but whether it was the cold occasional drops of rain or something else that made her hair stand on end, the young woman couldn't have said. Now she was not only afraid of the dark and the storm but of her guide—the woman she was trusting to bring her home alive from this fool's mission.

"I was in love once, when I was young." Usret had begun to speak again in a sad, dreamy voice. "But it didn't last."

"Come, come. You're still young. What? Thirty, if that?" Neferet said heartily.

She didn't want to yield to her fear. After all, Usret didn't seem to have the same premonitions about the dangers of the marsh that she did, although Neferet was increasingly suspicious that the weaver was at least moonstruck if not part of Tjay's criminal plot. More drops of rain began to fall.

To the pit with not looking afraid. "I'm going back, Usret. We won't see anything anyway."

Without waiting for the woman to offer to join her, Neferet turned and bolted back up the path, wild to get away. But it wasn't easy going. The storm was breaking. The wind hit her like a sudden slap, laying the reeds horizontal in her track, almost knocking her off her feet. The rain came down sideways with the stinging violence of a volley of arrows. She could no longer tell the flooded solid ground from the marsh. Her bare feet were up to their ankles in the swirling black water of the rain-pocked River.

Where's the path? Where in the name of all that's holy is the path? Her heart was hammering in her mouth. *You mustn't panic or you're a goner.* But it was dark now, and lots of reeds were broken by the wind. She couldn't find her way.

Khonsu the Traveler, help me! Great One, I swear, I'll never be cross with Mut-tuy again if you help me. May the crocodiles eat my toes if I do! May leeches plug up my ears! May frogs slither down the back of my dress!

She floundered in the direction she thought must be upstream and inland, splashing, stumbling, beating at the reeds. The only illumination was the lightning that blazed through the darkness, blinding white, at a frightening frequency, casting jagged shards of shadow. But there were no landmarks, just a featureless world of shuddering reeds lying down before her—and endless darkness.

The marshes aren't wide. Dry land can't be far.

Unless she was turned around completely, heading for the open waters of the River. At night. In a marsh full of crocodiles. A low wail escaped her.

Then, as suddenly as it had started, the rain stopped. The storm raced away at the pace of a bounding antelope. The battered reeds threw icy slingstones of water at her, but she was so sodden already it didn't even add to her misery. With a desperate gasp of effort, she burst ahead—out of the forest of wet papyrus and into open air. Before her, the blacker silhouette of the village huddled, sparking here and there with lamplight, against the faintly orange horizon. Overhead, the first stars were emerging and a slender crescent of moon. Crickets pulsed. The frogs that had seemed mocking in their own kingdom now played joyous castanets.

Neferet heaved an enormous sigh that emptied her whole body of the fear that had inflated it. "What about Usret, though?" she murmured, looking back uneasily at the dark marshes. She should wait to be sure the weaver was safe.

But the last person Neferet wanted at her side in the dark where no one could see was Tjay's sister. *She'll come out now. She knows the terrain.* Neferet ran up the gentle slope into the village and cast her eyes around desperately for Bener-ib and Mut-tuy.

By the time Hani reached the village, the sky had begun to look ominous. "I do believe we're going to have a rain," he said to Maya in some surprise. "Have you ever seen the cliff above Neb-ma'at-ra's mortuary temple? There's a pool up there that fills with rain, on those rare occasions when there is any, and it comes pouring down in a horsetail you can see from the city. It's a thing of beauty."

"I've never noticed," his son-in-law said, staring around. "Where do you suppose the girls would be?"

"I think Kem-sit's house might be a good place to start looking. I'm sure they've talked to her."

Hani led the way into the shadows of the trees, where evening was already settled in. A nightingale started its song then fell silent. The air was growing disturbingly heavy, and in the untidy yard of the mayor, the fowl had gone to roost early. A low "woof" greeted them from near the door, and Brute rose to welcome them, his curled tail waving.

"I guess we know where the girls are," Hani said, smiling with deeper relief than he would have liked to admit. Nub-nefer's worries had reminded him that they had passed beyond the innocent stage of identifying a dead man. There was somebody abroad who might well want to shut the young women up.

"Who's there?" called Kem-sit from within the house. She appeared shortly with a wooden spoon in her hand and an apron tied around her hips. "Oh, Lord Hani. Come in. I was pickling, but I'm finished. What can I do for you?"

"Have you seen the girls this afternoon, mistress?"

"Yes, they was all here a short time ago. They went off with Usret into the marshes to see where Hapu-seneb's body was thrown in. Lady Bener-ib and that young girl turned back. They're here now."

Hani exchanged a look with Maya. "Neferet's not back? The storm's coming."

Kem-sit shrugged, but it was a gesture more fatalistic than uncaring. "Tenacious one, your daughter." She must have noticed his anxiety because she attempted to reassure him. "Usret knows the marshes well, my lord—like everyone who was born and raised here. Besides, she helps her husband cut reeds for his boats. Lady Neferet may get wet, but she's not in any real danger of gettin' lost."

And can Usret also charm crocodiles and hippopotamuses? Hani smiled thinly. "Do you mind if we wait here for her? We'll stay out of your way."

"Oh, you ain't in my way. The others are in the kitchen." The mayor led the two men through her salon into the open-air shelter that served as a kitchen. Several crocks, lidded with flat pieces of limestone, stood against the wall. Bener-ib and Mut-tuy, who were squatting alongside them, jumped to their feet.

"Lord Hani," Bener-ib said, her high-pitched voice cracking with nerves. "Nef'et went on into the marshes with Mistress Usret. I'm so worried about her."

"I wanted to stay with her," Mut-tuy said, "but she made me go."

"I'm sure she'll be fine," Hani said with an assurance he didn't feel. "I'm told Usret knows the marshes well."

"She's so strange," said Mut-tuy distastefully. She widened her eyes and tilted her head, an artificial smile on her face, clearly imitating Usret.

Bener-ib elbowed her and said with unexpected fierceness, "Don't make fun of people."

Hani changed the subject. "Did you girls find out anything interesting this afternoon?"

"Not so much, Lord Hani. We never found the fisherman, but then Usret said she could take us to the sandbar he mentioned, so we set off. But the weather looks horrible." Bener-ib cast an uneasy glance up at the sky beyond the reed shelter. "I got scared, but Nef'et wouldn't turn back."

"We came up with a likely theory that may explain why Hapu-seneb found himself in the marshes that night." Hani recapitulated the scenario he and the other men had concocted with the help of Ta-em-resefu. "But clearly, whoever was supposed to take Ta-em-resefu the message to meet him there didn't do it."

"But instead took it to Tjay," said Kem-sit dully. She heaved a sigh.

Hani looked at her, and a light dawned. "Of course! That was undoubtedly what happened. And so it wasn't Ta-em-resefu who met him in the marshes but her husband, who had just been informed of her infidelity. Well done, Kem-sit! I think we've reconstructed the evening up to that point. And of course, the next step was the murder." He turned a beaming face on Maya, who looked properly impressed.

"Now we just need to find the messenger," Maya said. "He may have acted in complete innocence."

"Or she." Kem-sit stared grimly at Hani.

There was a pregnant silence, then suddenly thunder rumbled, like a heavy wagon rolling over a corduroy bridge. In the courtyard, outside the reed shelter, big drops began to fall.

"Do you say that because you know something, mistress?" Hani asked quietly.

"Not for sure, but it seems to fit." The mayor seemed increasingly reluctant to speak.

"And you mean who?"

"Usret."

This time, the silence was born of the in-taken breaths of the human listeners. Hani stared at the woman, not shocked but realizing with a jolt, as he processed the idea, how likely it was. There was only one hitch.

"Is she someone Hapu-seneb would have known? Would he have given her such a delicate mission to carry out?"

Kem-sit crossed her ankles and slid to the floor. She

nodded. Hani and Maya and the young women settled down around her.

"There's some history to all this you don't know." She folded her arms and considered the ground. "Ten or twelve years ago, she and Hapu-seneb were lovers."

A gasp escaped Hani despite himself, and the others exclaimed as well.

"Don't be surprised—she was plenty pretty when she was a girl, before she became so thin. They wanted to get married, although you can imagine the row his father put up. Eventually, though, it wasn't Khnum-em-heb that put an end to it but Hapu-seneb himself. Usret was always... different. Maybe he got tired of trying to read her, the way we all have to do. Then he broke it off. They seemed to stay friends, and you mighta said it wasn't that important to her. But she all but stopped eating. And I guess all her frustrated love and loyalty went over to her brother, who could always think of something for a willing slave to do for him. Maybe she thought of him as the one man who couldn't shake her off. In time, she found someone who would put up with her strangeness and got married to him. Far as anyone can tell, she's the perfect wife. But no children."

"*Yahyah*," whispered Maya, an expression of disgust on his face.

Hani's heart contracted with compassion for the woman rejected by her lover. But it spoke well of them both that they had remained on friendly terms. "Was there any kind of competition between her and Ta-em-resefu for Tjay's affections?"

"Not that I ever seen, my lord. She's been helpful and supportive of her sister-in-law in every way. She does tend toward his side in arguments between the couple, but she shows understandin' of Ta-em-resefu as well. I think she's a good person, just odd and awkward with her emotions. If she went to Tjay with Hapu-seneb's message for Ta-em-resefu, who could blame her? The man was tryin' to steal her brother's wife."

Hani nodded slowly. It was undoubtedly the moral choice if seen without nuance. And he suspected Usret saw life without nuance. The consequences of her bearing the tale to Tjay—the murder of Hapu-seneb—could hardly be laid at her feet. The law made it perfectly legal for an outraged husband to kill the man who cuckolded him, although he was supposed to put the woman to death too. Hani suspected that the latter harsh provision stopped a lot of men from exercising their right. But then it occurred to him that Tjay had tried to carry out that part of his sentence on his wife as well. Just what Tjay's punishment would be if they finally brought him to trial was hard to foretell. It might depend on how much his arrogance had alienated his neighbors, who would sit in judgment.

Another house-shaking roll of thunder boomed overhead, and the rain began to fall in horizontal sheets, splashing their legs even under the shelter.

Kem-sit got to her feet. "Let's go into the salon. It's gettin' dark. Them two should be back soon. And there's another thing you ought to know before they get here."

She lit a brand at the kitchen fire before the rain sent it hissing into extinction, then she led the way into the dark salon. There she set several oil lamps alight, and the group settled to the floor on cushions strewn around for that purpose. By the flickering lamplight, the mayor's face was as lined and grim as an old bole of an olive tree.

"This morning, Usret said to you all that Tjay would never have disguised hisself as a woman—he had too much dignity. Remember? But Lord Hani, when I'd told her what had happened to Ta-em-resefu last night, I didn't mention that the children had said he was dressed like a girl."

CHAPTER 13

HANI STARED HER IN THE eye, his heart stopped cold. They both understood that something not innocent lay behind that knowledge.

"Where could she have heard it?" he finally said.

"The only people present were Ta-em-resefu and me, you and your people, and the three children."

Hani pondered this. "It's possible that someone in the village observed him sneaking around, the same way Muttuy did. He might have said, 'Saw your brother last night. He was dressed in a shift. Ha ha.'"

But it didn't strike him as much of a likelihood. The whole village knew Tjay was being sought for murder. Kem-sit didn't seem convinced either. She lifted a skeptical eyebrow.

"Although," Hani said slowly, "we both know the greater probability is that she's talked to Tjay."

"Wouldn't surprise me at all."

"What if she's in league with him, Lord Hani?" cried Bener-ib in an anguished voice. "She's out there alone in the marshes in this storm with Nef'et. She could decide to… to put an end to our investigation, and nobody would ever know what had happened to Nef'et."

"It won't stop *me*," growled Mut-tuy.

Hani climbed to his feet. "I'm going out to look for them."

⸙

By the time Hani, Maya, and the three women had surged out the mayor's door, the storm was retreating, the starry night sky unrolling before their eyes as the clouds slunk away. The air was crystalline and surprisingly chilly. Frogs clashed their sistrums in a paean to their goddess—Kauket, raiser up of darkness.

Hani strained his eyes back and forth over the inky silhouette of the village. Kem-sit had thought to bring a lamp, but Neferet would have nothing. She could pass right by them without being seen.

"What direction will she be coming from?"

Kem-sit pointed. "See that black lump against the horizon? That's Usret's house. Just beyond there, the marshes begin."

Hani considered calling aloud, but he was afraid some people might have gone to bed. He would save that for a more desperate case—if the women failed to show up by the time the last light had drained from the west.

Breathing heavily, he lunged his way toward the River, Brute at his heels. Objects had been washed downslope and lay strewn here and there, barking his unwary shins. Behind him, he heard the women's stumbling footsteps and an occasional yelp, but his whole attention was fixed on the black wall of reeds.

Kem-sit pushed her way to his side. "This don't do much good at the back, my lord," she said, holding out the lamp before him.

The flame projected a frail puddle of orange light at his feet, swallowed up by the immensity of darkness. Night seemed to press him down, compacting him into something small and helpless. *Great Hidden One, bring her out safe.* The prayer breathed with his respiration, pounded in his blood. *Don't let anything happen to her.*

There was a wild rustling at the edge of the marsh, but all was in darkness. Did his eyes pick up a movement? *Yes!* A figure burst from the reeds, betrayed by its white clothing. Hani froze and held his breath. The little figure stopped for an instant then began to run toward the village. It was a female, stocky and broad-shouldered. Neferet. Brute's ears stood up, his attention fixed, his tail twitching.

"Neferet!" Hani shouted. "Over here! To the light!" Hani set off running himself, oblivious of the flotsam-covered field he was trampling. He wasn't built for speed, but he kicked off his sandals and fairly flew down the muddy, runneled slope, the dog galloping before him.

Neferet saw him at last. "Papa! Oh, Papa!"

They collided, and he swept her up in his arms. "My duckling! Thank all the gods you're safe!"

"I was so scared," Neferet panted, clinging to him. "You can't imagine how scared I was, with the dark and the storm and the crocodiles. And then I started wondering if Usret hadn't lured me out there to kill me. But I suspect most of that was just my imagination because it was so scary.

My feet were in the River half the time, and I could just picture a crocodile cruising up under the surface of the water and lunging at me, and I couldn't see anything at all. It was so incredibly dark. And then the wind started laying everything flat and nearly blowing me into the marsh. It made me think of Chaos, Papa, and how Sutesh is out to destroy order and light—that's exactly the way it was. I started thinking I'd never get out of there alive. And Usret was acting strange, and it was just too scary for words."

But Neferet being Neferet, excitement had already begun to replace terror in her voice. By that time, Bener-ib had reached them and thrown herself on Neferet. The two young women clung to each other in desperate relief, and Hani couldn't have said from which came the stifled sobs.

"I was so afraid! And so ashamed." Bener-ib sniffled. "I abandoned you just because I was frightened. If anything had happened, I don't know how I would have lived with myself."

"But nothing happened, my Sweet Heart"—that was what Bener-ib's name meant—"and here I am, safe and sound. I ran off and left Usret for just the same reason. She's completely alone in there, and it's pitch dark now."

"She knows the marshes well," said Kem-sit.

And as if conjured by their words, the reeds parted, and another white shadow emerged.

"Usret? Are you all right?" called her stepmother.

The weaver trudged in the direction of the lamp and stood before them, looking more skeletal than ever with her sodden shift clinging to her bones, her curly hair dripping in her face. "Lady Neferet, you got out without any trouble?"

"Yes, thanks. I'm sorry I panicked."

"Don't apologize. That storm was so freakish. You were completely right—we should have waited until morning."

"Let's get you women dried off," said Hani, strangely itchy in the presence of Usret, who stayed calm and smiling as if nothing unusual had happened. He asked himself if she had, in fact, had sinister plans for his daughter.

"I'll go on home, then. May the lord of the horizon give you good night." Usret turned and disappeared into the darkness. They could see the white ghost of her linen moving toward her house.

Hani and the others called out "Good night!" and set off back toward Kem-sit's. As soon as the weaver was out of sight, relief flooded him, even on top of that of having Neferet back sound. *And it's completely unfair. Usret's done nothing wrong. Still, I'm starting to wonder if she's a friend or an enemy.*

But he knew that malaise might have more to do with the hour and the place and the odd weather than with anything objective. Kem-sit trusted Usret, and the mayor had known her since childhood. *I'm as bad as Mut-tuy. I'm judging her ill just because she's odd.*

"Can I borrow a lamp from you, Kem-sit?" Hani asked. "We need to get back to the farm. I'm sure the family is wild with anxiety by now."

"Of course, Lord Hani. Take this one. I know my way back."

Thus armed against the darkness, Hani led his little squadron out of the village and through the vast black fields.

For a long while, nobody spoke. Puddles of water glittered under the light of the crescent moon as they passed.

Hani thought about what Neferet had said about Chaos and its lord. Every night, darkness came over the world like this. Ra poled his sun barque through a cosmic marsh, with black waters on all sides teeming with monsters. Great tempests of malice broke upon him. How terrifying it must be. And the dead shared that fear, helping the Lord of Light to gain the opposite shore despite every obstacle evil could throw against them. Hani's own mother would be there, her dimpled little hands only a cubit from the foul liquid as she rowed, her hearty laughter stilled in terror. A shiver twitched up his spine, and he was glad the women couldn't see. It would be hard to explain.

"It came to me out there that Usret must be working with Tjay. Kem-sit said she didn't know about Tjay's disguise through anything she had told her. That made me doubly scared." Neferet's buoyant voice suggested she was no longer under the weight of any fear at all.

"We don't know that she's working with him," Maya said. "But she was almost certainly the one who told Tjay about the rendezvous of his wife and her lover. Wouldn't you do the same for Pa-kiki if Mut-nodjmet were getting ready to run away with another man?"

Neferet was silent for a moment. "Probably. But not if I knew Pa-kiki was abusing her. I'd wish her good luck and Godspeed."

Hani smiled in the darkness. "That's a moral nuance I'm not sure Usret would comprehend."

"So where do we go from here, Papa Duck? Is it important to see the scene of the crime? I really, really, *really* don't want to go out to that sandbar again."

"I don't know. I think we already understand pretty

well what must have happened that night. Hapu-seneb was killed in the marshes. There would have been no need to drag his body any great distance, and nobody would have seen or heard anything, except for a chance witness like our fisherman."

"Now we just have to find Tjay and take him in to the council for trial, eh, Lord Hani?" Maya said.

"I think that's about it. I'm trying to think of a legal excuse for us to be involved in this action."

"You're the local landowner, Papa. It's probably your responsibility."

"You may be right, my girl. But I'd like to talk to someone with more experience than I have. Maybe Father would know. Or Ptah-mes, certainly."

A greatly relieved family greeted them when they arrived at the farm. Lamps were lit throughout the house, as if to hold back the darkness of fear, and Mama had kept a big pot of soup heating, not knowing how many hours would have passed before she saw her husband and daughter again. She and Sati rushed upon them—first Sati throwing herself upon her husband, then Mama upon Papa, and then everyone upon Neferet. Grandfather hovered, beaming, until he could squeeze in for a hug.

"Dear gods! Where have you been? That horrible storm struck, and we pictured you caught out in the fields in the rain, but then you still didn't show up." Mama grabbed her daughter's face between her hands and kissed her cheeks.

"It was quite an adventure," Neferet said, grinning, exhilarated by the attention and by her own near escape.

"Probably not as dangerous as it seemed at the time. Maya will have to add this to his 'Tales of the Traveler.'"

"But the Traveler was sitting cozily in Kem-sit's house," Maya said grumpily. He probably regretted not having come along. "This happened to somebody else."

Mama stared from face to face. "What exactly did happen? To whom?" Then she stopped Neferet with a hand. "Let's go into the salon so Baket can hear the story too."

But the women wanted to change into dry clothes, so everyone dispersed for a few minutes. Then they gathered once more in the rustic little salon, pulling stools and cushions around Baket-iset's couch. Mama and one of the kitchen girls had brought the pot of chickpea soup, and she was ladling it into bowls. The fragrant steam was like a rosemary-scented elixir of comfort. Neferet snuffed a deep breath before she lifted the bowl to her lips.

"This was a wonderful idea, Mama. Thanks. I can't even remember dinner."

"We didn't have any," Mut-tuy reminded her. "We just tramped around the village all afternoon."

Someone passed a pot-shaped loaf of bread, and Neferet tore a chunk off then handed it on to Bener-ib. Their eyes caught and held for a moment.

"We did learn something, at least." Papa recounted their theories about the involvement of Usret in her brother's affairs.

"And all this while, I was alone with her in the marshes, if you please! With a storm raging and our path flooded and crocodiles all around, climbing over each other to get at me, and me thinking, *What if she's been told to get rid of me?* And she was acting really strange. It was *so* weird."

Mama covered her face with her hands. "I'm glad I didn't know till afterward. Hani, how come you didn't go with her?"

"She'd left when I got there, my dove," he said penitently.

"And I abandoned her," Bener-ib confessed in a wavering voice.

"You mustn't blame yourself, my dear child. You did the prudent thing. Neferet should have followed your example." Mama looked at the night-haggard faces that surrounded her. "It's past time to go to bed, everyone. All the excitement will make you sleep. Let's reconvene tomorrow, all right?"

Sati and Maya headed off to their bedroom hand in hand, and Neferet and Bener-ib did the same. The others dispersed to their respective sleeping places. Neferet told herself, *I'm ready to drop where I stand. Bed, here I come.*

But it wasn't so easy to fall asleep after all. Neferet was wildly stimulated from all the strong emotions of the evening, and she lay on her comfortable straw mattress with her eyes wide open. Bener-ib breathed quietly at her side, sleeping the sleep of the innocent. Those who usually bedded down on the roof terrace had all retreated into the house after the storm, knowing that their pallets would get damp on the packed-clay roof, where water still stood. Indoors, the air was stuffy and chilly at the same time, and Neferet couldn't quite relax. She listened to the crickets. She listened to the frogs. She listened to some animal snuffling around in the yard outside and wondered what it was. Brute lay on the floor, an ear cocked but unengaged. Before long, Neferet began to imagine Tjay hunting her down, even following her to the farm, prowling around the low walls of the yard, crouching in the shade of the fig trees, climbing up to the high windows and sliding down into the darkened room with the sinister litheness of a cobra, his eyes glowing like coals. She grew more and more thoroughly awake.

The facts of the case began to parade before her mind. Everything made sense up to the involvement of Usret. But then nothing about the weaver made sense. Neferet still got the shivers when she thought about the strange conversation in the marshes. *Was she just an unfortunate crying for help from a medically trained acquaintance, or was she trying to keep me talking until she could kill me there, far from everyone's eyes?* A body could so easily be tipped into the water of the marshes and never be seen again.

She's at least helping Tjay. But what if she was more involved than that? What if she's the one who killed Hapu-seneb?

Slow down, Neferet cautioned herself. *There's no reason for you to conclude that except that you think she's odd. And nothing she says seems sincere.*

She tried to order her thoughts, wondering what would prove Usret's guilt or her innocence.

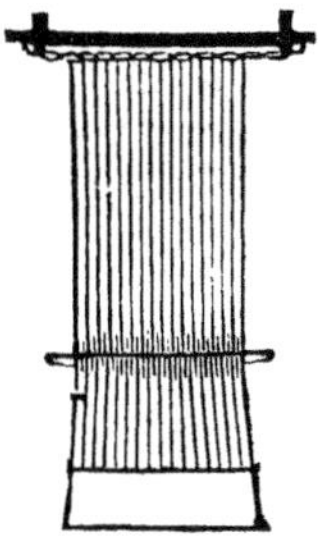

CHAPTER 14

Neferet couldn't have sworn that she ever fell asleep, except that rather late the next morning, she awoke. Bener-ib had already left the bed, and there were voices below in the kitchen. She pulled on a clean shift and wadded up the old one, still lying damp and muddy on the floor, for the laundry.

Rubbing her eyes, she descended the stairs slowly. The women were standing in the kitchen, talking as they dunked their bread in cups of milk. Bener-ib's gaze lit up at the arrival of Neferet, whose heart grew warm. *What a beautiful sight—someone who loves you.* With a pang, Neferet thought of Usret, who believed that no one loved her.

"Good morning, people. Where are the men?"

"They've gone back to the city, my love. That Khnum-em-heb showed up early this morning, and they all went back together. The children are still asleep, and so is Ta-em-resefu," said Mama. "Or rather, she's asleep again. She's been sick these last few mornings. I wonder if she isn't expecting." She gave her youngest a peck on the cheek. "The bread's a little stale, but it's fine in milk."

"I saved you one of the less stale pieces," said Bener-ib, proffering a chunk.

Neferet ladled some of the still-foaming milk from the big jug in the corner and closed the wooden lid. Part of her was still lying comfily in bed, but the hungry, awake part of her was gaining the upper hand.

"What's our plan for today?" asked Mut-tuy in what she no doubt intended to be a businesslike, grown-up voice.

"I have a theory." Neferet stuffed a piece of bread in her mouth, and silence followed until she'd swallowed it. "I wonder if Usret didn't kill Hapu-seneb."

"What makes you say that?" Sati asked.

Yahyah! Sati doesn't want to show it, but she's curious. "Usret had as much of a personal motive as Tjay. Hapu-seneb was a lover who had jilted her years ago. She pretended she wasn't mad about it, but every emotion she shows seems to be fake—so who knows? For twelve years, things are quiet. She hardly ever sees Hapu-seneb. Maybe she tells herself that he really still loves her—he never marries, after all. Then along comes Ta-em-resefu, her own sister-in-law, and steals him away from her. Maybe she already has it in for Ta-em-resefu because she's divided Tjay's affections. This is the last straw. She tells him that his lover girl is waiting for him in the marshes, then she jumps him and bashes his head and pushes him into the River. Then she goes after Ta-em-resefu. It all makes sense, doesn't it?"

The others stared at her, absorbing this scenario.

"You certainly have an imagination, my love," her mother murmured.

"Have we any evidence?" Bener-ib asked timidly.

But Mut-tuy looked skeptical. "I'd rather it was Tjay. I'd rather a man be put to death for the murder."

Neferet cast her eyes to the heavens. "Mut-tuy, my girl, we can't accuse him just because he's a man. We have to find the *real* guilty party. And we can't be blind to other possibilities just because they're one of us."

The girl twitched a shoulder in indifference.

Neferet said piously, "And he wouldn't be put to death anyway. It's legal for a man to kill an adulterous wife and her lover."

"Nef'et, do we have any evidence that it's Usret?" Bener-ib asked again.

"I can certainly vouch for the fact that she knows the marshes well. And what's more, she'd be keen to avenge her beloved brother's humiliation, wouldn't she?"

Nobody seemed to know what to say.

"It's only a theory," Neferet said defensively. "Though you have to admit, it makes sense of everything. And it makes better sense than saying Tjay was dressed up as a woman. It *was* a woman."

However, Mut-tuy still looked dubious. "But the children said it was 'Papa dressed like a girl.'"

Neferet tossed her head impatiently. "The grownups were all saying, 'It was Tjay, it was Tjay.' Of course the little girls assumed it was him despite the evidence of their senses. It was dark, after all. And it wasn't Tjay who told Usret that—he wouldn't have known that his daughters had seen him. She was trying to forestall questions because she *knew* the attacker had worn a dress."

"It sounds like you need to find more proof before you

accuse anybody," said Baket-iset cheerfully from her couch. "You'll turn up the truth before you're finished."

"Exactly. So, it's back to the village this morning, ladies."

They dispersed to their respective activities. The servants carried Baket's couch out into the shady side yard under the arbor, and the three *sunet*s were left alone.

"Nef'et, shouldn't we check in on the dispensary soon?" Bener-ib suggested. "I have patients who need to be followed, and you do too."

"The holidays are almost over anyway, my girl. What if we go back tomorrow? I'm sure that poor Khnum-em-heb and his wife want *ma'at* for the soul of their son."

Mut-tuy had already passed out of the room when Bener-ib caught at Neferet's arm and stared her in the eye. "You know, it could just as easily be Ta-em-resefu who killed Hapu-seneb."

Hani had awakened early. He loved the hours just after dawn before the day's heat broke, before the household was up. Sparrows twittered joyfully in the palms, bringing a big smile of contentment to his lips. He gazed out over the fields sparkling with water. In the distance, a pair of women were headed along the road toward the house—the kitchen girls, ready for their day's work. Inland, the sky was still blushed with rosy pearl. It would be a fine day, all memory of the bizarre storm effaced. Easy to forget that a killer still prowled the area.

He strolled around the vegetable patch, cast an eye at the beehives built into the wall, and greeted the geese and goats. Perhaps he could enjoy a leisurely day, forget about the murder case, and just tend to his farm. He wanted to talk to the foreman about getting a few cows. The holidays would be over very soon, and his duties would recall him to the Hall of Royal Correspondence.

Then Hani noticed a figure striding quickly up the path from the River—a middle-aged man on the heavy side, his short wig bound with a white scarf. As the visitor drew nearer, Hani realized it was Khnum-em-heb. Hani called his name. Khnum-em-heb looked up and, meeting Hani's eye, hurried his steps. Some distance from the yard, they clasped forearms.

"Lord Hani. I didn't know when you were returning to the city, so I took the liberty of tracking you down. Have you found out anything?" He forced a haggard smile so Hani would know he wasn't accusing him of sloth. His eyes were dark ringed, and he seemed to have lost weight so that his jowls sagged.

The poor man. "We have, my friend. But I'm afraid there's still no solid proof. It seems that Tjay probably murdered the man he considered to have cuckolded him, and he also made an attempt on his own wife. Neither act is strictly illegal, although it may depend on how the village council feels toward Tjay when they sit in judgment."

"Wait, Hani—are you saying that Tjay's wife was the girl my son was in love with?" Khnum-em-heb fell silent. Then he growled, clenching his fists, "Ammit take that ungrateful viper Tjay. I should have seen how jealous he was of Hapu-seneb. No sign of him yet, I suppose?"

"None since his attempt on his wife. He may no longer be in Waset."

Khnum-em-heb seemed to deflate, then he turned a pleading gaze on Hani. "I want to see Hapu-seneb, Hani. My boy—I don't care what state he's in at the embalmers'. The last time I set eyes on him… we argued. I can't bear to think my last words to him were angry."

He dropped his head as if to hide the tears that wet his lashes. "It was a special occasion. We had just given him a beautiful *weshket* collar of all colors. This sounds awful—I had seen Tjay wearing one and thought it was something Hapu-seneb would like, so I had a copy made. Maybe I was stoking their rivalry without knowing it. Maybe I did a lot of that. But he looked downright regal in it. Then afterward, we argued. It was the usual thing, about getting married. His mother said she hoped she'd live long enough to see grandchildren. And I said—oh, I don't even remember, but he got mad and said we were making his life miserable and that he wouldn't consider marrying anybody but this lady friend of his who was unavailable. And then I accused him of—but I don't want to remember that. He stalked out, and we never saw him again."

Hani's throat constricted with compassion, and he gripped the distraught man's shoulder in a gesture of solidarity. "If you're sure you want to, the high priest owes me a favor. He'll let you see him."

Khnum-em-heb clutched at Hani's arm. "Do you know if they found the collar with… with his body? His mother would like to bury it with him so he can enjoy it in the Duat. A little token of our love, you know?"

"I never saw it. It's possible the men who found him took it, but it's more likely that it fell off in the River, or when… if there was a struggle…"

Khnum-em-heb nodded, his shoulders drooping, hopeless.

"Listen, Khnum-em-heb, I need to get back to the city. If you wait a minute, we can go together to the Pure Place."

"I'd be grateful. My boat's down on the bank."

The two men tromped back to the farmhouse, where they found Maya and Mery-ra sitting in the shade of the fig trees, talking and eating their breakfast. They sprang up when they saw that Hani was accompanied by his visitor.

With a sorrowful expression, Mery-ra extended his arms. "May the gods console you for your loss, my friend."

Maya seconded the wish, and the weaver, his face twisted with the effort to hold back his tears, nodded.

Hani said in an appropriately subdued voice, "We're going down to Waset. I have some papers to sign, and Master Khnum-em-heb would like to visit the priests of Inpu. Do either of you want a ride? He's generously offered his boat."

"I'll go with you, my lord," said Maya, as Hani had foreseen. To his surprise, his father also expressed an interest in accompanying them.

Hani found Nub-nefer in the kitchen court, counting the jars of dried fish and checking to see if any of them had gotten wet in the storm. He called out, "My dove, the boys and I are going back to the city for a few hours. Khnum-em-heb showed up, and he wants to see his son."

She nodded sympathetically and murmured, "I hope this isn't a mistake, poor man. The lad will surely be in the *netjeri* by now, and if it changes a human body the way it changes our fish here..."

Hani shrugged fatalistically. She was right. After two

weeks, the corpse would be drying in a pile of desert salts. Later, the priests would do other things to bring it back to a lifelike aspect that the *ka* could inhabit, but the results of the uncompleted process could be shocking.

"He wants to tell the boy he loves him."

Nub-nefer made a tender noise, and Hani slipped back outside, thinking what a privilege it was to be married to such a woman. The rest of the household was silent. Maya and Mery-ra awaited him in a silence no less profound, while Khnum-em-heb stared at the ground, chewing his lip. What did one say to a man whom the bronze fist of the gods had so heavily smitten?

The four of them walked wordlessly to the riverbank and up the bouncing gangplank of the weaver's modest yacht. Like Khnum-em-heb, the sailors all wore the white mourning scarf. The passengers spent a gloomy hour standing at the gunwales, unspeaking, watching the banks slide by until the craft glided in to the city's bustling quay. Side by side, Hani and Khnum-em-heb walked toward the Pure Place, with Maya and Mery-ra in their wake.

The House of Inpu stood in the shadow of the much larger temple of Mut. It wasn't itself especially spacious, because most of the activity of the priests took place in the vast cellars hewn from the bedrock beneath. There, in the cool darkness, the priests of the jackal god carried out their ministry of preparing the bodies of the dead for eternity. Like death itself, they were both revered and feared.

At the modest pylon gate, Hani identified himself and asked to see the high priest Heri-har.

"He is serving the god right now, my lord," said the

young priest who received them. "But I'll tell him as soon as he's available."

They waited a considerable length of time, Hani beginning to tell himself he needed to talk Khnum-em-heb out of this. He almost hoped Heri-har would flatly refuse the request. Eventually, a lofty figure in priestly white approached, and even Hani, who knew the secret, was almost stunned into religious awe because the priest had every appearance of being the god Inpu himself. Set upon his shoulders was a black-painted cartonnage mask in the shape of a jackal's head that made him look inhumanly tall, with its pointed muzzle and sly eyes and ears standing up alertly.

"Hani, my friend," said a man's voice from within the head, and Heri-har lifted the mask off with some difficulty, revealing a sweaty face and a shaven human skull. "What can I do for you? Your lad won't be ready for more than a month."

It was hard for Hani to recognize the impish seven-year-old with two front teeth missing who had been Heri-har when the men first met in the House of Life. The future priest was almost expelled for a terrible act of mischief, but Hani covered for him and swore that he'd never left his room. That act of friendship had earned him the boy's—and then the man's—eternal gratitude.

"You got the message that the youth's identity has changed, right? He's Hapu-seneb son of Khnum-em-heb, and this is his father. Master Khnum-em-heb would like"—Hani dropped his voice and tried to convey, by his pleading tone, that he knew how unusual his request was—"he would like to see the boy, Heri-har."

The priest, too, spoke in an undertone as if to shield the others from the conversation. "But Hani, the body has been in the *netjeri* for a week. It's desiccated but not yet—how shall I say?—cleanly dry. And we haven't done any of the other things yet that give it a lifelike appearance. I'm afraid it will horrify the man, repulse him. That seems unfair to the Osir. I really don't recommend this."

Hani glanced at the grieving father, whose bloodshot eyes were fixed on him, beseeching. "He really wants it, my friend."

"All right. Because it's you." The priest said in a louder voice—somehow more liturgical—"The father of the Osir may view his mortal *khat*, but bear in mind that the process of resurrection has barely begun." He turned and gestured to Khnum-em-heb.

The weaver whispered, "Come with me, Hani."

Hani glanced back at Mery-ra and Maya, who stood watching with bugging eyes. Hani's heart was stuttering its protest—this wasn't something he wanted to do—but he understood that Khnum-em-heb might have need of his support.

The high priest led the way into a dark, echoing hall and thence to a steep stone staircase lit dimly by bracketed oil lamps along the painted wall. Hani noted the absence of soot on the ceiling. *Do they have some magical source of fire?* Heri-har repositioned his mask and descended carefully, the two men puffing in his wake.

The air seemed to grow physically heavier as they descended until the weight of the ancient city lay upon them. Before them, the cellars of the god opened out, cut from the living rock, supported by solid pillars, and pierced here and there by slim air wells that made the reeking atmosphere breathable—because it was laden with the stench of putrescence and throat-clutching chemicals and incense and resin—a brew of odors so thick that it gave Hani a sense of physically drowning. Here and there in the twilit darkness, priests and servants went about their work with devotion, stirring vats of foul-smelling liquids, bending over embalming tables where men and women lay in various stages of preservation. Some were submitting to the final artistic wrapping. The priests were so deft one would have thought they were winding a skein of thread, nothing more. Eerily, the same scenes were depicted, nearly life-sized, upon the painted walls, where the Lord Inpu himself presided over the merciful work of preserving the living home of the soul. It was marvelous and horrific at the same time. Hani wasn't sure if the shiver that passed over the hair of his arms was due to the chill or the sights around him.

Heri-har stopped just inside the second division of the underground hall, where a sloped embalming table stood unattended on lion feet. Upon it lay a long pile of crystalline white powder, damp in spots, more or less the shape of a man. An unspeakable dribble of pinkish liquid leaked through the drain in the table and into a runnel on the floor.

A wave of nausea rolled through Hani. He glanced sideways at Khnum-em-heb and saw that the man's face had grown gray. "Do you really—"

The weaver stopped him with a nod of resolution.

An embalmer priest approached, and at his superior's order, he began to clear away the powder at the top of the long pile. Carefully, he brushed it back until the twisted brown contours of a human face grew visible. Hani had an awful vision of a root vegetable cooked in the ashes.

Khnum-em-heb began to sob. "Forgive me, forgive me, son. Don't listen to what I said. I love you. I'm proud of you. Your mother and I love you with no conditions. No conditions. We'll cherish that girl for your sake. Don't leave us forever in anger. Oh, I hope you can hear me."

He reached out to touch the youth's face, but the high priest held back his hand. "You're not purified, master."

The weaver let out an animal howl of pain, and Heri-har discreetly turned him away from the table, where the attendant priest was covering the face once more with a bowlful of powder. Hani guided the staggering Khnum-em-heb through the icy cellar and up the stairs, in the high priest's footsteps. The temperature grew warmer as they rose until they stood once more in the summer of the human world, and the grieving father's cries dwindled away into exhaustion. Maya and Mery-ra waited for them in the temple court, looking unsettled.

"We'll take you home, my friend," said Hani to Khnum-em-heb. Over his shoulder, he nodded at the masked high priest. "I'm in your debt once more, Heri-har."

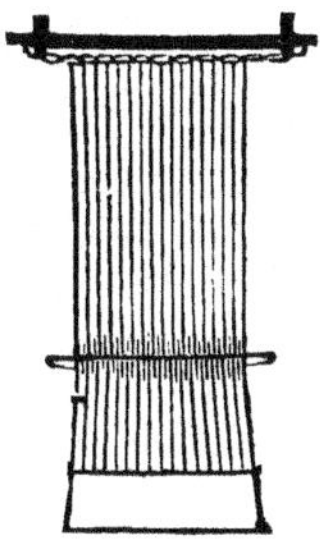

CHAPTER 15

THEY EMERGED INTO THE SUN-WASHED street. Hani staggered for an instant from the onslaught of the glare. "Can you walk, or shall I call for my litter?" he gently asked Khnum-em-heb.

Khnum-em-heb shook his head heavily. "I need to walk. Clear my head. How can I thank you?" He clutched Hani's arm. "I have some amulets I'll bring so they can include them with him. And jewelry that he liked. I hope we can find the collar. If not, I'll have another made. His mother is particularly set on that because he liked it so."

Good businessman that he was, the idea of practical things to do seemed to bring him to himself. Khnum-em-heb kept up an unbroken flow of monologue as they walked, as if the floodgates had been opened in the field of his soul. Much of what he said seemed trivial, but Hani knew it was important to let him talk. The man had plans for the boy's funeral. He wanted to do something for the girl his son loved, even though she was the wife of the boy's murderer—because "she must be a special person." Hani wondered uneasily how seriously to take this wish.

They left the weaver at the gate of his home, and he thanked Hani again, clutching at his hands. "You've been a great blessing to us in many ways, my lord. If there's anything my humble household can ever do for you, don't hesitate to ask."

"You've already repaid us by your contract with the king of Keftiu, friend. That has advanced our sun god's foreign policy—life, prosperity, and health to him."

It was nearly lunchtime, and Hani decided to head straight home rather than go to his office first. He thought longingly of the dried fish in the kitchen of the farm, but then Nub-nefer's comparison of fish and human bodies came back to him, and he revised his menu.

As they walked, he said to his father and Maya, "I didn't see Dapurazo this morning. Was he still asleep?"

Maya nodded and grinned. "He and Ta-em-resefu had a good long conversation last night after most of us went to bed."

Hani raised his eyebrows. "Interesting. He seems to be smitten."

"She's quite attractive, and I understand he's widowed." Mery-ra chuckled. "That would seal your contract with Keftiu, wouldn't it?"

They passed in good-humored silence through the southern suburbs until Hani's own gate came into view.

His father suddenly said, "What was it like down there, my boy? We heard Khnum-em-heb howling as if his heart would break."

"It was unspeakably unsettling. I never want to go there

again until I'm dead. I don't know how the priests stand it day after day." With his hairs still standing from the memory of the experience, Hani hammered on the gate, and Iuty opened. Old A'a, the former gatekeeper, sat in the background in the shade of the family shrine, beaming approval at the arrival of his master.

"Welcome back, my lord," said Iuty. "Has the whole family come back?"

"No, just us. They plan to stay until the end of the holidays, day after tomorrow."

"But the young mistresses are here, my lord. They just arrived, thinking you'd be here too."

Hani exchanged a look of surprise with Maya and his father. "They're here? Now?"

"That's what the man said, Papa!" said Neferet from the path to the house. She ran, laughing, to throw her arms around him with enough enthusiasm to knock a smaller man down. "Mama said you'd gone to the office. We came back to the city to check the dispensary and find out how the animals were doing, then we drifted here around lunchtime to see if you were eating yet. If you didn't show up, we were going back home to eat with Lord Ptah-mes. Then back to the farm. We have some more sniffing around to do in the village this afternoon."

"Maya and your grandfather and I just took Khnum-em-heb to see his son's *khat* at the Pure Place."

She gaped at him. "*Iyah*, Papa. Was it grisly?"

"*Grisly* doesn't begin to do the experience justice, my duckling. My respect for the servants of Inpu has just grown immeasurably."

"Come on in, and we can talk over lunch." She took

her father and grandfather by the hand and drew them after her. Maya followed, still looking a bit gray.

In the salon, Bener-ib and Mut-tuy were setting up the tables, while Brute stretched panting on the cool plaster floor like a foreman lazing while his team worked.

"Bring three more, people!" Neferet called. "Wait till you hear what Papa just did."

It appeared the kitchen girls had the day off since none of the family was expected back. So the three *sunet*s had undertaken to prepare lunch.

"Lentil soup," said Bener-ib apologetically. "I'm sorry it's so meager."

"But that's perfect, my girl," Grandfather assured her. "We've been eating like pigs at the farm. The fresh air seems to make a fellow hungrier." He patted his belly, which didn't look like it had been deprived of many meals.

Mut-tuy brought in an armful of flat loaves. Hani noticed that her eyes were red and teary. He shot a concerned look at his daughter then back at the orphan. "Is something the matter, Mut-tuy? Have you been crying?"

"They made me cut the onions," the adolescent said sourly, and to her evident annoyance, everyone laughed.

While they ate, Hani filled the young women in on the few things he'd learned from Khnum-em-heb. "If you see that collar lying around anywhere, bring it to me so he can bury it with Hapu-seneb. It had special sentimental value to the family."

"The only *weshket* I've heard about was Tjay's," Neferet said through a mouthful of soup.

"This one is a copy of Tjay's. Have you seen it?"

"No. Ta-em-resefu just said Tjay wasn't wearing it the night he allegedly killed Hapu-seneb."

Maya pounced on her. "Allegedly? You don't think he did it for sure?"

"Well…" She shot Bener-ib a conspiratorial look and snickered. "Actually, we've got another suspect now. It's only a theory, of course, but everything fits."

She described for Hani the whole elaborate reconstruction of Usret's actions and their motives.

Hani listened with a thoughtful pursing of the lips. "I suppose it's possible. But the most parsimonious explanation is often the right one. This seems a little complicated."

Mut-tuy asked sullenly, "What does parsimonious mean?"

"Simplest," Maya said.

Neferet looked offended. "I don't think the idea of Tjay dressing up as a woman is very parsnipfonious or whatever. Why couldn't it just be a real woman—Usret?"

"Or Ta-em-resefu," added Bener-ib in a small voice.

Everyone looked at her.

"But she couldn't have stabbed herself in the back, Ibet," Neferet said.

"We don't know that the same person committed both crimes."

"Two murderers?" cried Mery-ra. "Now, that's not parsnipfonious."

"What would her motive have been to kill Hapu-seneb? She loved him." Neferet stared at the lady of her heart.

Bener-ib, her face flaming, shrugged. "Maybe he'd betrayed her. Maybe he was going to drop her like he'd dropped Usret, and that's what he'd come back to tell her."

"Not parsnipfonious." Papa grinned. "You need to find evidence for some of these suppositions."

Neferet put her hands over her ears. "One suspect at a time, people. We haven't finished our investigation. At some point, there'll be some definitive piece of evidence. Then we'll know."

"I wish somebody would give me a silver *deben* for every hour I've spent on a boat during these so-called holidays." Puffing, Neferet climbed the steep bank below the family boathouse, Brute scrambling before her, while Bener-ib and Mut-tuy followed. She reached back to give the former a hand up. "I'd be rich."

"You are rich," said Mut-tuy with a snort.

That girl. Honestly. Neferet dusted her hands.

After their early dinner, the three had departed yet again for the farm. Now they marched up the path. The house, in its fringe of palm trees, shimmered in the late-afternoon heat against the distant line of mountains. Neferet intended to question Ta-em-resefu more closely then to go into the village and ask if anyone had seen Tjay in the settlement at all since his disappearance two weeks before. It seemed possible that he'd come and gone frequently, but they had to corroborate that. If he hadn't been there, he couldn't have killed Hapu-seneb or stabbed his wife. That would shift the presumption of guilt to Usret.

Their first objective was frustrated, however. Ta-em-resefu was out walking with Dapurazo somewhere along the riverbank.

"He's consoling her for the loss of her lover," said Sati with a little smile of mischief curling her mouth.

"He's a widower," Baket-iset said in the foreigner's defense. "He knows what it's like to lose someone you love."

Mut-tuy lowered her head but couldn't conceal the disapproval that knit her brows.

Mama, who was helping one of the household girls skein thread, had both hands held out before her while the servant looped and looped. "Ta-em-resefu is pregnant, as we suspected. She's sure it's Hapu-seneb's child."

"That's bittersweet. Papa said Hapu-seneb's father wants to do something for her. He'll be delighted to think she's carrying his grandchild." Neferet dipped a hand into the bowl of pistachios the women had been nibbling. "But it looks like we won't see her until evening. Come on, troops, let's head to the village."

The first person they saw there was Kem-sit, who was feeding her donkey an armload of hay. She waved as they passed.

"Do we need to talk to her at all?" whispered Bener-ib. "Should we pass our alternate theories by her? She knows these people better than we do."

"I'd rather talk to the villagers first and find out if anyone has seen Tjay. We may need to discuss such things with Kem-sit at the same time. She's the one who's going to sit in judgment on this case, after all." They stopped on the path that ran down the middle of the village parallel with the River. "I say we split up and go house to house. Ibet, you and Mut-tuy can take the houses above the road, and I'll take the ones along the River."

"I want to go with you," said Mut-tuy.

Annoyance ignited in Neferet's heart and flooded her face with heat. "Will you stop being so contrary, my girl? There are more houses above the road."

"But Usret's is by the River."

"You actually *want* to talk to Usret? You must be the only person in the Upper Kingdom."

"Yes. We've never actually confronted her about her brother and what she may be doing for him."

"And you think you'll get a straightforward answer?" Neferet gave a hoot of sarcastic laughter.

Mut-tuy, her cheeks flushed with anger and her eyes cold, bit her lip. Neferet flinched with guilt. Grownups who humiliated children weren't good people. Her exasperation had run away with her. She had to admit that Mut-tuy's rejection of Bener-ib had awakened a ferocious protective instinct. In childhood, poor intellectual little Ibet had always been the person the children chose last for their teams.

"All right, then. You can come with me, and I'll let you interrogate her. We'll meet right here at twilight. Ibet, you take Brute since you'll be alone. Is that all right?" Neferet whispered as they parted. Bener-ib squeezed her hand and nodded bravely. *She'd rather have somebody with her. A pox on that Mut-tuy.*

So Bener-ib and the mastiff set off toward the trees, and Neferet, with the orphan girl in tow, headed for the River. The first house they encountered was, of course, that of Usret. The bald husband was hacking away at a bundle of reeds with an ax, evidently engaged in building another boat. They were nice, plump little craft, something between a raft and a real boat. Papa had two that he used for cruising the marshes to look at birds, and they'd probably been made right here. The man gave Neferet and Mut-tuy a pleasant nod as they passed. Neferet, with the girl following, threaded her way through the littered yard and a flock of guinea fowl till they reached the door.

It stood open, but the fly mat was down. Mosquitoes whined around the visitors. Neferet slapped irritably and knocked. Almost before her hand had withdrawn, Usret was at the door. She seemed to be dressed for a festival, in a cheap but fashionable wig, with a faience collar on her shoulders. She'd even painted her eyes.

"Oh, excuse me. Perhaps you're going out. We just came by to ask you some questions." Neferet was thrown off balance by the transformation. Despite the gauntness of her face, the woman was genuinely pretty. The *weshket,* made of multicolored rows of variously shaped beads, was too broad for her—probably sized for a man—but that meant it covered her clavicles and fleshless shoulders. "Permit me to say, Usret, that you really look beautiful. What a pretty collar."

"Thank you," Usret said, beaming coquettishly. "A friend gave it to me."

"Your husband? Your brother?" *A lover? Mut, the mother of us all!* Neferet thought with a silent laugh. *This must be the most adulterous village on the River.*

The weaver opened her mouth as if to say something then changed direction. "My brother. Everybody who sees it wants one. Come in, won't you?"

Mut-tuy's eyes were round with the light of discovery.

Yes, my girl. This must be the famous collar of Tjay that Hapu-seneb's father had copied for his son—and the one that

Ta-em-resefu said he left at home the night he disappeared. If Usret has it, he must have given it to her later. He must have gone home and gotten it when his wife wasn't there. That means he's been back to the village.

But then it occurred to her that it was just as likely to be Hapu-seneb's collar. In which case, either Usret or Tjay had taken it directly from the body of the murder victim. His—or her—victim.

"If you're going out...?" Neferet said.

"Not for a while. Come in." Usret stepped back, and the two young women passed inside. "How can I help you, Lady Neferet? I hope you had no ill effects from our stroll in the marshes."

The vestibule was tiny and cluttered with what looked like old furniture or pieces of farm equipment stacked against the walls. Even the small shrine had things piled in the niche. There was a humid, unpleasant, mouse-haunted smell like that of a house that wasn't often cleaned.

Of course, they're close to the water. Nothing they can do about the damp. "Oh no. I'm fine. I wanted to ask you if you've seen your brother since the night he disappeared, Usret."

"Why, yes," she said with a smile that moved her mouth but left her painted eyes, which were suddenly suspicious, untouched. "He's well, thank you."

"So, he comes back to the village from time to time?"

"No, in fact. I visit him in Waset. That's where I'm going this evening."

"Could we go with you?" blurted Mut-tuy.

Neferet restrained herself from violence with considerable effort.

Mut-tuy forestalled her with a glare. "You said I could ask her questions."

"I'm afraid I can't invite guests along, much as I'd like to. I'm someone else's guest, my dear."

"Forgive her rather direct methods, mistress," said Neferet, directing a matching glare at her young partner. "She really is aware that what she just said was rude."

Mut-tuy, no doubt suspecting that her license to interrogate was about to be revoked, said in a rush, "Where does he live, Mistress Usret?"

"He has a house in Waset just like he does here. He's going to get a better job that earns him some of the respect he deserves. He's going to divorce Ta-em-resefu and marry somebody higher class."

"But at the moment, he has a murder charge hanging over him. That might make a prospective employer think twice about hiring him, no?" Neferet said.

"But he didn't kill anybody. Besides, he would have had every right to kill a man who was having an affair with his wife, Lady Neferet. That's what Kem-sit said."

"Only if he kills the wife too." Mut-tuy was watching Usret's face closely, but Neferet wasn't sure that anything it reflected was honest.

The weaver looked pleasant, as if they were discussing recipes. "His name will be cleared. You'll see."

"Do you know who did kill Hapu-seneb, mistress?"

"No, but it wasn't Tjay."

"How are you so sure?" Neferet persisted.

"Because he was right here with me that night. Ask my husband—he was here too."

The statement, made with utter assurance, dropped like a stone. An alibi. For both of them.

"For how long?" Neferet asked, trying desperately to save some part of their theories.

Usret shrugged, looking like a person who was simultaneously pleased with herself and trying to look humbly unsmug. "Overnight. He and Ta-em-resefu had argued, and he often came to talk to me when he was upset. We're very close. He left early the next morning."

"Did he have a boat here, then?"

"Yes. He used it to travel for his work. He had to go back and forth to collect piecework from Khnum-em-heb's weavers."

Her thoughts overturned, Neferet didn't know what to ask next. "Well, have a good evening. We may be back to ask you more things as we learn more. Certainly, we want to clear your brother's name if he's innocent."

"Thank you, Lady Neferet. I hope you can meet him sometime. You're educated. You would appreciate him."

Assuring Usret that she'd love to meet Tjay, Neferet exited the dark, fusty house, with Mut-tuy at her side. She stomped down the slope to where Usret's husband patiently whacked away at bundle after bundle of green reeds. "Excuse me, master," she called, catching his eye. "Could you answer a question for me?"

He straightened laboriously and made a kind of half bow.

"Do you remember the night the man was killed in the marshes? Did Tjay come to your house that night? Did he stay here overnight?"

The man stared at her, a perfect blank. She repeated,

more loudly and clearly. The boat maker shook his head and gestured first to his ears and then to his mouth, grinning apologetically.

"What? He's a deaf mute?" squawked Mut-tuy.

Neferet repeated the gestures, each time shaking her head. Then she lifted her shoulders in a questioning movement. The man bowed again, gesturing his agreement. She turned away in frustration. "Ammit take it! I can't believe this. A witness who can't hear or speak. What next?"

"Well, that's convenient, isn't it?" the adolescent said snidely. "'Oh, Tjay was here all night. My husband saw him. Just ask him.' There's only one problem."

CHAPTER 16

AS THEY DRIFTED TOWARD THE path that transected the village, Neferet said, "Usret's either telling the truth or lying. If this story is true, surely, someone else saw Tjay walking down here or setting off in the morning. I mean, a good-sized boat pulling away—somebody in a village of busybodies must have seen it. Let's keep asking people."

"Why didn't that Usret tell us about this right at the first instead of just saying, 'He's innocent'? If he had an alibi, you'd think she'd want everybody to know." Mut-tuy seemed to have taken the latest turn of the case as a personal affront.

"You know, I think somebody should watch Usret's house tonight to see if she really leaves for Waset. But we also need to talk to other people. There could be all sorts of information that nobody's bothered to tell us. I wonder where Tjay's boat was anchored."

They started north along the riverbank, then suddenly, Neferet stopped. "I've got to get that collar for Khnum-em-heb. I have a feeling it's Tjay's anyway. But Usret's not about to give it to me—she wears it."

"Weird, isn't it—to dress up like that for your brother? I think something strange is going on between them."

"That's their business. I just have to get one of those necklaces. I wonder if Ta-em-resefu would give us her husband's. We can try. Let's go to her house."

"But she's at the farm. And you said Usret has Tjay's necklace."

Neferet ignored Mut-tuy's second statement. She had a plan to find out which possibility was true. "Maybe her servants would accept a message from her brought to them by us." She gave the girl a devilish grin.

Mut-tuy whistled with the appreciation of a gourmet of underhand plots. "Let's go."

They arrived at the neat and prosperous residence at the other end of the village. They let themselves in the gate, and with a serious air, Neferet introduced herself to the housekeeper. "I'm Lady Neferet, the daughter of the landowner Lord Hani. As you know, your mistress is staying at our house."

The woman nodded.

"She knew I was going to be in the village this afternoon, and she asked me to give you an instruction on her behalf."

"Yes, my lady?"

"She wants the multicolored faience *weshket* collar of her husband—the one he always wears. Can you do that for me?"

"Yes, my lady, of course. Give me just a minute to find it. I know where he always puts it when he takes it off at night."

The housekeeper left the room. Neferet could hardly repress a triumphant smile.

"You're going to steal it?" Mut-tuy whispered conspiratorially.

Neferet acted shocked. "No! The necklace won't be here, my girl. Usret has it. I want to confirm that. Because if it were here, then the one she has on is Hapu-seneb's. And then we'd have to ask how she got that one. Did Tjay kill him and give it to her, or did she kill Hapu-seneb herself?"

"Isn't that what we're asking already?" the adolescent asked.

Neferet, not having an answer, heaved a sorely tried sigh.

Eventually, the housekeeper returned with—to Neferet's astonishment—a large, flat tapestry pouch. She laid it carefully in Neferet's hands. "Here it is, my lady. I trust my mistress is doing well. Do you know if she plans to return soon?"

"I don't think she knows what she plans to do yet," Neferet said. "As long as her attacker is still on the loose, she's afraid to sleep in the village."

"I understand. Please tell her we pray for her."

The *sunet* assured her she would, and with the pouch draped over her forearm, she led the way to Kem-sit's house.

"Seven-headed devils!" Neferet muttered, flummoxed, once they were out of hearing. "I was *sure* it wouldn't be there. This means that Tjay probably hasn't been back to his house since he disappeared." But of course, the worst of it was that now, they knew the collar worn by Usret was that of the dead man.

"Lady Neferet," hissed Mut-tuy, catching at the young

woman's arm. "There go some of those reed cutters. Maybe one of them could watch Usret's house tonight."

Neferet looked up, drawn from her disappointed reverie. Four men trudged past, heading upslope, loaded with bundles of papyrus that dwarfed the bearers beneath.

"*Yahyah*, people." Neferet planted herself in their path. "I'm Lord Hani's daughter. Could I tempt one of you to perform a service for me? I'll pay you well."

"I'll do it, Lady Neferet," one of the men said.

She thought he looked familiar and wondered if he'd been among the men who had found Hapu-seneb's body. "Go down to the reed-boat maker's house and hide out. Watch out for his wife and see if she gets in a boat and goes anywhere. If she does, stay around till she comes back. This may well keep you there all night."

"Usret's goin' somewhere?" said one of the others with a leer. "Who's the lucky fellow?" The men laughed unkindly.

The reed cutter handed his burden to two of his companions, who shared the extra weight between them, carrying it like an injured person. Still chuckling, the chosen spy took himself off in the direction of the River. Neferet watched him sidle noiselessly past Usret's husband, who was still bent over his task, and slip into the edge of the marsh.

Neferet reached out a hand to prevent the men from going on. "You others, has anybody seen Tjay since he disappeared? Does he ever come back to the village?"

The men looked indecisive and glanced one at another. Finally, the oldest of them said, "Ain't none of us seen him or his boat, my lady. But if we did... he wouldn't come back again, for sure."

The others murmured agreement. Clearly, village feeling toward the former weaving supervisor wasn't friendly.

"What about his sister—within the last two weeks, let's say? Does she often slip around the way she plans to do tonight?"

Another murmured confabulation met these questions. The old man finally said, "Now an' again, my lady. Mostly in the village, far's we know. Usually up to Kem-sit's."

And they think women are gossips. These fellows know every time somebody goes to the latrine.

"Anyone else you see sneaking around after dark?" Mut-tuy asked.

"Hapy the sandalmaker. Got hisself a little friend."

"My wife's gone to her sick sister's a few times."

"The mayor, now an' again."

"I been to see my grandchildren when their father's not home."

And so on. Twilight travelers were common, despite the mosquitoes, and no one person stuck out. Ta-em-resefu wasn't on the list. After the death of Hapu-seneb, she would have had no reason to go visiting.

"Thank you, then. If you see anything unusual, let Kem-sit know. All right?"

The men lumbered away under their rustling burdens, and Neferet watched with a sense of discouragement. She found a few more villagers at work in their yards or on their roof terraces. Some of them had seen no one. Others had noticed one or another of their neighbors out and about. But Usret was only one among many. No one had seen Tjay's big boat since he disappeared. If he'd returned, it had been on some less distinctive-looking craft. By the time

Neferet had interrogated the lower half of the settlement, the shadows were stretching long across the River. She and her apprentice headed back to the place of rendezvous, where Bener-ib and Brute were already waiting.

"Any luck?" Neferet called.

Bener-ib's discouraged expression gave her the answer. "It's not that nobody was seen going around after sundown. It's that *everybody* was. I guess the cooler hours of the day are exactly when people visit and make deliveries."

"How could anybody commit a crime in secret in this village?" Mut-tuy said in disgust. "Some old biddy is always watching."

"They could be covering for one of their own, but I get the feeling that neither Tjay nor Usret is well loved here. Somebody would surely have tattled on them." Neferet stroked her chin in thought.

Bener-ib, drooping, said, "I guess we wasted our afternoon."

For the sake of the others, Neferet kept up a facade of optimism, but she was frankly discouraged. Either the villagers were uniting against the city people and keeping their suspicious deeds to themselves, or nothing untoward had been spotted. Yet somebody had sneaked up Kem-sit's steps and attacked her daughter-in-law while she slept. Somebody had gone into the marshes on an assignation, and somebody else had followed them, with fatal consequences. Had no one really seen any of them except the fisherman on the sandbar?

I wish Papa hadn't gone back to Waset.

Mama was serving dinner when they reached the farmhouse—a ragout of chard and pork with dill seed.

Neferet laid the bag containing the necklace beside her stool. Her discouragement fell away with the first delicious whiff of the stew.

"Papa would love this," Neferet said enthusiastically as she served her bowl. She sucked her fingers appreciatively.

"How were your interviews this afternoon?" asked Baket-iset.

Neferet's face fell. "Nobody seems to know anything significant. Nearly everybody in the village sneaks around at dusk. And Tjay can't be proved to have returned since his so-called death. What kind of place is this?"

"Except that Usret says she's gone back to the city to visit her brother, you said. She didn't ever say whether he comes to visit her," Bener-ib said.

"Oh, thanks for reminding me, Ibet! That's the one interesting thing—she was wearing Hapu-seneb's collar."

Ta-em-resefu's face lit up with some emotion—hope? Longing? Fear? Neferet wasn't sure.

She turned to the weaver. "We brought back Tjay's collar, if the housekeeper should say anything."

Neferet explained about Khnum-em-heb's request, and Ta-em-resefu cried immediately, "Of course! I can't think of a better end for it. I'm sure it will look much finer on him than on Tjay, that dirty jackal."

"But how did Usret get Hapu-seneb's collar?" asked Baket-iset. "Was she the one who killed him, then?"

"That's what we can't figure out. She said a friend gave it to her, and we assumed that meant Tjay. She doesn't seem to have many other friends. You should have heard the way the reed cutters laughed at her. Yet she was really pretty when we saw her dressed up."

"It's sad," said Bener-ib, ever compassionate.

"Even animals cut one of their number out of the herd if it acts odd." Sati shrugged. "It's just the way things are."

Mama began consolidating the dirty bowls for the kitchen girls. "Well, tomorrow, we clean up the farm. Vacation is almost over, and I have to be back in temple service soon. It's time to return to the city."

"Can I help you, Lady Nub-nefer?" asked Ta-em-resefu, getting to her feet. Neferet knew she still felt her social inferiority to the women around her.

But Mama shushed her with a motherly smile. "No, my dear. You're our guest—and so is your little one. I wish Khuit was around to forecast whether it's a boy or girl, but actually, any of us can do it. We just have to wait until the moon's right. Besides, you've been injured."

It occurred to Neferet that Ta-em-resefu's sanctuary was about to evaporate. "You can come with us to Waset," she said, beaming at the weaver.

"Oh, no, my lady," Ta-em-resefu protested. "I mean, thank you, but I wouldn't dare take a chance on running into Tjay. I'll be all right in my own house. He doesn't seem interested in coming back, so he won't even know I'm there. I can hire somebody to guard us."

"Sleep inside, my girl. Don't risk the roof terrace. Do you want to borrow Brute?"

"No, no. The children need to get back to their normal life, and I have work to do for... for Lord Dapurazo. It doesn't hurt when I move my arm now. I can't thank all of you enough."

"Now, if we could just catch the murderer and put

Hapu-seneb's *ba* to rest..." Neferet spoke with a little too much enthusiasm to hide how low her optimism had sunk.

She didn't like being thwarted, and after two weeks, they still had only unproved theories about the killer's identity. She was sorely tempted to throw over the whole investigation. It was mostly the thought of Papa and Maya and Grandfather's constant warnings of doom that made her dig in her heels.

That evening, after much effusive thanks, Ta-em-resefu and the little girls prepared to head back to their home in the village.

"We'll go with you," said Neferet.

The little procession wasn't very talkative as the late sun strung their shadows across the fields. The children were happy to be returning and seemed to interpret that move as a signal the danger was over. They skipped and sang around the women's feet as they walked. Brute padded stolidly at their side, but his eyes never ceased to comb the surrounding fields for peril. As for the adults, Neferet suspected they were all thinking the same thing: *I hope this is safe.*

When they entered the gate of the property, things were quiet.

"Should there be any servants here?" Neferet asked, looking around. The cicadas carried on as if nothing could possibly be the matter on such an evening, but the hairs on her neck were uneasy.

"No," Ta-em-resefu said. "I told everybody but the housekeeper they were off until I returned, and the housekeeper leaves in the afternoon. Nobody sleeps here."

The door wasn't barred, but the weaver assured them

that was typical when no one was home. The three *sunets* crowded in after her. An air of abandonment lay over the house sunk in dusty twilight. A thump made everyone flinch, but it was just a tomcat jumping down from the high window. It trotted, meowing, to the children, who exclaimed over it and petted it while the cat slid in and out between their little ankles. Neferet realized she missed her own animals.

"Thank you again for everything," Ta-em-resefu said, her tense face finally relaxing into a smile. "You've been so good to us."

Neferet and Bener-ib gave her a hug, one after the other. Neferet said, "I'm just sorry we haven't been able to solve the mystery of Hapu-seneb's murder. But we will—don't worry. Stay safe, my girl. Let us know if you need anything."

The three sunets waved goodbye and left, carefully closing the door behind them. Neferet heard the bolt slide in. *Good. She's protected now.*

They made their way across the small garden toward the gate and were letting themselves out when Brute emitted a low growl that rippled his floppy lip. His great lionlike head swung back toward the house.

All at once, from within, a shrill scream broke the stillness of evening and just as suddenly ceased.

CHAPTER 17

Neferet froze and stared at Bener-ib in horror, her heart leaping into her mouth. Then, as one, the three turned and rushed back to the doorway. Neferet pounded and jerked at it, but of course, it was barred from the inside.

"Mut, the mother of us all!" cried Bener-ib in a shaky voice, her hands to her mouth, her eyes bugging. "It's Ta-em-resefu!"

"We have to break it down or get in some other way." Neferet looked around but saw nothing they could use as a ram. The door was sturdy and new—it wouldn't go down easily.

From within the house, all was ominously silent.

"How did that cat get in?" asked Mut-tuy.

"Through the window, but how, by all that's holy, do we get up there?" *How did the cat get up there?* Neferet forced herself to be calm, to think things through. There was a sycomore fig tree, with heavy branches that brushed the wall, but still, the window was near the level of the salon ceiling. It would be a dangerous climb, and not every branch that held a cat could support the weight of a person.

"Wait, Nef'et—I found a ladder!" Benner-ib dragged the thing awkwardly from against the garden wall.

It was nothing more than a crude fruit picker's ladder—the trunk of a slender sapling with holes drilled into it, through which rough rungs had been shoved. Neferet could picture it turning as she climbed, leaving her hanging from the underside. But every second might be critical—there wasn't time to look for anything else. Ta-em-resefu and her girls might already be dead. Neferet propped it against the lowest limb of the tree, where it was still well below the level of the crucial branch.

She hissed, "Hold this, people, so it doesn't turn. I'm going up."

"Wait," cried Bener-ib in a panicky voice. "You'll need a rope or something so you can get down after you're inside. You can't jump down like the cat."

"Hand me the ladder after I'm up on the branch. I'll drop it down inside. Hurry!"

They held the rungs of the primitive ladder, trying to hold it steady when her weight wanted to spin it at every step. It would have made better sense to send one of the smaller girls up, but she didn't want to risk their lives. Neferet's heart was banging inside her. She quickly realized that the rungs pressed against the limb at the top kept it from turning completely around, despite the stomach-in-the-mouth sensation of losing balance, and some of the terror ebbed out of her. Finally, she swung a leg over the branch and laboriously pulled the ladder up behind her, panting and huffing as it scraped against the bark and caught again and again on twigs. The bare soles of her feet tingling with the precarity of her perch, she padded outward on the dipping branch, holding onto the parallel one above her. When she'd gotten close enough to the window, she went through the exhausting process of raising the ladder yet again. She had a splinter in the web of her thumb and was dissolving in sweat by the time she put the foot of the ladder through the opening and let it drop. The thud reverberated with frightening volume. *So much for the element of surprise.*

Below her in the deepening twilight, the two young women stood staring up through the leaves, their eyes round and anxious. "Hurry, Nef'et! Hurry!" Bener-ib urged, almost dancing with nerves.

Whispering a prayer, Neferet ducked low and slid a leg through the opening. The space was divided in two by a wooden grille intended to keep out intruders, but being considerably smaller than the average man, she was able to squeeze through. The top of the ladder was cubits below the window. She held onto the frame and let her body slide down the wall until she was hanging, then she found the rung with a groping toe.

"Open the door for us when you get in," Mut-tuy called in a stage whisper.

"Mut-tuy, go get Kem-sit," Neferet called.

The room was dark. It was also empty. But Neferet could hear a man's voice holding forth from upstairs. Her whole body twinged with fear as she let her weight settle on the top rung of the ladder. It rocked then stabilized.

Just don't fall over. She inched her way down, palms pressed against the wall for support, her feet painfully feeling for each knotty rung. At last, she touched the plaster floor and stood, panting in relief. *Now to let Ibet in.*

But before she could run across the salon to the door, sandaled footsteps clattered down the stairs. Into the room burst a man. He froze at the sight of her, looking just as shocked as Neferet felt.

"Who are you?" she cried. "What are you doing here?'

"I live here. What are *you* doing here?" He eyed the ladder, his brows contracted with outrage.

All you dear gods—this must be Tjay. He's come back. "What have you done to Ta-em-resefu? We heard her scream."

"I think I've had enough questions from a housebreaker, woman. Off my property." He took a menacing step toward her, then comprehension dawned on his face. "You're that *sunet* who's been snooping around, aren't you? Usret told me about you. I have one thing to say to you—I haven't killed anybody. And I want you out of my private affairs. Do you hear? Clear out and stay away."

Neferet looked him up and down. Despite the growing darkness, she could see the general resemblance to Hapu-seneb and understood how his wife might have mistaken the description of the corpse for his. Both men were curly haired and in their thirties, with slender build, medium height, and coppery Theban complexion. Tjay was good-looking—despite the expression of wrath—with dark brows, a firm jaw, and a well-shaped mouth. Neferet could see a strong resemblance to his sister. Poor Ta-em-resefu had been deceived by the attractive packaging into falling in love with a vile specimen.

"So, if you're not guilty of anything, how come you disappeared all at once? You just left your family behind."

"I don't owe you any explanations," he said curtly. "Out." But then he seemed to change his mind and stepped between her and the door. "No, wait. You know I'm still alive. Maybe you need not to be."

Neferet's stomach fell ominously. "I-I thought you said you weren't the killing type," she said, trying to put a little sass in her tone despite the fear she felt.

"No, I didn't say that. I said I'd never killed anyone. Not even that jackal bait Hapu-seneb, the double-crossing turd." He bared his teeth in an icy smile. "There's always a first time, though."

Oh dear. Where's Papa when I need him? She swallowed with difficulty.

"Ta-em-resefu!" Tjay yelled.

The woman came hastily down the stairs and stopped in surprise at the sight of Neferet. Her expression was tense, and tear streaks marked her cheeks.

"Did you ever find it?" he asked his wife, never taking his eyes from Neferet.

"No, Tjay."

"Well, get a rope first. I want to tie this housebreaker up. Then you can go back and look for the collar."

Neferet forced a brittle laugh. "That multicolored collar? Hapu-seneb's wearing it."

Tjay took a step toward her, his fists clenched. "I thought he was dead. What do you mean by that?"

"I mean I gave the collar to the priests of Inpu. Hapu-seneb will have it for eternity. He got your wife, and now he has your favorite piece of jewelry."

"Ammit take you!" the man shouted, beside himself. "Who gave you the right to interfere in my life like this, you shaven-headed bitch?" He turned to his wife. "Is this true?"

Ta-em-resefu shrank under his glare, not answering. But her silence *was* an answer. Tjay broke into a string of furious curses.

Not quite close enough to Neferet to strike her, he grabbed his wife's arm instead and gave her a savage shake. "I suppose you knew this all along, didn't you? Didn't you? You just pretended to look for it."

She whimpered and tried unsuccessfully to twist away, but he had her by her injured arm.

"*Iyah*, be careful there!' Neferet cried, outraged. "The woman is pregnant." She tried to insert herself between the pair, but Tjay struck her back.

"Yes. And whose child is it, eh? Get me the rope, you whore."

He slung Ta-em-resefu away from him with such force she staggered. She fled into the back of the house.

The two of us together might be able to overpower Tjay, but she's so cowed she wouldn't dare stand up to him, Neferet thought feverishly. She didn't like this talk of killing. He might be making empty threats, but he might just as easily be angry enough to do it. No matter what he said, he could well have killed Hapu-seneb in a jealous rage.

A furious rain of knocks, so ferocious the door panel bounced, made Tjay whirl.

"Ibet, my girl? Don't come in unless you have someone with you!" Neferet yelled.

Tjay's features twisted in a snide smile. "Unless she has a battering ram, I don't think she's coming in, do you?"

Neferet cast a desperate glance at the door from the corner of her eye. Could she rush it and pull up the bar before Tjay fell upon her? It seemed unlikely.

But an unexpected voice from outside shouted, "It's Kem-sit! I have several men with me. What's happening, Neferet? Is Ta-em-resefu all right?"

"Come in through the window, Kem-sit!"

Tjay was upon Neferet before she could draw another breath. He grabbed her by the upper arm and cuffed her in the face twice. "Shut up, you she-hyena."

Tears of pain sprang into her eyes despite herself. Neferet held up her other arm to block his blows. Then she stretched out a foot and jabbed at his ankles, knocking him off balance, and the two of them fell in a painful heap.

Spluttering with rage, Tjay crawled upright, still holding her in a bruising grip. Neferet danced around as wildly as she could, but pain limited her movements. She had no doubt he would break her arm if he needed to.

"That does it," he growled between clenched teeth. "Ta-em-resefu, damn it. Bring that rope."

The weaver crept toward them, holding a frowsty length of rope such as one might use to secure an animal. Her face was a mask of fear and reluctance. Tjay grabbed the rope from her and jerked it around Neferet's neck, knotting it and immobilizing her. Then he grabbed her elbows behind her in the crook of his own and wound part of the length of the cable around them. Finally, he pushed her roughly to the floor and knelt on her flailing feet, tying them with the other length of the cord so that she was arced backward and any movement choked her. Ta-em-resefu cowered a few feet away.

"Ta-em-resefu, my girl, open the door!" Neferet gasped. She could hear scraping and grunting outside the high window. Perhaps the men had found another ladder. But it would take time. "Open the door quick!"

But Tjay snarled, "Make a move and she's dead, Ta-em-resefu."

The weaver covered her face with her hands and wept. Silence fell, punctuated by Neferet's and Tjay's panting.

"Get me a knife from the kitchen." When his wife was slow to respond, he shrieked, "Now!'

He's losing control of himself, Neferet thought, her heart in her throat. *Where is Kem-sit?*

Ta-em-resefu disappeared again. From the floor, Neferet said defiantly, "You're about to commit a terrible mistake, Tjay. There's no place you can hide where *Ma'at* won't find you. You think you're heading off to a new and better life, but you're wrong. If you kill me, you'll be a hunted fugitive for the rest of your days."

"Shut up."

"I bet you've got a lady friend, haven't you? What's she going to think? 'He's not just an adulterer but a murderer of women too.' What a sweetheart."

"I said shut up. Ta-em-resefu, what's taking you so long?"

She appeared behind Tjay in the doorway from the kitchen, a long, oft-sharpened knife in her hand, her eyes haunted. Neferet swallowed hard. That blade would soon be sliding into her body, severing her blood vessels, and rupturing an organ unless she could think of something fast. *Come on, Kem-sit. Where are you?*

As if in answer, hammering resounded from the window. Kem-sit's men were trying to knock the frame out. Tjay glanced away from Neferet long enough to be sure the weaver had brought the knife, then he turned back to his prisoner, afraid to let her out of his sight for an instant.

He held out a hand. "All right, woman, give it to me handle first."

Ta-em-resefu approached fearfully.

"Give it to me, I said!" Tjay waggled his fingers impatiently.

His wife took a few more tottering steps, raised her hand, and plunged the knife into Tjay's back. He croaked out a strangled cry and turned, his eyes popping with astonishment. Then he crumpled silently to the floor, a spreading stain of carmine disfiguring his fine linen shirt where the point protruded from his chest.

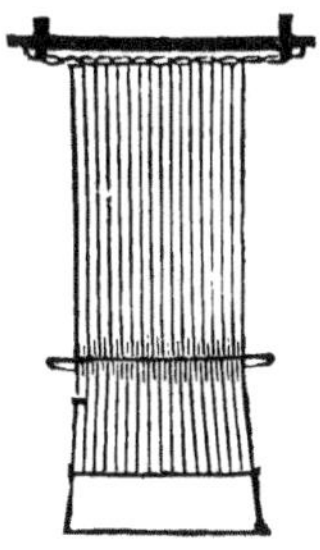

CHAPTER 18

TA-EM-RESEFU STOOD FROZEN AND STARING.

"Cut me loose, girl!" Neferet shouted.

The weaver fled. Neferet howled a curse of disappointment. But a moment later, Ta-em-resefu ran back with a smaller knife and sawed the rope at the prisoner's back. A wave of relief swept over the young *sunet* as she stretched out her legs and slipped the bristly noose from around her neck.

"Well done, Ta-em-resefu." She staggered to her feet and yelled, "Forget the window! I'm going to open the door, Kem-sit."

She flew through the vestibule to the door and raised the bolt. The mayor burst in with two middle-aged men at her back. They stopped as they saw Tjay folded on the floor.

"Is he dead?" Kem-sit's eyes took in the pile of rope at Neferet's feet.

"I'm pretty sure," Neferet said. "Although I haven't examined him yet."

"Good job, Lady Neferet." Kem-sit smiled dryly, like a person who was happy but didn't want it to be too obvious.

But Neferet said, beaming, "It wasn't me, mistress. It was Ta-em-resefu. She came through when I needed her."

Kem-sit pushed past the corpse on the floor and threw her arms around Ta-em-resefu, who was still standing, dazed, behind Tjay. "My poor girl. What happened? He found you here?"

The younger woman nodded. "He was here when we came. I barricaded the children upstairs so they wouldn't come down. I need to let them out." Together, she and the girls' grandmother headed for the stairs.

But one of the men called out, "What should we do with Tjay, mistress?"

Over her shoulder, Kem-sit said in a hard voice, "Throw him in the River. He's done enough harm."

They picked him up between them and sidled out through the door and away.

At that very moment, Bener-ib and Mut-tuy burst into the house, Brute at their side. Bener-ib flew to Neferet and hurled herself into her arms. "Oh, Nef'et! Thank the gods you're safe!"

Neferet crushed the little physician to her, tears of relief wetting her eyes. Life had never seemed so sweet. She saw Mut-tuy standing behind, looking lost and a little sullen, and she opened an arm to the girl and drew her into the embrace. "May the gods reward both of you. Your help came just in time. Tjay was getting ready to kill me."

"We told Kem-sit, like you said, and she rounded up the next two men she saw to come help," Bener-ib said breathlessly. "Then we went on to the farm to tell your family. And your father was there. He's coming, but we were faster."

Brute sniffed the spot occupied until recently by Tjay's body. The packed earth was dribbled with blood. Kem-sit and Ta-em-resefu descended from the staircase, the little girls pattering alongside, hanging onto their hands. Ta-em-resefu still looked stunned, but her normal color was returning. The need to appear calm for the children had clearly taken over. She and Kem-sit settled onto the two stools.

"Tell us what happened," said Mut-tuy avidly.

"We arrived, and the door wasn't bolted, but Ta-em-resefu said that wasn't unusual. This is an honest village, after all, not the city." Neferet still had Bener-ib by the hand as if she might evaporate like a sweet dream.

Ta-em-resefu said in a faint voice, "He was already inside the bedroom when I entered. It scared me half to death, and I screamed."

"We heard you." Neferet nodded.

"He was looking for that collar of his—the one you took for Hapu-seneb. I told him I had no idea where it was."

"Perfect!"

"Then he made me look for it upstairs, and he came downstairs. He... he was rough with us, insulting me in words I didn't want the little ones to hear. He described the sex he had with his new lady friend and taunted me about Hapu-seneb. He kept saying things like 'I could kill you right now, adulteress.' I was terrified."

"As the poor girl has been for most of her married life," said Kem-sit blackly. "But Ma'at sees all."

"What's going to happen to me now, though?" Ta-em-resefu turned fearfully to her mother-in-law. "I've murdered somebody."

But Neferet spoke up. "It wasn't murder. You were defending me. In another second, he would have killed me."

At her side, Bener-ib blanched.

Neferet continued the story with her own entry onto the scene and how Ta-em-resefu, who'd been under Tjay's power, had turned on him. "It was *sooo* brave!"

A man's deep voice called urgently from the vestibule, "Neferet! Are you all right?"

"Papa!" She sprang up and ran to the door of the salon, where her father caught her up in a desperate embrace. At his back stood Maya, Grandfather, and Lord Dapurazo. Everyone was grinning in relief except the foreigner.

"Is Mistress Ta-em-resefu safe?" he asked anxiously.

"She is. And she's a hero besides," Neferet said, effervescent with excitement.

They crowded back into the salon where the others sat. Ta-em-resefu popped to her feet at the sight of the man of Keftiu. He went directly to her side but seemed to grow shy. Instead of grabbing her in his arms, he took her hand, kissed it, and pressed it to his heart. But there was no mistaking the look that poured from his eyes, flowing over the weaver like warm date syrup.

Somebody's in love.

"What's happened here? Where is Tjay?" Papa asked, dropping to a seat on the cushions.

Neferet launched into the story for the second time.

"That was a little too close for comfort, my girl," said

Grandfather at the end of the recital, raising his bushy black eyebrows. "Didn't Brute protect you?"

"We had him stay outside the door, as usual. But I think that's not such a good idea after all."

"He came with us to Mistress Kem-sit's," said Bener-ib apologetically. "I should have left him with you."

"But he couldn't have climbed in the high window with her anyway, people," Mut-tuy said dryly.

Neferet suppressed a flash of annoyance. She felt she had a right to forget certain details after an evening of such drama. But she said nothing. Sometimes, Mut-tuy was too quick for her own good.

"How is it you were at the farm, Papa?"

"We came back to help your mother and Sati pack up for the end of the summer. With all the children around, it was hard for them to get anything done. I knew you were interviewing people in the village, so we didn't start to worry until it began to get dark. We were actually on our way when the girls ran into us." Papa squeezed her around the shoulders. He showed admirable self-restraint by not saying anything further about danger.

"So, did your interviews elucidate the murder of Hapu-seneb at all?" asked Maya.

"Not so much, but I'm pretty sure it was Tjay, even though he denied it. He didn't have any scruples about doing away with me, and how much more the man who humiliated him."

"And what about the attack on Ta-em-resefu?" asked Grandfather. "Did he admit to that?"

"Admitting to any wrongdoing wasn't Tjay's style," Ta-em-resefu said bitterly. "But it had to be him. He'd killed

Hapu-seneb, and he would've been eager to punish me. It would have made him safe from prosecution, too, wouldn't it?"

Everyone absorbed this likelihood soberly.

"You can sleep safe tonight, mistress," said Dapurazo in a gentle voice to Ta-em-resefu. "That bastard will never bother you again."

"I don't know. I feel like Tjay's angry ghost will be abroad tonight," the weaver murmured.

"Would you like me to stay here, just in case?" Dapurazo asked. "A little protection might be a good idea. And the girls may still be frightened."

Papa and Grandfather exchanged amused looks, and Maya raised his eyebrows knowingly. Neferet held back a snicker. *Men are so transparent.* They left Dapurazo to guard the family, and everyone else walked to the door with Kem-sit.

The mayor thrust out a hand like a man, and she and Papa grasped forearms in a firm clasp of gratitude. "Thank you, Lord Hani. Thank you all for everything you've done to try to make things right. You should be proud of your daughter and her friends."

"Oh, I am," Papa said, his voice unsteady with emotion.

The family set off into the moonlit summer night, Brute at their heels.

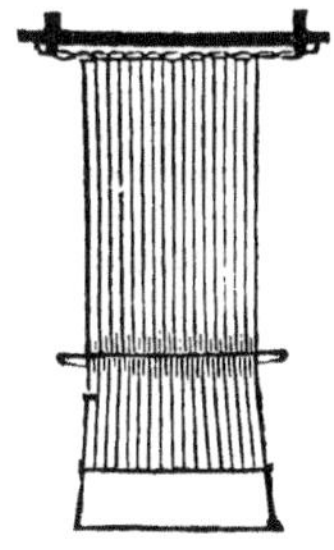

CHAPTER 19

THE NEXT DAY, A SMALL delegation of reed cutters appeared at the door of the farmhouse before the entire household was even up. Neferet, who was sitting with Bener-ib in the shade with a bowl of carob pods in her lap, put down her pods and jumped up to intercept the men.

"Lady Neferet," said the eldest, bobbing a bow, "Shu, here, watched Usret's house all evenin' and all night and said nobody never left. Nobody came neither. No boats puttin' in anywhere near an' nobody walkin' around. Just her husband—at some point, he went inside. An' she come and stood in the door for a bit."

"How was she dressed, Shu?"

He look nonplussed, then shrugged. "N-Normal. I'm not sure what you mean."

"Dressed up fancy?"

"No, my lady. Normal."

She thanked the men and gave them the bowlful of carob pods she'd been preparing to scrape. "That's helpful information. We're grateful. Here—treat your children with these."

They bowed appreciatively and thudded off down the path directly to the River, eager to start their workday before it got any hotter. She watched their heads disappear over the steep edge of the bank.

Neferet conveyed the information to Bener-ib. "So, she was lying after all. But why was she all dressed up, then?"

Bener-ib's pointed face grew sad. "That was Hapu-seneb's collar. If she still loved him, she may have been… I don't know what to call it. Fantasizing about him. Dressing up for him while nobody was around. Maybe she really had nowhere to go and just wanted to pretend someone who loved her was waiting for her."

"I'd like to know how she got that collar if Tjay hadn't been back to the village."

"Just because no one saw him doesn't mean he hasn't been back, Nef'et."

"But wouldn't he have gotten his *weshket* if he'd come back? It seemed to symbolize his aspirations for himself." Neferet heaved a sigh. She still lacked a satisfying sense of conclusion about this case. It was like being sent away from the table before the fruit was served.

She was still gnawing on the unresolved parts of it later that morning as she and the lady of her heart helped Mama pack.

"The only thing that worries me is what Usret will do when she finds out it was Ta-em-resefu who killed her brother." Neferet was stacking freshly washed clothes into the chest in her parents' bedroom. The family was due to depart for Waset just before noon.

"She seemed surprisingly unmoved the first time she thought he was dead—I mean, considering how she idolized him," Bener-ib said, handing her a pile of folded breechclouts.

"She's a hard one to predict."

"Should we pay her our condolences?" Mut-tuy was folding Mama's shifts on the bed, smoothing out the least wrinkle so they'd be fresh looking when the family returned.

"Not a bad idea. If Qen and Shu-roy have left us any flowers, we can take her a little bouquet."

"Tiry's turning four about this time of year."

The adolescent had said nothing about her three-year-old sister's birth date. Neferet rolled her eyes. "Could you have given us some warning, my girl? She'll have to learn a new number." *And now everybody's busy with packing.*

"That's all right. She doesn't know what day it is. She'd be perfectly happy to say 'three' for the rest of her life."

"Good thing she's not a god, or we'd have to throw her a party," Neferet said dryly. She thought about the redoubtable toddler with her amazing lungpower and the ability to pass through a room like a cyclone in the desert, leaving it in shambles. *Maybe she's a god of chaos.* "If we're going to the village, let's go before it gets any hotter."

They left the folding on the bed, and Baket's cat, Pamiu, appeared from nowhere to make himself at home on top of the immaculate shifts. Brute jumped up and followed them downstairs—he hadn't been much interested in feminine domestic duties. They gathered a scruffy armload of Papa's flowers from the farmyard and set out down the path through the fields.

Perhaps it was her optimistic imagination, but Neferet

had a sense that the temperatures were going imperceptibly down. They were in the midst of what passed for autumn in the Southern Kingdom, after all. A fresh, dry breeze floated past, bringing the smell of herbs and fruit. It was almost time for the grape harvest. Some people might already have begun.

The village, buzzing with cicadas, drowsed under the white sun of late morning, faintly blurred with humidity from the River. A man trudged down the middle of the road, with yoked jars across his shoulders, singing. It seemed like the most peaceful little place in the Two Lands, yet three acts of violence had split the calm in only a few weeks.

The young women turned toward the water and followed the slope to Usret's house. Her husband was lining up sized reeds, ready to start another boat. He waved as they passed. The door was open, the mat rolled up.

"Usret? Are you here?" Neferet called, pushing her way through the crowded vestibule.

Usret materialized out of the twilit darkness, a mourning scarf around her head. She looked serious but not crushed with mourning, despite the disheveled hair and torn strap. "Ah, Lady Neferet."

They trooped into the tiny salon in her wake. Here, too, there was an air of the midden, with used-up artifacts of daily life piled all around. To their surprise, Kem-sit and Ta-em-resefu were already seated there, become a part of the decor that overflowed almost into their laps. Their hostess cleared a few dusty cushions of their loads and bade her guests be seated.

"Lady Neferet, Lady Bener-ib," said Kem-sit in her deep voice.

Ta-em-resefu nodded, her face glowing with joy despite the appropriately sober absence of a smile.

"We've come to offer our condolences," said Neferet, settling herself among the clutter with a distaste she hoped was concealed.

Usret watched her face with unnerving attention, but she seemed neither angry nor deeply sorrowful. "How very kind of you," she said with a fleeting smile. "We've already mourned him once, of course. Although it turned out to be a false alarm."

Bener-ib extended the flowers. "The children messed these up, Usret, but they're heartfelt. We know how close you were to Tjay."

"Aren't you nice, though. The worst shock was that it was Ta-em-resefu. I've always thought of her as a friend." Usret extended a fleshless hand and laid the bouquet in her lap. She shot a look at her sister-in-law that was devoid of any rancor. "Who'd have thought she had such anger in her."

Ta-em-resefu said nothing, just looked down at her hands. There was no way she could have explained what she had suffered.

"I understand Tjay wasn't very nice to her through the years." Neferet shifted uncomfortably. A tool of some sort was poking her in the back. "And she was defending our lives. He was about to kill me."

"Oh, I doubt he really would have."

"He tried to kill her, too, remember?" Neferet prodded.

Kem-sit added, "She wouldn't have felt safe as long as he was alive."

"It wasn't him." Usret looked at Neferet almost in pity.

"He wouldn't do something like that. How would he have known she was sleeping at Kem-sit's house, anyway?"

Neferet found it annoying that Tjay's sister still refused to hold him responsible for anything. *She helped make him what he was.* "You could have told him," she said pointedly but managed a smile. "Ta-em-resefu and Kem-sit told you everything."

Usret lowered her eyes and smiled, too, as if she had a secret.

"Was it you who attacked Ta-em-resefu?" Mut-tuy blurted.

Neferet barely had time to register embarrassment before Usret said, "Yes."

Suddenly, it all fell into place. Tjay had sent his willing slave to do the deed in his place. Papa in a dress. Someone familiar to the children. And when everyone kept saying it was Tjay, that had seemed to explain why the little ones knew the figure they'd glimpsed in the darkness.

"She just told us," Kem-sit confirmed, still in a peaceable voice.

"But why, Usret?" Neferet said, confused. "You called her a friend. She was nice to you."

"I had nothing against her. But she had humiliated Tjay. It's a man's right to avenge his honor."

"And he sent his little sister to do his dirty work in his place?" Neferet could hardly suppress the contempt she felt for such a person.

"No. He never said a thing. But I had heard Kem-sit say the law permitted a man to kill his wife's lover if he killed the wife too. I just wanted to make it legal."

"So, you knew Tjay had killed Hapu-seneb?" asked Bener-ib.

"Not really. He would never do such a thing. He didn't have to." Usret's demeanor was too bright and cheerful for a discussion of the death of human beings. She paused as if waiting for the young women to ask her what she meant, and when they said nothing, she added, "I killed him."

Neferet exchanged a look with Bener-ib. She saw Kem-sit and Ta-em-resefu stiffen.

"I found Hapu-seneb lying in the marshes. He'd been hit on the head, but he was still alive. You know, it was a moment of real communion. I had a real feeling he loved me better than Ta-em-resefu after all. I held him in my arms as he died, and he reached out for me. That's something special, isn't it? He told me to keep his collar."

Ta-em-resefu was gaping as if she didn't know what to believe. Kem-sit looked frozen.

For her part, Neferet was chilled. "Y-You didn't go for help?"

Bener-ib murmured, "We could have trepanned him, Usret—lifted the broken pieces out of his skull. We might have been able to save him." She spoke gently and without judgment, as if to a small child.

"But, my lady, he deserved to die. He had humiliated Tjay. I was Tjay's hands, don't you see? Tjay wasn't around, but I was his hands to make good his legal right. Ma'at had spoken. No point being sentimental about it." Usret didn't seem at all angry. She spoke in the most matter-of-fact tone imaginable.

Dear gods, woman. Neferet suppressed a shudder. *I thought you loved Hapu-seneb.*

"What did you tell Tjay that night when Hapu-seneb asked you to be his messenger?" asked Bener-ib in a voice soft with compassion.

"I told him about Ta-em-resefu's infidelity but not about the rendezvous in the marshes. I was afraid he'd confront Hapu-seneb, and if they fought, he might be hurt. I planned to take care of the adulterers myself. Kem-sit had said that it wasn't against the law as long as you killed them both. That's why I attacked Ta-em-resefu too. She's a nice girl." Usret smiled at her sister-in-law, who was staring, mouth wide open in disbelief. "I wished her no harm. I wished Hapu-seneb no harm. But they had sinned against Tjay, humiliated him. He's a proud man. Ma'at demanded reparation."

Usret smiled reasonably. She seemed convinced of what she'd said. And to let an injured man die wasn't altogether the same as to kill him or even to try—especially if Usret thought he was expressing his love for her. Neferet knew quite well that Hapu-seneb wouldn't have been conscious after the terrible impact.

"It must have been Tjay who struck Hapu-seneb the first blow, though, right?" *Please let it be Tjay,* Neferet prayed. *He's dead, and it would be so much easier to close the case with the killer dead.*

"Oh, no. I hadn't told him about the rendezvous, remember? Whoever struck him didn't kill him. I did."

Neferet felt no sense of resolution. *What do we do now? Do we turn her over to Kem-sit for trial?* A woman had set out to avenge a wrong against her flesh and blood. Part of Neferet felt she should applaud her willingness to act. Part of her feared for a world where everybody righted their own wrongs. She turned to Kem-sit and Ta-em-resefu—the would-be victim and her family. Ultimately, it was up to them whether Usret went to trial.

Kem-sit stood up, and the others followed. "Usret, Ta-em-resefu is healin' nicely. If she's willin' to forgive you, I suppose we can forget about the attack on her."

Ta-em-resefu seized her sister-in-law's hand. "You know I forgive you, Usret. I didn't die, and you… you were doing what you thought was right."

"So, that leaves Hapu-seneb." Neferet bit her lip and said hesitantly, "Usret, are you *sure* you didn't hit him yourself? No one else knew he would be there if you hadn't told Tjay. There were no witnesses. We wouldn't be mad at you if you did it."

Usret shook her head tranquilly, but Kem-sit looked uncomfortable. She said finally in a flat voice, "No, my lady. Usret don't lie. If she goes to trial, I'm not sure the council will pardon her. They see her as one with her brother, who wasn't much liked." She drew a deep breath. "There *was* a witness. Me. I know she didn't hit him. Because I did."

Everyone stared at her, stunned. Neferet could hardly believe her ears. "Are you defending someone?" she squawked, thinking of Ta-em-resefu.

But the mayor shook her head gravely. She caught Ta-em-resefu's shocked glance and lowered her eyes. "It was a terrible accident. I was trying to kill Tjay."

Bener-ib said gently, "Perhaps you can tell us the whole story, Kem-sit."

The mayor cleared her throat. "Usret had told her brother about Hapu-seneb's affair with his wife. I understood that she'd also told Tjay about the rendezvous in the marshes. Of course, she had *not* told Ta-em-resefu, as she was supposed to, so to my knowledge, the person who was actually gonna meet Hapu-seneb was Tjay. I think we can safely say his intention woulda been to kill Hapu-seneb. I saw a perfect chance to clear Tjay out of his wife's way, to give her and the girls a chance at a happy life, at last, with a man who really loved them. And to pay that crocodile spawn back for all the pain he'd gave his father and everyone else over the years."

Her mannish voice trembled with suppressed rage. "I hid in the reeds and waited for Tjay to come. After a while—it was darker by then than twilight—I saw a man comin'. He had a little lamp, although he carried it low, so I couldn't see his face well. But he was wearin' that *weshket* collar that Tjay always wore. I let him pass, and then I sprung on him from behind and bashed him with a big rock I'd brought—one of the ones I use to prop the loom. He didn't have on a wig, and I got him good. Then I slipped away without even lookin' at him up close. I didn't know it wasn't Tjay until you mentioned the scar on his wrist." She hung her head but raised it again and stared bravely at the others. Her weathered face seemed to have aged ten years. "The gods've punished me for taking the law into my hands. I've spoiled Ta-em-resefu's happiness after all."

The younger woman threw her arms around her mother-in-law in a gesture of forgiveness. "You couldn't have known. It was dark."

"My eyes isn't what they used to be."

Neferet felt emptied of breath, as if someone had punched her in the stomach. This was a turn of events she had never foreseen.

"I guess I'll turn myself in to myself," Kem-sit said wryly. "I'll have to recuse myself as magistrate, and the council will judge me."

"And I'm sure they'll take into account the torment that awful Tjay put his family through all these years," Neferet said comfortingly. "Everyone in the village knew him. Why, you were saving Ta-em-resefu and the children's lives, probably. It was a tragic mistake that made Hapu-seneb the victim."

Does the fact that Kem-sit probably took a gleeful satisfaction in seizing the life of a man she thought had cost her husband his count against her? Neferet remembered saying, not long ago, that the right action didn't have to be painful to count as good.

The three took their leave, and Neferet led the way back upslope toward the village in a pensive mood. Brute followed along, his drippy tongue lolling.

The next morning, Neferet awoke in her bed at Lord Ptah-mes's house. The long holiday was over, and so was the summer. Bener-ib had already slipped downstairs, leaving the mosquito net folded neatly back, and the slashes of sunlight descending from the high window suggested that the day was well underway. Neferet sat up and stretched luxuriously with a loud roar—Papa always swore it was more satisfying that way—then swung her feet to the floor. *Back to the dispensary today.* It would be nice to see the three old dogs and Cheetah again. And no doubt there would be patients to tend. She looked forward to it.

But then she remembered she had one more unpleasant

duty to tend to. She needed to return Hapu-seneb's collar—or rather, its prototype—to his family. The thought of the bereaved parents sobbing brokenheartedly in her presence was enough to curdle her fine mood.

The young woman slipped off her sweaty night shift and unfolded a fresh one from the clothes chest. Rubbing her eyes, she descended the stairs and meandered toward the kitchen then remembered that at Ptah-mes's house, one didn't break fast standing at the kitchen door. Her vacation was over.

The steward glided up to her. "Lady Bener-ib is in the garden pavilion with the master of the house and your father and grandfather, my lady. Can I bring you some bread and milk?"

"Yes, please." *Papa is here*, she thought in delight.

She heard his beloved voice and trotted the rest of the way down the gravel path. Papa, Lord Ptah-mes, and Lord Dapurazo were discussing some business matter, a scroll unrolled before them. Grandfather leaned back in a low-backed chair and hummed an off-key tune. Bener-ib was seated on the edge of the porch, drinking her cup of milk.

"Papa Duck! How is it you're here so early in the morning?" Neferet gave her father a big hug and seated herself next to the lady of her heart.

The others laughed.

"It's not as early as that, little duckling. Dapurazo and I had some details about customs to work out with the Master of the Double House here. Then I told him about Usret's part in the attack on Ta-em-resefu. I hope you don't mind me passing on that story."

"Well, do we have something to add to the account!"

she said dramatically. "Wait till you hear this." And she described for the men what Usret and Kem-sit had told her, complete with different voices and an abundance of theatrical gestures.

Papa looked troubled. "The poor soul. I hope Usret's testimony may reduce Kem-sit's charge to attempted murder. I hate to see such a good, conscientious public figure punished."

"Punished?" Grandfather said. "The council won't punish her, Hani. They'll probably give Kem-sit the gold of honor. She'll be the first woman to wear the *shebyu* collar. And the Golden Mosquito."

"What's that?" Bener-ib asked.

"It's for acts of valor carried out in the marshes." Grandfather gave her a wink.

"Actually"—Papa laughed—"I think at least one queen has worn the *shebyu*. But what we're trying to say is that she's not in any real danger from her peers, who like her well. It's possible the council will acquit Usret, too, because of the personal nature of revenge, but of course, she wasn't the offended party."

"Not literally his 'hands,' as she seemed to think," Ptah-mes said. "It will depend on the goodwill of the council."

"But I don't think she knew she was doing anything wrong. Ta-em-resefu isn't pressing charges. Why should Usret have to go to trial?"

"I'm sure your father will take all of this into account."

Neferet looked from Ptah-mes to Papa, confused.

Papa said reluctantly, "Ptah-mes tells me that as the landowner of the village, it's my duty to preside over a trial when the mayor has to recuse herself. Kem-sit is the defendant, so it's up to me to conduct the trial."

Neferet exchanged excited looks with Bener-ib. "That's wonderful, Papa. They all respect you and will do whatever you say."

"I won't be there to tell them what to do, little duckling, just to preside. I'll recapitulate the known facts before they vote. Kem-sit will be judged by the elders of the village. People who know and like her."

A maid approached silently and set a small table at the young woman's side. Upon it, she placed a blue herringbone-glass cup of milk and an exquisitely fresh small loaf. She left as soundlessly as she had come.

"Do we know everything about the two cases, then?" Papa asked. "I'm sure the council will be lenient toward the women. If Ta-em-resefu doesn't press charges, that means Usret probably won't even go before the judges."

"What about Hapu-seneb's family, though?" Bener-ib asked. "Do we tell them who killed their son?"

Neferet's good cheer curdled. "Oh, right. What if they go after Kem-sit?"

Papa said, "I don't know the wife at all, but Khnum-em-heb has impressed me as a good man. He's expressed a desire to take care of his son's lover, and he wants the grandchild to be part of his life. But I'm not sure about this. He was roaring for vengeance. He'll probably plead for a harsh penalty."

"Maybe, without actually saying so, you should encourage him to think it was Tjay who killed Hapu-seneb," said Lord Ptah-mes. "Tjay's dead, and no consequences can touch him."

Neferet nodded forcefully. "Tjay *would've* killed Hapu-seneb. He didn't have any scruples about killing me. I've got to take Hapu-seneb's necklace to them today. I'll let them know how the case turned out—sort of."

She turned to the merchant from Keftiu and asked with a twinkle in her eye, "And what about Lord Dapurazo?"

Papa threw back his head and laughed. "There's the fortunate part of this all."

Dapurazo, his cheeks reddening and a grin of sheer happiness splitting his face, said, "Mistress Ta-em-resefu has consented to marry me. We're going to set up an entrepot here and export fine Egyptian linens to my country then import some of the fancy-woven heavy woolens from mine. I understand they're popular here for rugs and awnings. I can't thank you enough for all your help, Lord Hani. I never could have done all the official filings without you."

"With our young sun god's blessing—he'll be getting a cut. This is still as close to the Hittite style of commerce as I'm aware of here—private merchants dealing with private merchants abroad." Papa clapped the foreigner on the back, his little eyes crinkled with benevolence.

"As the treasurer, I can only express my enthusiasm for the arrangement," said Lord Ptah-mes, a wry quirk twitching the corner of his mouth. "Our friend will be paying customs in both directions."

"This all ended well, then. The only sad note is poor Hapu-seneb. But then, Dapurazo and Ta-em-resefu wouldn't have gotten together if he hadn't died." Neferet smiled but felt a little pang of sorrow. *Do joys always have such a high price?* Out of nowhere, she thought of Baket-iset.

Her somber reflections were interrupted by the children's nurse, who appeared around the corner of the pomegranate bushes. She had the baby in one arm and dragged Tiry at her side with the other hand. At her back, Mut-tuy scuffed along.

"Oh, excuse me." The nurse started to back away, but Neferet called her back.

"What is it, my girl?" Neferet asked.

"I wasn't sure whether to take the children to the dispensary this morning, my lady. Mut-tuy keeps saying yes, but I didn't know whether the regular schedule had started up again yet or not."

"Oh. We probably won't go until this afternoon." Neferet turned to the others and grinned. "Everybody tells me it's already late." She held out her arms to Tiry, who toddled over and climbed into her lap. "Somebody's got to learn a new number. Somebody is four now."

"How old are you, Tiry?' asked Bener-ib, holding up four fingers.

"*Hamtau*," the little girl answered with a big grin. Three.

"No," Neferet said, tickling her belly with four fingers. "This many fingers is four—*yifdau*. So, how old are you?"

"*Yifdau*?" Tiry seemed uncertain. In fact, she didn't seem to like this new number, holding it out on the tips of her lips.

"Yes! Good girl!" Bener-ib applauded and kissed her on a chubby cheek.

"How old are you again, Tiry?" Mut-tuy pushed.

Her sister grinned naughtily and held up four fingers. "*Hamtau.*"

Mut-tuy tossed her head in despair. "You're so dumb, Tiry. *Yifdau, yifdau.*"

The men laughed.

"I look forward to having children of my own," said

Dapurazo, enchanted. He was so happy he probably would have been ecstatic over cleaning the baby's bottom. Papa and Lord Ptah-mes, whose children were grown, smiled.

"You'll never stop worrying about them, even when they're adult men or women," Papa said, shooting a glance at Neferet.

She cast her eyes up to the heavens just to let him know she understood what he meant—*Don't do dangerous things.* "I know, I know, Papa. We're careful."

That afternoon, while the nurse led the orphans to the dispensary, Neferet took the *weshket* collar in its tapestry pouch, and she and Bener-ib set off for Khnum-em-heb's house. Papa had specifically asked to accompany them. He made it clear that it had nothing to do with protecting the young women but was only out of a sense of sympathy for the grieving weaver—he wanted to be able to offer at least the small comfort of this memento to a man he'd come to admire. He joined the two *sunet*s outside Ptah-mes's gate, and together, the three of them made their way through the stifling city lanes to the weaving workshop with its modest attached residence. A lugubrious gatekeeper in a mourning scarf let them in, and within a few minutes, Khnum-em-heb joined them in the work court.

"Lord Hani, my friend," he said with a strained smile. "How good of you to come. I want you to understand that you're all invited to Hapu-seneb's funeral when the time is accomplished. Lord Dapurazo, too, of course, if he's still here."

"We're honored," Hani said, clasping the man's forearm

in a grip of solidarity. "I'm sure Dapurazo will be too. And he'll most certainly be here. He plans to settle permanently in our city, in fact." Hani explained the man of Keftiu's plan for an entrepot. "And he's going to marry Tjay's widow. He'll be sure your grandchild has a good life in a loving family and that he grows up knowing the weaving trade."

Khnum-em-heb's eyes overflowed with tears, and his lip trembled. "May the gods bless him," he croaked. "To take on another man's child like that. I hope he'll consider himself part of our family too."

"I'm sure he will. He's a good man."

Neferet felt her own eyes grow misty. It always melted her when men cried. "We have something for you, master," she said, holding out the jewelry pouch.

From his awed and touched expression, Khnum-em-heb suspected what was in the fold of tapestry. He took it reverently and opened the flap, exposing the collar in all its beautiful rainbow of colors. A sob escaped him as he clasped it to his breast. "How can I thank you, Lady Neferet? This will make the boy's mother so happy. It was a gift of love. Now Hapu-seneb will wear it for eternity—our gift over his heart."

Neferet impulsively threw her arms around the weaver. Then she stepped back, not wanting to embarrass him. Behind her, Bener-ib blew her nose. *She's always so tenderhearted.*

"We, uh, we think we know who killed your son," Neferet said in a lower voice.

But to her surprise, Khnum-em-heb held up a hand. "Don't tell me, my lady. Hapu-seneb was not a vengeful boy, and my wife and I are trying to put this behind us as he would have. I don't even want to know the wretch's name. Just see to it that justice is done to him, I beg you."

A wave of relief washed through her. She didn't have to lie. "The gods have already punished him—don't worry."

Papa watched her speak with a proud, quiet smile, and gave her a wink, but it was a serious one. All at once, she realized she knew exactly what his words that morning had meant. It was more than *Don't do dangerous things*. It was *Parents never stop loving their children. Not ever, no matter what they do or how big they are.* Pa-shedu hadn't given up on the ungrateful Tjay. Kem-sit was still kind to Usret, however strange and confused she was. The cowed Ta-em-resefu had found the strength to protect her little girls. Khnum-em-heb and his wife were remaking themselves completely to be worthy of their son. And Papa and Mama? The heavens couldn't hold the vastness of their love.

Neferet's nose twinged dangerously, and she slipped an arm around her father's waist.

THE END

Did you enjoy this book? Here is a sample from the next *Hani's Daughter Mystery*, ***Wheel of Evil***.

CHAPTER 1

"AND THERE GOES THE LAST patient of the day," said Neferet, collapsing against the gate of the dispensary in relief. "It seems like every child in the neighborhood fell off something or got stung by some insect today."

Bener-ib, the woman of her heart and her fellow physician, smiled shyly. "I think we saw *more* little ones today than live in the whole neighborhood."

"They must have been coming in from all over the City of the Scepter!" Neferet whooped with laughter, imagining a great parade of naked children marching from all quarters, converging on the little house in the working-class neighborhood of Waset where the two young women had their infirmary.

Their apprentice, Mut-tuy, with a fourteen-year-old's determination to be contrary at all costs, said sourly, "Nothing interesting, though. Just stupid booboos."

"Ah, but that gave you a chance to practice your skills, my girl," Neferet reminded her. "You got to clean and bandage cuts and apply plasters and all sorts of things. Were you expecting to trepan somebody's skull on your first day of actual practice?"

Mut-tuy rolled her eyes, a gesture she had perhaps copied from Neferet but which she had perfected at its most dismissive. Bener-ib tried to hide a grin. She and Neferet exchanged a look of understanding. They had been adolescents not so many years ago themselves and were still young enough at twenty-five to remember what that awkward age was like.

But even more, they understood the hurtful few years the girl had undergone. She and her brothers and sisters were orphans—or nearly so. Their father, a goldsmith, had been murdered, and their mother had run away, leaving her children behind. The younger siblings thought she was dead, but Mut-tuy was old enough to suspect the truth of that cruel abandonment. She refused to act grateful to the two *sunet*s for adopting the family.

"Shall we tell Nurse to gather the troops and all march on home, then? I think I wouldn't object to an early supper. I hardly even remember lunch."

"I'll see to it that the animals have food and water," Bener-ib said, turning back to rear of the house.

Neferet headed into the small walled garden, where some neat beds of simples tried to grow, despite the rowdy games of the children. The nurse, a cheerful, buxom young woman not much older than her employers, called the youngsters to attention and scooped up baby Baki, who was toddling relentlessly after Brute the mastiff. Baki was obsessed with trying to unroll the dog's curly tail.

"Has the night guard not come yet?" Neferet asked the day guard, who was still squatting against the wall whittling, an activity in which he passed much of his time. It had been a long while since anything had threatened the serenity of the dispensary, but everyone still remembered last year's violent attacks. It seemed like a good idea to have an armed presence at all times, just in case. After all, Neferet's husband, Lord Ptah-mes, was the Master of the Double House—the treasurer of the Two Lands—and one never knew when some disgruntled taxpayer might try to take his wife or adopted children hostage. Not to mention the young woman's propensity for getting involved in murder cases.

"No, my lady. But he should be here any minute now," the man replied. "Don't worry. I won't leave 'till he comes."

The three graybeard dogs that helped the guard keep order swarmed eagerly when Bener-ib returned, a plate of scraps in her hand. She divided it among their dishes and checked the water. Cheetah the cat acted uninterested. She had brought them an enormous rat that afternoon.

Meanwhile, Nurse was having no luck getting the orphans to line up for the walk home.

"All right, people," Neferet called above the noise of the rowdy youngsters. "Good children first in line and naughty ones last. We're heading to Mama and Papa's house."

Predictably, everybody mobbed forward, trying to be first in the queue. Even four-year-old Tiry pushed her baby brother to the ground and squeezed ahead of him, leaving him sitting, squalling, on the gravel. Hu-may, a gentle thirteen-year-old apprenticed as a goldsmith, finally went to the back of the line and picked up the little one, carrying him to the front.

That boy's too sweet for the real world, Neferet thought, touched.

Nurse shouldered Tiry and off the small pack set, heading for the southern suburbs of the great city where Neferet's parents lived. Mut-tuy, as usual, had nothing to do with her brothers and sisters, instead walking with the two young doctors. At their side paced Brute, his small eyes scanning the lane for danger.

"We're going to eat at Lord Hani's house?" asked Bener-ib as they walked.

"Might as well. Lord Ptah-mes is still off hunting with the king. He won't be back until tomorrow at the earliest." Ptah-mes's ancestral mansion was an enormous, gorgeously furnished, and cold dwelling, and Neferet was eager to get away to the warmth and informality of her childhood home whenever she could justify it. Her marriage was a most unconventional one. Ptah-mes, her husband—her father's friend—let her do whatever she wanted, making no demands upon her. After the loss of his first wife, Neferet's presence had kept his suitors at bay, and being married to him provided a respectable cover for her relationship with Bener-ib.

"I thought the king was a little boy. How is it he's hunting?" Mut-tuy said, in a disinterested-sounding voice.

"I don't know if he's actually taking shots, but like any boy would, he loves to go out in a chariot and chase after gazelles or whatever they're tracking. The grownup courtiers will bring back enough game for them all, I'm sure. Lord Ptah-mes is a good shot with a bow."

"I hate to think of killing those beautiful animals,

although I understand people have to eat," said Bener-ib sadly. She was always tender-hearted.

"Papa won't hunt for just that reason."

It was deep into the season of Peret, and the cool winter sun was already oblique, evening shadows stretching long across the narrow lanes and broad processional ways as they passed. Neferet regretted leaving her tufted linen cloak at the dispensary.

Bener-ib, as she so often did, seemed to read her thoughts. "Do you want to share my cloak, Nef'et?"

"Thanks, my girl." Neferet snuggled next to the smaller woman and drew the panel of heavy cloth around her shoulder. *Better. Everything's better shared.*

By the time the little party, with its chattering vanguard, pooled at the cheerful red gate of Papa and Mama's house, the evening was sinking into brassy gold and purple. A scud of dry plane leaves rustled in the street along the wall. Neferet hallooed and pounded on the panel, and almost before she had withdrawn her fist, the gate opened.

Papa stood there beaming. "I thought it was you. Ptah-mes is still with the king, isn't he?" He folded Neferet into a huge hug and then Bener-ib and Mut-tuy.

The younger children piled noisily into the garden without stopping to be greeted, sweeping the nursemaid along. Neferet's mother cried out happily from inside the house, "Look who's come!"

Papa's grin faded and he said quietly, "Uncle Pipi's here. He hasn't said anything yet, but I have the feeling he's in trouble again. If he hints about a loan, my duckling, don't offer him anything. He has to learn to get himself out of trouble, and I don't want Ptah-mes to feel he's responsible for my family's imprudences."

Imprudence was the word. Father's brother Pipi, his junior by four years and hence a man in his early fifties, was still a big ten-year-old when it came to managing his finances. He seemed to reel from one costly obsession to another which his salary as a low-level scribe in the foreign service couldn't support. There had been the horses, then boats. Who knew what he had gotten excited about now? Neferet felt downright adult by comparison to her feckless uncle. She heaved a sigh and shot Papa a complicit look of hopelessness.

"Understood, Papa Duck."

While the children marched upstairs to games on the roof under the eye of Nurse, the two *sunet*s and their apprentice followed Papa into the salon, where the family had gathered. Mama and Aunt Nedjem-ib and Baket-iset were there, and sure enough, Uncle Pipi, "in the flesh and plenty of it," as Grandfather would say. He and Auntie jumped to their feet, bursting with life and loving enthusiasm, and welcomed the girls with open arms and shouts of happy laughter.

Pipi could almost have passed for Papa's twin, but a little younger and a good bit fatter. He was broad and squat, with a smiling, square-jowled face under close-cropped hair; small, friendly brown eyes; and a wide grin, marked by a space between the front teeth. Nedjem-ib looked surprisingly like him, with wild, frizzy hair and a comfortable air of perpetual untidiness. As a child, Neferet couldn't have asked for a more loving and indulgent pair of relatives. They had let her do anything.

"Where are the boys?" she asked. The couple's youngest sons were twins and as undisciplined as their parents.

Nedjem-ib said, "They're at Mut-nodjmet and Pa-kiki's house for dinner. They wanted to see their sister and the baby." Their oldest daughter was married to Neferet's next-oldest brother and had just borne Pa-kiki his third little girl.

"Speaking of dinner," said Mama, "your father was hoping for an early supper. I hope you girls won't object."

Neferet laughed aloud. "You read our minds!"

It was just too chilly to eat in the garden, so Mama had the servants set up small tables in the salon, upon which they set the pot-shaped loaves of bread, big bowls of dressed endive, and lentil soup.

"Where's Grandfather?" Neferet asked, as they tucked into the food.

"At his lady friend's house," said Mama with a smile. "I'm sure they're eating something more elegant than lentils."

"No apologies needed, my dove." Papa winked at his wife. "It may be more elegant, but it couldn't be more delicious. This is my idea of a perfect winter meal." He mopped up a bit of salad sauce on his bread.

"How is your practice doing these days, girls?" Aunt Nedjem-ib said around a mouthful of endive.

"Busy, Auntie. Every child on our block had a splinter, a scrape, or an insect bite today. Mut-tuy got to set her hand to some bandaging."

"That must have been fun," Uncle Pipi said enthusiastically. "I've always wanted to be a doctor."

Neferet caught her father's eye. *Sekhmet have mercy—is this his latest passion?*

Mut-tuy disabused him. "It was boring."

The others laughed. But Neferet noticed her parents exchange uneasy glances.

Papa said carefully, "We missed you at the farm this summer, my brother."

"We were at our own farm!" Nedjem-ib gave a shriek of laughter and elbowed her husband. "Right, Pipi?"

Pipi forced a smile, and his chubby face grew crimson. "Yes, well. Farming wasn't all it was made out to be." He turned to Papa and said in a pitiful voice, "It's a lot of hard work."

"It is indeed," Papa said with no sign of rebuke. "So, you bought a farm? Where is it?"

"Too far away. It wasn't practical at all. But land is so expensive near the city." Pipi looked suddenly dejected. "It seemed like a good idea, but you have to hire so many people to maintain it. And it was lonely out there, with nobody around. It… it didn't work out. We sold it a month or two ago."

Mama said innocently, "I'm sure you turned a nice profit, at least."

But Nedjem-ib hooted. "Dear gods, no. We were flayed alive, weren't we, Pipi? But we're well out of it, say I."

"It probably sounds stupid, Hani, but I know we're always butting in on your family at the farm. I mean, Father left it to you, and he probably wonders why we're always there too."

"Hardly. He wondered why you *weren't* there last summer. It's for the whole family, Pipi. He turned it over to me to administer because, as you've found out, it's a lot of work. But it's still his as much as it is mine. And yours too. You know you're always welcome—it's part of our childhood."

"That's what I told him," said Nedjem-ib, shaking her head. "But he wanted to play landed gentry."

As soon as Neferet had grown old enough to pick up on such things, it had become clear to her that Uncle Pipi felt like he was always in competition with Papa—and losing the contest.

"But enough of that," Papa said kindly. "How are the children?"

The conversation turned to Mut-nodjmet's baby and the rate at which the twins were shooting up. Gradually Pipi's good cheer returned, and he seemed to have forgotten about the debacle of the farm. But sometimes, when the conversation lagged, his smile drifted off and a haunted expression veiled his humor-crinkled eyes.

Papa's right. Something's going on. Neferet shot a surreptitious glance at Bener-ib, who appeared to have noticed too.

"How is your husband, my dear?" Aunt Nedjem-ib said to Neferet. "As busy as ever?"

"Fine. He does work a lot. But right now, he's hunting with the king and a group of courtiers."

"He's the handsomest man." Nedjem-ib sighed dreamily, then poked Pipi. "After you, of course."

But Pipi seemed to be interested, not offended. "Hunting, you say? I guess they need good chariots for that."

Papa said blandly, "I suppose so. I suppose chariots always need to be good. They move at great speed."

Neferet had experienced a hair-raising ride in Ptah-mes's chariot only a few months before, and she could vouch for the terrifying speed at which they moved. "They're so flimsy! It's amazing they hold together."

"They have to be light so the horses can pull them without tiring," Papa said, watching his brother closely.

Pipi's little eyes had grown bright with attentiveness, and he leaned forward as if he couldn't wait to jump into the discussion. "A good chariot-maker could ask almost anything he wanted for his work," he said, with the air of revealing a great secret. "It's a wonderful business to invest in."

A sudden silence descended on the party as they realized they had discovered Pipi's latest passion.

"How exactly does one invest in an artisan's workshop?" Papa asked after a moment. "Isn't it just a master and his journeymen and apprentices, the same as with any business?"

"Yes, but if some investor provided him with supplies and an up-to-date workshop and a list of clients, that would be worth a cut of the profits, wouldn't it? And the margin of profit is very high, Hani. The supplies are cheap—it's all in the skilled labor. Think of the number of rich men like Ptah-mes who want a topnotch chariot for hunting. Think of the army—why, they must use thousands, and they're always getting wrecked and have to be replaced." Pipi was fizzy with excitement.

At his side, Nedjem-ib rolled her eyes. "I told him anything that seems too good to be true probably is."

"Do you mean you've invested in some chariot-maker's workshop?" Papa said neutrally.

Suddenly Pipi looked hunted. He cast his little eyes back and forth, as if there might be spies all around. "It's complicated, brother. I… I need some advice."

Ever discreet, Mama rose. "Ladies, let's adjourn to the terrace, shall we?" She called for the servants to carry Baket-iset's couch, and she and Nedjem-ib trooped away to the staircase. "Neferet? Are you girls going to join us?"

But Neferet didn't want to go—things were just getting interesting. She hemmed and hawed.

Bener-ib got to her feet and took Mut-tuy by the hand. "We're coming, Lady Nub-nefer." She gave Neferet a significant look as she sidled around the table with the adolescent in tow. *Stay if you want*, it seemed to say, *but our presence would just embarrass your uncle.*

What a ripe fig among women, Neferet thought gratefully. *How have I deserved her?*

Once the others had disappeared up the stairs, Papa laid a hand on his brother's shoulder. "What's going on, Pipi? You seem troubled by something."

The younger man slumped in dejection. "It sounds so easy, doesn't it? Easy gold. But it's turned into a nightmare, Hani. How could anything so simple have become so complicated?" He seemed to have forgotten about Neferet's presence altogether.

"Start at the beginning."

"Two months or so ago, a friend came to me with a sure business proposition. He knew a chariot-maker who wanted to expand his business but couldn't afford to find a bigger workshop or hire more men. My friend was going to help him financially in return for a share of the profits, but he wasn't very rich himself and thought that if several of us went together, the artisan could make more vehicles and hence more profits. Perfectly straightforward."

Papa nodded encouragement.

"I had all those *debens* from the sale of the farm in my hand, so I thought 'Why not?' There turned out to be six of us investors, each of us putting in a modest amount. But there wasn't much profit coming out at the end. It's not so easy to scale up a skilled craft like that. And I guess the real problem is that the market's limited. How many people are rich enough to own a chariot and team? I suggested selling to the army, but it turns out they've got their own workshops."

"Of course," murmured Papa. "So, have you pulled out of it?"

Pipi looked up at him with stricken eyes. "That's the problem, Hani. I can't."

"What do you mean?" Neferet cried despite herself. "Did you sign a contract?"

"Sort of. But… but it's worse than that." Uncle Pipi buried his face momentarily in his hands, and when he raised it again, his lashes were sparkling with tears. "Hani, my friend tried to pull out, and the next day, he… he was dead."

Oh no, thought Neferet, dread creeping up her spine. *Uncle has gotten involved with some rough characters.*

"Maybe it was coincidence," said Papa hopefully.

"Oh no. They came to see me too. Said, 'We hope you're not thinking about backing out, because see Pen-djehuty here? He may have died of something contagious, and you could be the next to catch it.'"

Papa grunted, his optimism melted out. His drawn-down eyebrows spoke of how troubling he found this news. He considered his lap.

"Dear gods, I have a wife and children!" Pipi wailed. "These people might hurt them somehow to pressure me. I'm trapped."

"Who is this 'they'? Not the artisan himself surely."

"No. At least, I don't think so. There are these men who came to talk to us and to see we signed the contract. They collect the *debens* every week. They get the supplies and things the artisan needs to keep working. I don't know who they are, or what they have to do with the workshop. I don't so much as know their names."

"Who are the other investors?" Neferet asked. "Do you know them?"

"Not at all. I don't even know their names except for one. He's a scribe in the chancery, but that's the only thing I know." Pipi groaned and cradled his head in his hands. "I've got to get out. I can't afford to spend any more on this thing. I needed that farm gold to pay back a loan. I thought this would earn me some quick *debens*, but it's just getting thrown down a hole."

A discouraged silence stretched out. Papa and Neferet exchanged a look of gloom. Finally Papa said reluctantly, "I'll try to help you, little brother, but it sounds to me as if you've gotten involved with the underworld."

Pipi stared up at him, wide-eyed. "You mean demons and things? Oh, Hidden One help me!"

"No. I mean criminals and things. Thugs. Assassins. Black marketeers. May the Hidden One help you indeed."

ACKNOWLEDGMENTS

The author gratefully acknowledges all those who have helped her in the production of this book. To the wonderful women of my writers' group, for their critique and encouragement, my thanks. To Lynn McNamee and her editorial team at Red Adept—Jessica, Sarah, and Kim—profound gratitude (and Lynn, for so many other forms of help). To the flexible and talented gang at Streetlight Graphics for the cover and map. To my cousin and her husband, my technology guru: thanks, guys. And most of all, to my husband, Ippokratis, who put up with the months of fixation it takes to write a novel, many, many thanks.

ABOUT THE AUTHOR

N.L. Holmes is the pen name of a professional archaeologist who received her doctorate from Bryn Mawr College. She has excavated in Greece and in Israel and taught ancient history and humanities at the university level for many years. She has always had a passion for books, and in childhood, she and her cousin (also a writer today) used to write stories for fun.

Today, since their son is grown, she lives with her husband and two cats in northern France, where she gardens, weaves, plays the violin, and dances. And reads, of course.

OTHER TITLES BY N.L. HOLMES

THE LORD HANI MYSTERIES

Political intrigue and mystery in Akh-en-aten's Egypt

Finalist, Best Series of 2021, Next Generation Independent Book Award

Finalist, Best Series of 2022, Chanticleer Independent Book Awards

Bird in a Snare (2020) Grand Prize, Chaucer Award 2021 for best historical fiction before 1750

The Crocodile Makes No Sound (2020) Gold Medal, Adult Fiction, The Wishing Shelf Book Awards 2022

Scepter of Flint (2020)

The North Wind Descends (2020)

Lake of Flowers (2021)

Pilot Who Knows the Waters (2022)

THE *EMPIRE AT TWILIGHT* SERIES

Free-standing personal dramas with a touch of intrigue, set in the Hittite Empire

The Lightning Horse (2020)

The Singer and Her Song (2020)

The Queen's Dog (2020)

The Sun at Twilight (2021)

The Moon That Fell from Heaven (Red Adept Publishing, September 2023)

The Mountains of Freedom (Red Adept Publishing, *Vella*, coming soon)

THE *HANI'S DAUGHTER* MYSTERIES

Neferet carries on the family curiosity in the reign of Tut-ankh-amen with cozy mysteries

Flowers of Evil (2023)

Web of Evil (January 2024)

Wheel of Evil (July 2024)

Printed in Great Britain
by Amazon